CLOSE YOUR EYES

ALSO BY
TERESA DRISCOLL

Recipes for Melissa

Last Kiss Goodnight

I Am Watching You

The Friend

The Promise

I Will Make You Pay

Her Perfect Family

Tell Me Lies

CLOSE YOUR EYES

TERESA DRISCOLL

Text copyright © 2024 by Teresa Driscoll
All rights reserved.

Published by Thomas & Mercer, Seattle

www.apub.com

Amazon, the Amazon logo, and Thomas & Mercer are trademarks of Amazon.com, Inc., or its affiliates.

ISBN-13: 9781662523144
eISBN: 9781662523137

Cover design by Dan Mogford
Cover image: © Dmitry Schemelev / Unsplash; © Silas Manhood / Arcangel

Printed in the United States of America

CLOSE YOUR EYES

PART ONE

CHAPTER 1

SALLY – Day One

She will come to regret the tussle in the shop more than anything else in her life. Very soon she will lie in the dark, replaying every word. Every expression on her daughter's face.

But in the moment in Freda's Fashions, Sally Hill can know none of this. In the moment, all she knows is she is stretched. And tired. And running very late.

'Can I try this on, Mummy?'

Sally turns, phone in hand, to see Amelie holding up a green dress on a hanger.

'Sorry, darling. We don't have time.' Sally's gaze is straight back to her phone, scrolling for the party invitation. Amelie's being picked up from home by one of the other mums. But Sally can't remember the timings. *Four or four thirty?*

'Don't you like it?' Amelie turns to check her reflection in a mirror on the shop wall, holding the dress against her body and tilting her head.

'It's very nice but we've really got to go. Come on. Put it back.' Sally frowns. Pick-up time is four. They're even more pushed than she feared. Sally starts leading the way through the central aisle of

Freda's Fashions. It's on Maidstead High Street, half an hour from home on a good day. But it's not a good day.

Tuesday afternoon. Big crowds. Half-term traffic. They've been in town for a birthday present. Sally bought Amelie a new outfit *last* week and no way is she getting another one today. She turns to find her daughter hasn't moved. 'Come on, Amelie. Put it back.'

A woman in a black mac turns as Sally raises her voice. Sally feels a momentary sweep of guilt. The green actually looks very nice against Amelie's dark hair but that's not the point.

'I want to try it now, Mummy. *Please.*'

'I told you. We don't have time. Put it back.' Sally is aware of the woman in the black mac still watching them, eyebrows raised now. She wishes she could tell her to mind her own. *You try getting a wilful eight-year-old in and out of town inside an hour.*

At last Amelie puts the dress back on the rail, huffing her disapproval and following Sally, head down.

'We'll come back another day.'

'Yeah. *Sure* we will.'

'Enough of the attitude. I wanted to come into town yesterday for the present, remember. You were the one who left this until the last minute. Now come on. Let's get going.' Sally keeps marching the length of Freda's Fashions and through the front doors where her phone rings.

Sally stands still, Amelie a step behind, just in front of the shop. The screen confirms it's Laura. The mum doing the party run. 'I need to take this, Amelie. It's about your lift. Wait there. I need a better signal.' Amelie rolls her eyes, folds her arms and leans back against one of the doors, right knee bent, foot flat against the central pane of glass.

Sally takes a few paces until two bars emerge. 'Hello, Laura. I'm in town. Running late.'

'Sorry, doll. Emergency here. Turned my ankle. Can't drive.'

Much later with the police, Sally will say she was on the phone for just a few minutes. But this will turn out not to be true. The reality is she's drawn into the logistical nightmare of being asked to step up as eleventh-hour party taxi to four girls across the South Hams, juggling a myriad of WhatsApp messages about who to pick up from where. And warning everyone she's running late . . .

By the time she turns to check if Amelie's still in her strop, the doorway to Freda's Fashions is empty.

No Amelie.

Sally frowns. She glances around, looking for Amelie's bright pink hoodie. No sign along the High Street. She walks back into the shop as a new thought lands. She hurries right through the central aisle to the changing rooms at the back. There's just one curtain closed, and she swishes it open, fully expecting it to be Amelie with the dress.

'*Excuse me!*' An older grey-haired woman in her underwear stares daggers.

'I'm so sorry. I'm looking for my daughter.'

Sally retreats to double-check the other cubicles. Empty. She walks around the rest of Freda's Fashions but there's no sign of Amelie anywhere. A wave of cold now passes right through her.

Next door there's a bakery cum café. Maybe Amelie needed the toilet? She's not supposed to go to the toilet on her own but she's in a mood, remember.

Sally checks the three cubicles in the café's restroom. Also empty. The wave of cold turns to something else. A dread she for some reason recognises . . .

The next few minutes spiral into a blur. Sally marches from shop to shop, casting around for a flash of pink and calling Amelie's name over and over. Finally she loops back to Freda's Fashions and clutches an assistant's sleeve.

'Have you seen a girl in a pink hoodie? Dark hair. Aged eight but tall.' She signals Amelie's height with her hand. 'Looks more like nine.'

'No. Sorry. Do you want us to—'

Sally doesn't let her finish. Suddenly can't seem to even hear properly. She turns and makes for the High Street again, calling Amelie's name much louder. *Amelie. Where are you?* She goes back in the café next door. And the chemist. And the shoe shop. She trips on a step. People are starting to stare.

The panic now coursing through Sally is making her feel sick, and again she is conscious of the familiarity – this same nausea – and realises it's from a dream. Dreading this *very* thing happening. Yes. One of her nightmares . . .

'It's OK. We'll find her, love.' A stranger's voice. The tone is gentle, and Sally looks up to see a short woman in a stripy jumper leaning in towards her, then reaching to touch her arm. 'She's probably just popped into one of the other shops. My daughter does that all the time. Hides. Thinks it's funny. Might she have gone to the toilet?'

The woman's waiting for a reply but it's as if she's behind a screen. Two feet away but on the other side of some invisible, frosted glass. Voice dimmed. Image blurred. The stripes on her jumper *moving*.

'The toilet? Might she have gone to the toilet, love? We could check all the nearest loos—'

Sally is still feeling sick and closes her eyes to block the rolling stripes on the jumper. She tells the woman, eyes still clamped shut, that she's already checked the café toilets. 'She's eight. Dark hair. Pink hoodie . . .'

The woman offers to help search but Sally's voice out loud sounds strange now – echoey as if under water. And how can this woman help? She opens her eyes – *sorry, sorry* – and turns away

6

from the stripes to keep marching from shop doorway to shop doorway – *Amelie. Are you in here?* – as she takes out her phone and tries Matthew's number. It clicks through to answerphone.

A couple more women start following Sally, offering to coordinate the search. They mutter about checking the whole High Street, shop by shop. *We need to be methodical.* And then another much taller woman in a red coat breaks away from the huddle to match Sally's strides, marching right alongside, asking if it's maybe time to call the police? She's calm, this woman. Practical. Voice steady. Eyes grave.

The woman lowers her voice and asks again, 'Do you think it's maybe time we called the police?'

Sally suddenly stops walking. Back straight. She realises in this instant, rock still with the blur of bright red alongside, that she should have done this already. She's not dialled 999 out of blind fear; not wanting to face it. The seriousness. Clinging instead to the life raft of hope that any second now there will be a happy ending – *There you are, lovely girl. I've been frantic.*

'How long's it been?' The woman in red again.

'Ten minutes. No—' Sally checks her own watch to see it's more than twenty. 'Much longer. I've been a bit all over the place—'

'Right. The police then? Yes? Just to be on the safe side?'

'Yes. Please call the police. Please do that now.' Sally feels her stomach surge again, afraid she's really going to be sick. Right here. 'I need to try my husband again.'

'OK.' The woman in red pulls out her own mobile from her pocket and starts to dial. 'Right. You phone home. I'll get help.' She turns to speak into her phone. '*Police please*' then back towards Sally as she waits. 'What's your daughter's full name? And do you have a picture if they ask?'

7

'Amelie Hill. Eight. She doesn't normally wander off.' Sally holds up her own phone for face recognition. 'It's been twenty minutes at least. Tell them it's serious. I'll sort a picture.'

Her phone opens. *Come on, come on.* She wonders as it rings if Matthew will blame her. As she in this moment blames him.

His number goes straight to answerphone again. Sally waits for the bleeps this time, nails pushed hard into her other palm. 'Amelie's gone missing. I've tried everywhere. The police are being contacted. I'm on Maidstead High Street. Just up from Boots. Call me.'

The woman on the phone to the police suddenly raises her hand for her attention. *Yes. I have the mother with me now.*

But Sally's mobile rings just as the woman in red steps closer. Sally signals that she needs to speak to her husband first.

'Where on the High Street, Sal? I'm leaving now.' Matthew's trying to keep his tone steady. 'How long's she been missing? You sure she's not just looking in a shop. Just—'

'No, she's gone, Matthew. *Gone.* I've looked everywhere. People are helping me. I've been looking for a while.' She can feel both her hands starting to shake again. 'I'm about to speak to the police.'

'Dear God. OK. I've got this. I'll call Mel. Stay on the line—'

'I'm sorry. I can't. I need to speak to the police right now.'

She rings off to take the stranger's mobile. Her voice robotic as she shares more details, answers the questions, imagines the police form being filled out, all the while the echo of voices all round still calling her daughter's name. A bigger crowd gathering now. Some of them wanting to help. Some just standing, gawping. A few holding their own children just that little bit closer. Toddlers bundled back into pushchairs. The paranoia like a cancer. Straps strapped. Babies held tight.

'They're on the way,' Sally says, handing the phone back to the woman. 'They say to wait here. Do you mind waiting with your phone? They're going to ring again in a minute. They wanted my number but I went blank. I'll give it to them when they ring back. Sorry. Stupid of me—'

'It's fine. I'll wait with you. Hold on to my phone. Now – we need to get you somewhere to sit down. A hot drink. Can someone get a drink?' The practical woman, the kind, middle-aged woman, back straight, is widening her eyes at the group, glancing about and then back at Sally. 'You drink tea? Yes?'

Sally nods and a man signals that he'll fetch the drink. 'With sugar,' adds the woman in red, and next she's steering Sally by the arm towards a bench near a department store. 'You need to sit down. You look very pale.'

As she allows herself to be guided to the bench, Sally realises just how capable this woman is and her kindness and steadiness are all at once both essential and unbearable. Sally's legs seem to give way as she sits. The woman grips her arm tighter.

The stranger's phone suddenly rings in Sally's hand. A male voice. 'Hello. Is that Mrs Hill? I understand that your daughter Amelie is missing. I realise this must be very frightening but I promise that we're going to help you.'

'Thank you. My name's Sally Hill. My daughter's just eight and she never wanders off. *Never.* My husband, Matthew Hill, is ex job. A private investigator. He's recently agreed to rejoin the police force. There's been some media coverage. He's had some very difficult cases in the past, both in the force and as a private investigator. I've always worried something might happen' – she pauses – 'to our family.'

'And why's that, Mrs Hill?' His tone has changed. 'Have there been problems before? Specific threats?' A pause. 'Are you saying you think someone's taken Amelie? That she's been deliberately targeted?'

'I don't know. I don't know.' Sally says this to comfort herself. But it's a lie. Because she does feel that she knows. Deep down she fears that's *exactly* what's happened. For weeks and months she and Matthew have been arguing over whether it was safe for him to rejoin the police force. After the threat all those years ago. But mostly because of all the nasty letters every time he's in the papers . . .

Once upon a time it was Matthew who was afraid. She the one longing for a child. *We are allowed to be happy.*

And now?

Still she can hear the voices of strangers calling her daughter's name. And then come little dots of black on the periphery of her vision.

She tries to fight it – *not now, please not now* – but the dots grow bigger and the voice on the phone gets weaker. Distant. 'I'm sorry. But I'm feeling a bit faint—'

And then she's sinking. Falling. And all around her becomes a complete blur, the voices fading, as she spirals down. Deeper and deeper. The same words following her into the blackness.

Amelie. Gone.

This thing she's feared. Dreaded. Dreamt about. This thing she's known deep in her gut all along. His fault? Her fault?

How wrong she was to believe they were safe now.

Too late.

Amelie is gone.

CHAPTER 2

MATTHEW – DAY ONE

Matthew Hill dashes from the small flat adjoining his office back to his desk.

'I'm sorry but I have a family emergency. I'm going to have to go. Reschedule this.' He's grabbing his jacket from the back of his chair as he speaks, checking the pocket for his car keys. His head says there will be an update any minute to say that Amelie has been found. Hiding. Pranking. *Sorry to panic you.* But his heart, pounding out of his chest, says he will *never* forgive himself if he's wrong.

He has to go. *Now.*

But the girl doesn't move.

'What about my mother?' she says. 'Trying to find . . . *my* . . . *mother?*'

Her crestfallen expression underlines everything he suddenly realises is wrong with his life. Has *always* been wrong with his life? The push-pull of family versus work. The work as a PI always so full on.

The girl looks as if she may cry. She's a mother herself, apparently, but looks too young. Nineteen. A kid with a kid. Her email said her mother left the family when she was eight and Matthew's only had time to take the most basic of details.

'I'm sorry but I really do have to go. I have your number and I promise I'll update you as soon as I can. Either to fix another meeting or to suggest someone else who can help you.'

'But I've come a long way. Are you saying you can't take the case? I've got money. I told you I can pay.'

'I'm so sorry but this really is an emergency.' He's moving towards the door, heart still pounding and his head spinning. *Who to call first? Mel Sanders?* 'Look. I'm going to have to close the office. Ask you to leave.' Still the girl doesn't move. '*Immediately.* I'm so sorry.'

At last she slowly picks up her own jacket and moves to the door, passing through just ahead of him, huffing in frustration. Matthew locks the upstairs office door behind them and calls out to remind her that the staircase is steep. On the street, he checks that the main door is properly closed and repeats that he'll message and update. The girl looks genuinely shaken still. 'So what's the emergency?'

'I'm sorry. I can't say.' He mutters more apologies then marches to his car on a nearby meter.

As he pulls away, he sees in his mirror the girl staring at the car, her face white. He feels guilty but what to do? No choice.

Sal is always complaining he gets it wrong. Job before family. Once – a shiver goes through him as he remembers – he left his wife and daughter on Maidstead High Street to investigate a shooting nearby. He was the first official on the scene. It helped. But he will never forget Sally's face. *Don't leave us. Please don't leave us . . .*

It took years to build Amelie's confidence to go back into town. And now *this.*

Matthew rings Sally as he drives. Answerphone. *Damn.* She must still be talking to the police. Or maybe they've found Amelie

12

and she's soothing her? He tries to hold on to that thought, that hope, that picture in his head, but it won't stick.

Should he wait? Not wait? Be optimistic? Or catastrophise? *Sod it*. He speed-dials Mel Sanders.

'Hi, Matthew. What's up?'

'I've got a situation, Mel. Might need your help.'

Matthew feels his heart pumping even faster as he changes through the gears. Melanie Sanders is the best police officer he knows. Old colleague. Old friend. They trained together years back. When he left the force over a traumatic case, Melanie tried to dissuade him. Since he set up as a private investigator, they've remained good friends and he's helped, both unofficially and officially, on a few of her cases.

'Right. Shoot.'

'It might be nothing. It might resolve, but Amelie's gone missing. Sal's just phoned from Maidstead High Street to tell me. I don't know how long she's been gone yet. But Sal's speaking to local uniforms.'

'Jeez.' A pause. 'And def *missing*?' Her tone is immediately into professional gear.

'Haven't confirmed details. Like I say, I don't know how long. But Sal wouldn't call the police unless—'

'OK. I'm on it. I'll see what I can find out once it's official. Where are you?'

'In the car, just left Exeter. On the way to join Sally. Praying it's a false alarm, a prank. A mistake.' A pause. He lowers his voice. 'But between us, I'm worried it's . . .' He breaks off.

'Course you're frightened. Anyone would be. But you know how this goes. In most cases they turn up very quickly. And meantime I'm on this. I'm *with* you, Matt.'

Matthew feels a sweep of an emotion he can't quite identify. It's not relief. There can't be relief until he gets the call to say that

13

Amelie is safe, back with her mother, that it's all been a terrible mistake. That Sally is sorry for frightening everyone. But until that call comes, at least he has Melanie Sanders, the newly appointed head of CID in Cornwall, on his side. She may now work in the wrong county, technically, but she has strong history in Devon. *Contacts.* And for now she's the best he's got.

'Just thinking aloud, Matt. You're not worrying this might have anything to do with—'

'No. No.' He pauses. She means him rejoining the police. It's been in the papers. He's set to help build Mel's new team in just over a month. 'Well, I mean it's highly unlikely. Right?' He's glad that she's said it first. The truth is he *is* worrying this has something to do with him – his recent decision – but he needs to shut that thought right down. 'No. I can't go there yet, Mel. Let's pray for a mistake. A misunderstanding. Going to ring off now. Try Sally again.'

CHAPTER 3

SALLY – DAY ONE

'Hello, Mrs Hill. Can you hear me?'

As Sally comes to, there's a face leaning close to her. A blonde woman. Big red glasses. For a moment, she can't work out what's happening.

'Can you hear me, Mrs Hill?'

'Yes, yes I can hear.' And then the punch to the gut. '*Amelie. Oh God. I need to find my daughter.*' She tries to sit up, but a hand is pressed firmly on her shoulder.

'Please try to keep still. Just for a minute. I'm a doctor. You fainted but I can see from your movement that your neck's fine. Just take it gently. Breathe slowly for me. That's it. When you're feeling a bit better, we'll sit you back up on the bench.' A pause. 'Do you have any pain anywhere?'

Sally's so confused. Still groggy. She turns her head to find she's on her back on the pavement. Her hand flat on tarmac. The woman who helped her earlier, the one in the red coat, is holding her feet up off the ground. Instinctively she puts her hand to her face, worrying if there's an injury. But there's no pain. No cuts. 'No pain.'

'Good. Your colour's improving. This nice lady grabbed you as you went down. Thankfully broke your fall. It was probably the stress. And shock.' The doctor's glancing at the other woman, the one who called the police. She tells her that it's OK to slowly lower Sally's legs to the ground and Sally starts to remember more. The black dots. The sense of falling.

'Good. Your colour's good. You feeling a bit better? Ready to get back up on the bench so I can check you over?'

Sally nods and lets the two women help her very slowly back on to the seat just as two police officers, a man and a woman, appear.

'You Mrs Hill?'

'Yes. My daughter. Amelie. Has Amelie been found?'

'Sorry. Not yet, Mrs Hill. We're asking in the shops. No news yet. But we're here to help you. Now, first of all, we need to make sure you're OK. Do you need an ambulance?' The female officer's frowning as she speaks. 'Because I can put in the call but I have to warn you we still have really long delays—'

'No, no. I need to stay here. We need to keep *looking*. To find Amelie.' Sally starts casting her head left and right, annoyed to be stuck. Seated.

'She fainted but she's fine. I'm a doctor. Just making sure nothing's broken.' The blonde woman gently feels Sally's arms and legs, one by one, then asks her a series of questions. Does her head feel OK? Does she have any pain? Has this happened before? Is her head hurting at all?

'No, no. I feel fine now. Never mind me. We need to find Amelie.'

The next few minutes are spent sharing details with the two police officers of how Amelie suddenly disappeared. There one minute. Gone the next. 'I was on the phone but not for long.' Sally describes Amelie's clothes again and explains that she's checked all the nearest shops. A couple of women step forward to say they too have coordinated a check with staff in about a dozen shops on the High Street. Nothing so far.

The male police officer quickly steps away to talk on his radio. Face grave. His expression once again sends cold shooting through Sal. She shivers and the doctor says she will stay for a few more minutes to make sure she's OK but will need to leave then. On shift at the hospital.

Sally repeats what happened. How they were in town to buy a present. They were tight for time. Amelie was grumpy there was no time to try on a dress she liked.

Sally explains about her phone ringing. The friend bailing on the party lift. Her daughter standing just *behind* her, outside the clothes shop.

'I wasn't on the phone long at all. But when I rang off, Amelie wasn't there. Gone. *Vanished.*'

The female police officer is writing all this down as her colleague confirms that back-up is on the way and that he'll start door to door officially. Or rather shop to shop. Sally shows them a photograph of Amelie on her phone, which they copy. A smiley shot from just last weekend. Lunch by the river. Amelie's beaming in the picture. She'd fed the ducks. The thought of it – the happiness, the normality – absolute torture now.

Sally repeats that she's already tried all the nearest shops.

'Does your daughter have a phone? You've tried ringing her?'

'She's eight. She doesn't have a phone.' Sally tries to control her tone but the irritation and the panic's like a wave moving through her whole body again. She mustn't let it overwhelm her. Mustn't faint again, but she wants people *looking for Amelie*. Not standing around, talking. 'We've said no to a phone before secondary school.' She doesn't add that it's caused arguments; a couple of Amelie's friends have been allowed phones already.

'Does she have a favourite place in town? Somewhere she might have gone?'

'No, no. She's not allowed to shop on her own.'

'And where's your car? Might she have gone back to the car, looking for you? If she wandered. Got lost. Couldn't see you.'

Sally can't believe why she didn't think of this herself. Her car's on the second floor of the multistorey. It could be as simple as that. Amelie must have somehow lost sight of her, got disorientated, and has gone back to the car park.

And then there *he* is suddenly, striding down the High Street towards them. Matthew.

'Any news?' Her husband's face is pale. He's trying to keep his tone calm but his eyes are terrified.

She shakes her head, watches his face darken, and then his arms are around her and she has to fight the panic. And the anger. And the sense of fury. With him. With herself. With the world.

'I haven't checked the car park yet. They're saying she might have just gone back to the car. I didn't think of that. She's never done that before. Do you think she's just at the car?'

CHAPTER 4

MELANIE – DAY ONE

'Hey there. How's it going?' Melanie on speakerphone tries to keep her tone neutral. The traffic's busy. A car in the middle lane blasts its horn and she tweaks the volume button on the steering wheel.

'Er, it's going fine my end. Just tying up a few things. But you sound stressed and I can hear traffic, so now I'm worried.' Her husband Tom lets out a sigh. 'You don't ring in the middle of a shift unless it's bad news. Especially the last day before a holiday. So hit me with it. Why are you in the car? What's happened?'

Melanie bites into her bottom lip. Her husband could write a book on the *long-suffering* woes of being married to a detective. He's used to the crazy hours. The calls in the middle of the night. But this crisis crosses all the lines. They have a large Airbnb booked for the following morning for the rest of half-term. A trip with his brother and his family. New Forest. Change of scene. A much-needed mini break for all of them.

Technically this is an admin day. She's supposed to be tying up loose ends in the office ahead of the holiday.

'This is a very big ask, Tom – *very big* – so I'm just going to spit it out.' Melanie feels cold suddenly despite her thick jumper and immediately contradicts herself. Can't find the words. Thinks instead of their son George packing his toys last night.

'OK. So this is agony here, Mel. How about you just give it to me straight. What's happened?'

'Right. So I'm on the road to Devon and if you insist, I will turn around. This isn't a fait accompli.' He says nothing so she plunges on. 'A girl's gone missing, Tom. Aged eight. It's looking serious. A possible abduction. You know that the first forty-eight hours are absolutely critical. They're short-staffed in Devon. My promotion and transfer to Cornwall is a part of that pickle. And the thing is – I want to give them those forty-eight hours. Give the case its best shot.'

'Oh – no, no, no. Mel. You don't even work in Devon any-more. I don't understand. It's awful that a girl's missing. Dreadful. But you can't take the whole world on your shoulders. This is not your problem. Not your case. I'm sorry but I'm putting my foot down. We're going on holiday.'

'It isn't that simple.'

'Yes, it is. You choose us. You turn around and you choose us. Me and George.' He sounds both angry and determined and this is not like Tom.

Melanie feels her throat clamp, close to tears. She takes a couple more long, slow breaths. Doesn't want to say it as if avoiding the name will make it untrue. She finds her head twitching slightly, like a tic, as she speaks. Fighting tears. 'It's Amelie, Tom. It's Sally and Matthew's Amelie.'

'Oh, dear God – *no*.'

The silence that follows is horrible. A terrible cavern in which unimaginable things happen. Pain and loss and unbearable fear. Melanie and Tom and Sally and Matthew are friends. Kitchen suppers and outings with the kids. She knows that Tom will be doing right now precisely what she's been doing since Matthew rang.

Imagining the horror of their George missing. Mirroring the fear and the dread that must be driving Sally and Matthew completely insane.

'But *how*? Amelie? I don't understand.'

'OK. So this is where I am, Tom. It's been two hours since she was last seen in town, in Maidstead, with Sally. Not a whisper. Not a sighting. It's completely out of character and we simply don't know what's happened. If it's an accident or, more sinister, a random crime or something linked to Matthew's work. As a PI or when he was in the force. All the departments are short-staffed everywhere. I'm the only one with the right experience who's supposed to be on leave. I'm free. Devon's stretched. So I've offered to step in as SIO as a favour.'

'But you know Amelie. Surely that's not allowed? Surely that's a reason for you not to get involved?'

'We're not related. And I've said I'll do this for time off in lieu, not overtime, as a favour to the force. It's not like knowing a suspect. No strict conflict of interest, so they're thinking about it. I have a meeting with the suits when I arrive. I sense they'll bite my arm off, but I've said I need to speak to you first.'

Melanie pauses, noticing a lorry creeping closer to her left. She pulls out into the fast lane but misjudges it. A blast of a horn from a white van behind. She has to press hard on the accelerator, heart quickening.

'What's with the horn? You OK?'

'Sure. I'm fine.' She's not. Mel realises she needs to try harder to concentrate on the road. The problem is she's afraid to tell Tom *all* of it. She waits a few moments until it's safe to return to the middle lane and pulls back her speed again.

'There's something else,' she says at last. 'I may have messed up.' Dark thoughts are already tumbling through Melanie's brain. Dive teams. A helicopter. Checking the list of local sex offenders.

21

Digging up all of Matthew's past cases. Who's still inside? Who's at liberty? But also this new and terrible question haunting her. *Dawn Meadows* . . .

'What do you mean – messed up?' Tom's voice sounds wary now.

'You remember Dawn Meadows. That woman who wrongly blamed Matthew for her son's death. When he left the force?'

'Of course.' They'd talked about it often enough. Years back and also more recently when Sally was worrying about Matthew rejoining the force. Dawn had made some nasty threats once. But it was nearly a decade ago.

'And you remember the hate mail, the anonymous letters every time Matthew's been in the papers?' Matthew had been on some big cases as a PI. Several made the news.

'You're worrying me now. I thought you said the letters were all investigated. They were not from Dawn. And not taken seriously. Just green-ink warriors. All ancient history. Nothing for Sally and Matthew to worry about.' It was true. Dawn had been visited twice years back and no evidence found. She was on file as angry but harmless. Matthew's set to join Sally's team in less than six weeks. The decision made. All the agonising over Dawn Meadows in theory behind them.

'So the thing is' – Melanie pauses, hardly able to say it in this new context – 'another anonymous letter came in. Addressed to me. After Matthew was in the paper again about rejoining the force. To help me build my new team in Cornwall.' Melanie's throat is dry again. She has to cough.

There's quite a long pause.

'I got Forensics to check it. Nothing. No prints. No leads. So I just' – Melanie can feel tears blurring her eyes – 'I just put it on file with the others.'

'Oh, right. Goodness.' Tom's tone has changed completely.

'It's worse, Tom.' She has to wipe her eyes with the back of her palms. 'I didn't tell Matthew.'

'Oh dear God. Why *not*?'

'I didn't want to worry him unnecessarily. I really didn't think it was a serious threat. I mean, we'd discounted the Meadows in the past. There were no useful forensics, so I didn't want to rake all that up again . . .' She doesn't add that she didn't want to spook Matthew. Make him reconsider his decision to work with her, especially as Sally was never keen.

'And now you think . . .'

'Now I don't know *what* to think—' Mel breaks off. 'Except we have a very different and dangerous new context, so I have to find Amelie. And I have to interview Dawn Meadows again.'

'You don't really think it's her, do you? That she's taken Amelie?'

'For the record – no, I don't. But I'm not going to sleep until I make absolutely sure. Check for certain that I haven't made a wrong call . . .' Her voice trails away.

There is another long pause.

'OK. So I understand now.' Tom sounds really shaken.

'So can I take the case?'

He doesn't answer. Melanie checks her mirrors again, then the clock on the dashboard. 'Do I keep driving or do I turn around?'

'If it was George—'

'Matthew would drop everything to help us, no question. You know he would.'

'OK.' Tom lets out a long sigh. 'So you go and you find her.' His voice breaks and he coughs. 'I'll take George tomorrow and you join us when you can. Yes?'

Melanie's suddenly fighting tears again, which she feels angry about. Because this case needs her at her professional best. Top of her game. Not this. Not . . . so . . . scared.

'Are you going to be all right, Mel?'

'Honestly?'

'Please. This is me.'

'I don't know, Tom. It feels very confusing. The new letter and then this happening.' Another punch to her gut. Pure fear. Picturing again the helicopter and the search teams. Imagining the incident board with Amelie's photograph right in the middle. 'What if I can't fix this? What if this is my fault? What if this is because I put pressure on him to help me build the new team—'

'If you can't find her, no one else can either. And this is *not* your fault.'

'You think?'

'I know. OK, so you should have told Matthew about the new letter. You know that. And you do need to tell him *now*. Put it right. But it's unlikely to be Dawn Meadows as you say. And the new letter doesn't make any of this your fault.'

'I will tell him.' She means it. But she deliberately doesn't say when. She wants to find Dawn Meadows first and make sure it really is nothing to do with her.

'So how are they holding up? Sally and Matthew?'

'They're not.'

'Sorry. Stupid question.'

'Sally's refusing to leave the car park in town in case Amelie looks for her there. We need to get her home but it's all very distressing.' Another pause. 'Matthew's with her but they're saying she may need sedation.'

'Jeez. How awful for them. I can't begin to imagine. Will you give them my love once they're home?'

'Of course. And you tell George I'll speak to him very soon. Don't tell him about Amelie yet, though you may need to keep him away from the news. We'll have to decide very quickly whether to go to media appeal tomorrow. Put her picture out. I'll let you know when that happens so we can prepare George.'

There is another long pause and finally Tom asks what she's been dreading.

'So this new letter that came in. What did it say?'

'Usual rambling. Nasty. But no worse than before.'

This isn't true. Fact is, and this is why she is silently crying again, Melanie remembers the anonymous letter exactly. The previous notes about Matthew – all with individual words cut out of different magazines – were addressed to the chief constable. And the media. This one was addressed to her.

> Matthew Hill is a child killer. You take him back on
> your team and you will all be sorry.

CHAPTER 5

MATTHEW – DAY ONE

'Stay away from me! Don't anyone come near me! I'm *not* leaving!' Sally is alongside her car in the multistorey, thrashing her arms around to prevent anyone coming close.

'OK, darling. OK.' Matthew puts his palms up in a signal of surrender and glances at the policewoman who does the same. The officer steps back but Matthew – completely broken to see his wife like this – tries again to very slowly and very gently edge forward. He wants to take her into a hug. To try to soothe her. But Sally is like a trapped animal.

'No. No. You don't *touch* me. No one is to touch me.' Sally's eyes are still completely wild. She backs away towards a concrete pillar. She feels for it with her right hand and then her body seems to weaken so that she slides her back down the pillar until she is sitting on the dirty floor. Next, she begins to cry again, huge waves of sobbing. Unbearable to witness. 'I am staying here. I am waiting for Amelie *here*.'

They've been like this for the best part of an hour. Paramedics have come and gone and, according to the policewoman, are still standing by, but out of sight now. Sally is refusing a sedative.

When they were first driven to the multistorey in a patrol car, Sally had become almost alarmingly upbeat. She had it in her head that Amelie would definitely be at the car. Upset and lost. But safe. *That's all that's happened. A misunderstanding.* She bolted from the police car as soon as it stopped near her own. She seemed to get a glimpse of something near one of the exit doors and ran across to the stairwell, shouting Amelie's name. But it was an older teenager in a darker pink hoodie who shrugged her away. Looked confused. And also a bit scared.

Between them, they checked Sally's car and looked into every vehicle across the whole floor and that was when Sally became completely hysterical as if her brain simply couldn't cope.

Matthew looks again at his wife. He's said 'no' to medics forcefully giving her a sedative injection; she would never forgive him. But he needs to get her home safely and is at a complete loss as to how.

He feels the vibration of a text to his mobile and removes it from his pocket. Mel Sanders. It's looking hopeful she can lead the investigation. *Good.* And staring at his phone, that's when he gets an idea.

'Listen, Sally. Melanie's going to help us. To lead the search. But we need to get you by the landline at home. *Urgently.* Amelie knows the home number. If she's lost and tries to ring – to borrow a phone or asks someone to call us – that's the number she'll give. And she'll want to speak to you.' He should have thought of this before. They taught Amelie their landline number years back, but she doesn't know their mobile numbers. Too many digits.

'Your husband's right. We need you at home. By the phone,' the policewoman says. 'So how about I arrange for a police officer, one of the search team, to be stationed right here by your car in case Amelie turns up here. I'll wait until they get here. And you can be right by the phone at home?' The policewoman gets on her radio to make this request officially so that Sally can hear.

Sally frowns. She looks very confused, casting her head this way and that. 'I don't know. I don't know.'

'If she rings, she will want to speak to you, darling.' Matthew feels a frisson of discomfort at the deceit – the straw he prays she will clutch – when deep down, he's lost all hope of something innocent going on here. If Amelie were merely lost, someone would have helped her by now. Phoned the police or approached one of the search team crawling all over town.

At the thought of this, the serious place they're really at, he feels his chest clamp tight. He breathes in deeply, very deliberately. Two long breaths, in through his nose to steady himself.

'OK. I'll go home,' Sally says quietly at last, her tone defeated. 'But no tablets. No sedative. I need to be awake. You mustn't put me to sleep.'

'No one is going to do that, Sally. Now come on. Nice and gently.' At last she lets him approach, dissolving into more sobbing as he helps her up and leads her towards the stairwell. 'My car's one floor down. I'll drive you in my car.'

Half an hour later, not far from home, with Sally silent and slumped alongside him, her head leaning into the passenger window, Matthew is in a daze too. There are too many thoughts crowding his brain. And so much pain and fear crushing his heart.

He is thinking the most terrible thing of all. The new and unexpected possibility that this might all be his fault.

He is thinking of his beloved daughter, his feisty and funny and entirely unpredictable Amelie, and at the same time remembering the precise moment all those years ago when he pledged *never* to have children.

He was in a car then too. Older car, younger Matthew. Parked outside the inquest that changed his life. In that moment, he'd meant it – the pledge. The pact with himself to give up on the idea of parenthood. It wasn't so much that he thought Dawn Meadows would really follow up on her threats. It was more that he needed to punish himself. He didn't feel he deserved to be a parent because Dawn Meadows was no longer a mother . . . because of *him*. And as a young man, it didn't feel too terrible. Or impossible to make that decision. Did you really need the whole family package to be happy?

But that was before Sally, the thunderstorm of Sally. The shock – yes, like a clap of thunder through a dark sky. Bright and magnificent but frightening too.

He turns his head to his wife and takes in the pallor of her skin. 'We're nearly home.'

'I'm still not sure we should be going home.' Sally's voice is barely a whisper. He has no words to comfort her, so afraid that if he says the wrong thing she will become hysterical again as he drives.

Mel has messaged again. It's all official now; she's definitely taking the lead on Amelie's disappearance. He cannot bring himself to even shape the word 'abduction' in his mind. But that's where he fears they are. And he wishes he didn't know the stats; that they don't have long before . . .

Mel's new message says there's a big murder inquiry still ongoing elsewhere in Devon – all the county teams stretched to the limit – so her offer to help was snapped up. She'll message with an update as soon as she can.

There's a family liaison officer assigned already, heading to their home to meet them. Matthew's priority is to get Sally there, back under their roof and under the care of the FLO and maybe their doctor too. Only then will he be able to leave his wife's side and liaise with Mel properly. Get involved. *Do* something.

He feels a terrible pull deep in his stomach as he thinks of her again. His Amelie. Twirling in her new ballet outfit, practising for her exam.

Watch me, Daddy. What do you think?

Alongside him, Sally closes her eyes while Matthew's mind travels back once more to that inquest. The curse. The pledge.

◆ ◆ ◆

He was just a young police officer when it happened. Already making a name for himself. Destined for CID but still doing shifts in uniform, waiting for a vacancy to come up.

On his way back to his car near the end of a shift, he saw a child bolt from a shop ahead of him. Just a kid. No more than eleven or twelve. Matthew – tired and especially conscious of the boy's age – was of a mind to let it go. Check the CCTV the following day to try to find the kid and maybe give him a talking-to. Put him straight with a warning. But the shopkeeper appeared right after the boy. He spotted Matthew across the street and started pointing and shouting for him to give chase. Said the boy had stolen. *Go after him. Go after him. What are you waiting for?*

Shopkeepers back then always wanted action. Prosecution.

Matthew would give anything to go back in time and try to calm the shopkeeper down. Promise to check the CCTV and try to find the kid later. To deal with it all calmly. And appropriately. But put on the spot, he did the only thing he felt that he could do. In public. In the moment.

He ran after the boy . . .

He thinks of the independent inquiry that followed. The questions from the police panel. In the end, he was exonerated of any blame. He was told that his job and his future were safe. He was also offered counselling.

But none of that helped because the bottom line is the boy died. Not because he had stolen. Made a juvenile mistake. But because Matthew chased him and he got scared.

He was just twelve years old. A boy who lost his life over two packets of cigarettes.

The problem is the boy ran around a corner and at first Matthew did not realise the geography. Matthew shouted for the child to stop. Not to be afraid. *I just want to talk. If you stop we can just talk.* But then the boy cut through to an alleyway that led, at the far end, to fencing on to railway sidings.

Matthew remembers the seriousness of the situation dawning on him very fast. He stopped running to try to defuse things. He called out. *No. Stop. Not the railway. It's not safe. Look. I've stopped. I'm not chasing you.* He kept still and put his hands up, but the kid didn't turn round. Instead, he scaled the fence and, despite Matthew's warnings, he jumped down on the other side and immediately darted across the line.

The *live* line . . .

Matthew glances at his hands on the steering wheel. The scars at his wrist.

Getting ready for the inquest, he changed shirts twice, trying to find one with longer sleeves to conceal them. He didn't want the mother to think he was looking for any sympathy for himself.

Matthew was badly burned trying to help the boy. He broke protocol. He was supposed to wait for the line to be turned off. But how could he?

He will never forget the smell.

He saw a long, thick branch not far from the track. It had been raining slightly so wouldn't be dry enough to be safe, but what the hell. He used it to prod, ever so quickly, to push the boy's body away from the live rail.

There was a jolt as he felt the charge trying to pass from the boy's body to his own. A flash and a burning to his right arm and hand. *Damn. No good. No options.*

◆ ◆ ◆

Naively Matthew had hoped that at the inquest the mother would listen to how hard he had tried to help. To stop the boy. To save the boy. But he was not a parent then. He did not understand that particular kind of love. He did not know what he knows now; that the love for a child is all encompassing. Irrational and completely overwhelming. So he underestimated just how terrible it would be to sit in the same room as a mother who so bitterly and completely blamed him for the loss of her only child.

Matthew turns again to take in his wife's face. Grey. Broken.

The verdict had been death by misadventure. Matthew was exonerated by the coroner. Afterwards the mother, Dawn Meadows, stood up and started shouting. First, she cursed the coroner, then the system. Her husband, aided by an usher, tried to steer her from the court. But it was messy. Ugly. Harrowing. She kept on shouting, thrashing her arms and then outside the court she cursed Matthew, pointing at him.

She shouted that she hoped he would never sleep again. She hoped that he would never become a parent. And then she changed the curse.

She said, 'No. No. I hope you *do* have a child and I hope that child dies so you will know what this pain truly feels like.'

Matthew feels a punch deep in his gut as he remembers the terrible feeling that swept through him as she shouted.

◆ ◆ ◆

So is this linked to him? Amelie gone. Linked to his work? His life? That mistake. That *curse* . . .

Fact is, he made a decision, sitting in that car after the inquest, to leave the force and never to have a child.

But then he met Sally. And after the rollercoaster of guilt in the early days of their relationship, he changed his mind.

She changed his mind. *We are allowed to be happy.*

He can't regret having Amelie. The joy that is their beautiful, innocent and perfect Amelie.

But when the weird letters started, even Sally got spooked. They were never pinned on the Meadows. But what if they've all underestimated Dawn Meadows? Were wrong to dismiss her as harmless?

He turns again to find that Sally still has her eyes closed.

His biggest fear now is that this is somehow linked with what happened all those years ago.

Which means this could be his fault . . .

CHAPTER 6

MELANIE – Day One

'Why am I hearing divers may check the canal? Is there something you're not telling me?' Matthew's face, across the table, is ashen as he speaks first.

It's late evening now and Melanie has arranged this update in a hideous café near Maidstead police station. She checks her watch, trying not to let him see just how up against it she feels. That ticking clock.

Also – her dilemma.

'Right. So I promised to be straight with you and I will, Matt, but before we talk about the dive team, you need to make me a promise too.'

Matthew shrugs, eyes uncertain now.

'They're only letting me take this case because I'm not related to Amelie. They do know I know her. That you and I are friends. It's not ideal but fact is a lot of people in the force remember you. They care about you and, in the context, they need me on the case. And providing I'm careful and do everything by the book, we're OK.'

'I'm hearing a but?'

'You can't be involved, Matt. Not directly. Not out there. With the official police inquiry. You're the parent and I get that you're going through hell. But I've promised them I won't let you up close. Interfere. I'm going to find her, Matt, but I can't have you going rogue on me. Interfering. Going anywhere near witnesses or anyone else on your own.'

She means Dawn Meadows but she doesn't say the name yet.

He doesn't reply. He has his nails dug into his palms and she watches him move his hands to his lap.

'I can't just sit back and do nothing, Mel. My daughter is missing. Any parent would be out there looking.'

'I get that. And it's fine to be helping with the general search; to be checking with all of her friends. Her favourite places and all of that. But I'm here to tell you that you have to promise not to act on anything I share with you from the inquiry. Anything sensitive. I have to be sure I can trust you. That we have an agreement. That you won't go off-piste on me. Anywhere near *anyone* we want to speak to.'

Still he doesn't reply.

'I need the promise, Matt. Please.'

'OK. I promise I won't do anything without telling you if you promise to keep me in the picture. Tell me everything. However tricky. Leave no detail out. Agreed?'

Mel feels herself colour. She's not ready to tell Matthew about the more recent anonymous letter. She's escalated the search for Dawn Meadows. She's got Forensics checking the letter again. But she can't face Matthew's reaction. His anger. His judgement. Not until she knows more. Also she's worried he'll go after Dawn Meadows himself.

'Agreed,' she says.

'Now please, Mel. Let me know where we are tonight. Why are the dive team setting up?'

'And how did you hear about that?'

Melanie put the dive team on alert just an hour ago and hadn't expected Matthew to know yet. A water search was normally only approved if a missing person was seen going into water. Melanie was sticking her neck out, authorising it this early on.

'Someone called me, Mel. A mate. I don't want anyone getting in trouble so you know I'm not going to say who . . .'

'OK. Fair enough. But I don't want the press knowing about the dive plans yet.'

'Understood. But they'll find out soon enough; they always do. And you do know this is going to break Sally. She'll see it on the news. I won't be able to keep it from her. So what's going on?'

He's already told Melanie about the state Sally's in. The doctor's been out and Sally finally agreed to a sedative but the mildest of doses. There's no family living nearby and so she's with the family liaison officer, a nice and very experienced woman, but it's obvious Sally won't sleep tonight.

'So is there CCTV pointing to the canal? Please. Tell me straight.' Matthew is unblinking, his eyes pleading with her. It's killing Melanie to see him like this.

'No. The dive team is purely precautionary. Me needing to discount the canal.'

'But why so soon?'

'OK. So, we've got nothing useful from CCTV so far. From the shops or the High Street. We picked up Sally and Amelie walking around the centre of town earlier but nothing beyond them going into Freda's Fashions.'

'That's where Amelie saw the green dress she wanted to try on?'

Matthew's been over and over the details with Sally. Why there wasn't time to try the dress; why Amelie was peeved.

'OK. No judgement. And I share this with love and as your friend. But from the records, Sally was on the phone outside the shop quite a bit longer than she realised.'

Matthew's face changes as if physically hit.

'Like I say, no judgement and I don't think it's helpful to share this with Sally.' Melanie feels anxious. Sal is her friend too. 'We've all been there. It's easy for time to run away when you're on the phone.'

'She said it was just moments.'

'And I'm sure it felt like that to her. But it looks like it was long enough for Amelie to get bored. To get fidgety. So one of the theories, one of the possibilities, is that Amelie went back into the shop to check out that dress again. While her mum was distracted. The reason I'm sharing this with you is we haven't picked Amelie up on any other town centre cameras after that point. Freda's Fashions doesn't have CCTV near the changing rooms. Privacy – blah blah. So we're still checking all the cameras we can find. There's a lot of footage to go through but so far – nothing. It's a hell of a mystery.'

'So why the canal? The dive team on standby?'

'Like I say, there's nothing specific pointing to the canal. No evidence per se; I'd tell you if there was. But there's a direct walkway behind the High Street to the canal and the external CCTV at the back of Freda's Fashions has been tampered with.'

'What do you mean tampered with?'

'Someone put a bag over it, Matt. It's a high camera. They must have climbed up on to a wall to do it as far as we can see. But it means we don't have footage to discount Amelie being on the towpath behind the shop, alongside the canal. There's a rear door to Freda's Fashions. It's a fire door. Alarmed. Supposedly just for staff emergencies but one of the first uniforms on site opened the door and no alarm went off, so it's just possible Amelie used it. Not likely – I'm not saying this is my theory – but it is possible. So we have to check it; I'm just ticking boxes, Matt. Because we can't pick her up on any other cameras and because I can't confirm she wasn't by that canal—'

'Dear God. What are you saying? You think Amelie took the dress? Bolted out the back door. Fell in the canal?'

'No, no, Matt. I'm not saying that's my theory; I'm just doing my job and discounting things. One by one. So that we can work through the list of possibilities rationally and methodically and find out where she is. What's really happened.'

Sally watches Matthew's face change again. He looks down at the table, his expression appalled, then back up at her, this terrible new fear in his eyes.

'This will kill Sally. The dive. Seeing the divers on the telly. I don't think it's occurred to her to worry about the canal. Christ. I don't know if I can handle the thought of this.' Matthew looks away and has to take deep breaths in and out. Melanie observes his right hand, back on the counter and shaking. The plastic tabletop is dirty. Needs a wipe. She finds it almost unbearable. His shaking hand by the sticky marks of someone else's coffee.

'Take a moment, Matt. Breathe slowly. Remember that I'm just trying to rule out every possibility. I don't have any firm evidence suggesting Amelie has fallen into the canal. That's not what this is. We have ground teams out checking every garage, shed, outbuilding. Everywhere. She may have hurt herself. Got trapped somewhere by accident. Who knows? But I've put the dive team on standby too, waiting for my clearance. If we have no leads from the ground search, no sightings or CCTV overnight, I'll order that sweep of the canal. They'll do a grid search. It's not that deep, so I'm hoping it won't take too long. It's just to *discount* that possibility; to know precisely where we are as we move on.'

'Why would someone disable that camera?'

'It could be nothing to do with Amelie. Someone up to no good. Dealing drugs on the canal path. Who knows what?'

'Do you think she's been taken, Mel?'

Melanie's shocked he's said it so bluntly. So soon. He looks shocked himself as if he didn't mean to say it yet.

'I don't know what's happened to her but I'm going to find out, Matt. I'm going to find her for you.'

'And you're going to check the Meadows? Dawn Meadows? Yes? Tonight? As soon as possible? I mean, you remember what she said at the inquest. The letters.'

She's been dreading this. The discussion about Dawn Meadows. Melanie and all of Matthew's friends tried so hard all those years ago to change his mind about leaving the force after she cursed him at the inquest. No one believed what happened was his fault. *Any one of us would have done the same.*

'I'm going to check *everything*, Matt. You know how this goes. You know the job. You know the list I'll be working through.'

'Including the Meadows? Asap? Top of your list?' He's leaning in, checking her expression.

'Including the Meadows. Yes. We're already on that.' She wonders if he can read her face. Tell that she is holding something back.

Matthew looks relieved and she doesn't add that it's not straightforward. No current address for the Meadows. Driving licence details out of date. Neighbours having no idea where they moved. She doesn't tell him about the new letter, even though Tom is right: she should have told him the moment it came in.

She thinks of Matthew and Sally's home. The extension to their open-plan kitchen with the huge sliding doors on to the garden. All the suppers they've shared there. The clinking of wine glasses. The fairy lights strung around the room at Christmas time, Amelie and George laughing and playing. She imagines Sally all alone there now, the family liaison officer trying to persuade her to get some sleep.

'There's something else I need to ask you. Something difficult.' She takes a long, slow breath. She has been dreading this above all else. 'I wouldn't ask if it wasn't really important, Matt.'

He doesn't speak and so Melanie plunges on.

'The dive will attract more media coverage, which is a good thing so long as we control the narrative. Someone must have seen Amelie. There's been some good coverage online already. We've sent out media appeals for the late news. People want to help. There's a list on social media with people offering to join the search. But tomorrow, if we have no news, we need to step up a gear with the coverage. I've talked about this with the team and we're all in agreement. We need *everyone* checking their phones. Their selfies. We need everyone who was in town and especially in Freda's Fashions to see Amelie's photograph. To help us find her.' Mel tucks her hair behind her ear. 'So I want to do a press conference tomorrow afternoon. In time for the evening news.'

'A press conference?' He sits up straighter. 'OK, yes. Good idea. I can do that.'

She looks away for a moment and then straight at him.

'It's better if it isn't you, Matt.'

She holds his gaze as his expression changes, the horrible truth dawning.

'Oh no, no, no. I can't ask that of her. No way. Sally's not up to it, Mel. If you'd seen her in the car park.'

Melanie can't begin to know how much it must hurt. The pain. The waiting. She doesn't want to do this, but Matthew knows how this goes. If the roles were reversed, he would be saying the exact same thing: *Get the parents on camera . . .*

'Please let it be me.'

40

'You know why that's not a good idea.' Melanie still believes it's a long shot for Dawn Meadows to be involved. But just in case, it's too dangerous to put Matthew on television. 'We don't know this has anything to do with Dawn Meadows but she *is* a suspect. And if she's involved, it could be triggering to see you on television. I'm not risking it.'

'Right.' Matthew looks away, closes his eyes. 'But I don't know how I can ask this of Sally.' He speaks very slowly. 'Imagine it. Up there – in front of the cameras . . . On her own?'

He squeezes his eyes tighter. 'It'll kill her.'

CHAPTER 7

SALLY – DAY ONE

Sally is lying on the sofa near the sliding doors looking out from the kitchen on to the empty swing in the garden. She's clutching Bunny, Amelie's precious pink rabbit, and puts it up to her nose.

It's not a good smell and in the past she teased Amelie about this. Begged her to let her pop Bunny in the washing machine again. But in this moment the stale smell of dust and old dirt brings a new wave of guilt.

Sally feels tears coming again. What was she thinking, worrying about how a toy smelled? What did it even matter? She breathes it in again and pictures her daughter holding it tight in bed at story time.

'Do you want a cup of tea? Or coffee?' The voice is from across the kitchen. The FLO – family liaison officer. Milly or Molly, Sally can't remember.

'I washed this rabbit once. I shouldn't have done that.'

'I'm sorry?' Milly or Molly frowns and Sally wishes she could ask her to leave. Wants to be alone. But Matthew said he's not allowed to liaise with Mel unless Sally has someone with her. In case there's news. A phone call. An update.

Or maybe they think she might harm herself if she's left alone? Is that what they think?

'This rabbit. Amelie's rabbit. I washed it once and she was furious.'

Sally remembers Amelie's face at breakfast. She was about three, maybe four, and Sally had secretly washed Bunny overnight, expecting her daughter to be pleased to see the pink fur all bright and fluffy again. She wasn't. *It smells like the washing machine now. I hate you.*

'Mine's like that over his whale. He has a large, blue, furry whale. Stinks.' Milly or Molly has tilted her head, the kettle whirring into action behind her. 'I put it in the freezer sometimes. That's supposed to help with germs apparently.'

Sally feels a small smile deep inside – she hadn't realised the policewoman was a mother – but the smile doesn't reach her face, her muscles frozen somehow. She looks up to take in the FLO's expression. Soft. Sad.

'I'm sorry. I didn't catch your name properly. Is it Milly?'

'Molly. Don't worry. It's the shock. Brain fog. I'll make more tea. Yes?'

'Thank you. So you have a son?'

'Two boys. Six and eight.'

'Right.' Sally feels her lip quivering, fighting the jealousy. A rage that this woman's sons are home safe, one of them tucked up in bed with a blue, furry whale while Amelie . . .

She felt the same jealousy when she messaged all the mothers taking children to the birthday party Amelie was supposed to attend. She was grasping at straws, hoping there might be someone who knew something. *Had Amelie mentioned anything to any of her friends?* It drew a blank. The mothers were in shock. Sally told them to go ahead with the party. Not to frighten the children. But

43

in truth, it broke her to think of it. The games. The balloons and the cake. Amelie's party bag unclaimed.

The kettle clicks. Molly puts a tea bag in each of two mugs and pours water in both. Sally can almost hear Matthew saying *the milk should go in first*. They used to argue about that but not anymore. He always drinks coffee these days.

'My husband's a bit of a coffee snob. Not fond of tea.'

'Yes. I noticed the machine. Very impressive.' Molly glances at the espresso machine in the corner. Gleaming chrome. Sally remembers Amelie watching her father frothing milk for a cappuccino.

When will I be allowed coffee?

'I can't imagine what you're going through, Sally, but I promise you we have the best team doing everything they can. We're going to find her.'

Sally finds herself nodding. 'It's the not knowing,' she says finally.

Tiredness overwhelms her and she lies back down along the couch. She closes her eyes, suddenly aware of wetness on her cheeks. She hadn't realised she was crying again but finds that she doesn't care. She hears Molly's footsteps and the click of a mug being placed on the small table in front of her, but she does not open her eyes. She has no energy left to be polite or brave; to be anything at all. In her mind she can hear Amelie's voice and the words she cannot bear: *Where are you, Mummy?*

CHAPTER 8

MELANIE – DAY ONE

It's late and dark. Melanie zips up her puffa jacket. She has two layers underneath but is still surprised at the cold. A bitter wind. She reaches into her pocket and is relieved to find gloves, putting them on as she approaches the dive team's van.

Melanie has Raynaud's syndrome – a condition that makes her fingers and toes go white in the cold. She was once offered tablets by the doctor but didn't bother. She manages the condition with gloves and good socks but she hates it if people see when she forgets to wrap up. Ugly fingers. Like the digits of a corpse.

She pulls the wool of the gloves up her wrists and glances around. Further along the bank there's a team of three, one of them already in a drysuit, the others checking the equipment, all in animated discussion. Good. There will be tests and risk assessments and all manner of palaver before anyone can go in the water but it's good they're getting ready. No sign of any gawpers, or worse, media, but she's not sure how long this will go unnoticed. Dive teams always draw a crowd.

The van doors open and she recognises the dive supervisor immediately. He looks older than she remembers. Hasn't seen him in a while. Less hair. More lines.

'I thought you didn't like the cold?' He's smiling and Melanie smiles too, but not for long. And not a real smile.

'I appreciate this, Ed. Cracking on so quickly for me tonight. I know it probably feels a bit early in the investigation but I can't move anything forward on this one until I know. With that CCTV camera disabled.'

'Sure. We all have kids, Mel. I wasn't short of volunteers. It's not a huge stretch of water and it's not that deep.'

Mel again turns her head to take in the divers, just visible from her angle along the bank. She wonders how they manage this with family life. The long hours. The cold. The dark.

It was the cold and the Raynaud's that put her off that one time forever ago that she volunteered for an introductory day, fresh out of police college. She had wondered if she might try for the dive team herself, maybe even pitch for the full course. But no. One day was quite enough.

'You remember that training day you did with us?' Ed's looking at something on the computer screen inside the van as he speaks.

'How could I forget? Never been so cold in my life. I have no idea how you do this.' Melanie's fingers took an age to return to a normal colour that day but she's surprised that Ed remembers. He didn't mention it on the phone when she asked him for this favour. To turn out the team as fast as possible.

'You would have got used to it. The cold. We told you that.'

Melanie pulls her coat tighter around her. 'Doubt it. So how are we doing?' She resists the urge to look over his shoulder, instead putting her gloved hands in her pockets.

'Just finishing the pre dive checks and then we'll put the first diver in. As I say it's not too big an area so we'll get going and keep you posted.'

'And it's OK to work in the dark like this? You don't need to wait for first light? I don't want to be making it more dangerous—'

'Like I told you on the phone. Visibility down there is so bad with the silt, it makes very little difference. It will be a fingertip search so we may as well get cracking. Let the family know one way or another.'

'Exactly my thinking.' Melanie wants this canal ruled out so she can crack on. There's nothing from the ground teams and no one home at the last-known address for Dawn Meadows in Cornwall. Neighbours still saying they moved long ago. Priority now is to find the Meadows and check all those on the local sex offenders' register. Plus the press conference for a big media push.

'You want a brew? Just making tea for the gang.'

'No thanks. Still prefer coffee. The good stuff.'

'Well, I won't offer you instant then. It's one of those giant economy packs.' He's smiling again as he finishes up on the computer.

'I'll just say hello to the guys before they go in.' Melanie nods and steps down from the van to move along the canal bank to the team now testing the safety line for the first diver.

'DI Melanie Sanders. In charge of the investigation.'

They all turn their heads to acknowledge the introduction.

'Ma'am. Good to see you.' It's the team member not in a dry-suit who's speaking.

'You can call me Melanie. Just wanted to thank you for this and to wish you the best. Always difficult when it's a child missing.'

The three men all nod and Melanie watches them continue with their preparations. She suspects only one diver will go in initially. There are rules about how many are in the support team on the bank and each piece of kit has to be meticulously checked.

She still remembers vividly her introductory day. She was taken first to a swimming pool for stamina training. Fifteen lengths and then various exercises with the air tanks. One of them involved sitting on the bottom of the pool, wearing weighted belts, sharing air from a single tank, the mouth piece passed from one to another. It was designed to prepare you for a possible emergency if air in one tank ran out or a system failed. She was told to keep calm but she remembers the panic, holding her breath and counting as she passed the mouth piece over to the next person.

After the swimming pool stint, she was taken with the team to a reservoir to watch the complex set-up procedure. That was when Ed, more junior back then, turned up to show her all the equipment checks and explained the on-site rules. She wasn't allowed in the water but they let her try on a full drysuit and even getting changed was freezing. Awful. She spoke to everyone about how they managed. The cold. The dark. Did they get afraid underwater?

She realised pretty quickly, white fingers and all, that it was not for her, but she knew it would be useful for her other plan – a future in CID – to understand how the dive teams worked.

'I think I'd get claustrophobic.' Melanie finds that she's saying this aloud, alongside the canal, just as she did all those years ago on that introductory day. 'And much too cold. I admire what you do. I want you to know it's appreciated.'

'Thank you, ma'am.' The guy on the bank smiles. 'Melanie, I mean. We'll do our very best for you.'

Melanie nods and walks back along the bank to the van, poking her head around the open door to say goodbye to Ed.

'I'm off now. My thanks again for this. You've got my mobile? Ring me the minute you get anything. Anything at all.'

'Sure. Are you staying at a hotel? If I can't get the mobile.'

'Technically. Strictly between you and me, I might have a sleeping bag in my boot so try the office if you can't reach the mobile.'

'So the rumours are true?'

'What rumours?'

'Workaholic. Grapevine says you're supposed to be on holiday.'

'Yes, well. He's a friend.'

'So what's he like, this Matthew? I googled him. How he left the force. Sad.'

'Yes, it was all very unfair. He was a great officer.'

'And how's he holding up?' Ed's tone and expression are much more serious now.

'He's one of the good guys, Ed. And he's *really* struggling.'

'Tough for you then? Being his mate, I mean.'

Melanie doesn't answer. Just nods. She turns to the water. She pictures Amelie at her last birthday party, playing in the garden. George and Amelie squealing with delight at the small bouncy castle set up on Sally and Matthew's lawn.

She watches as the breeze makes ripples on the dark surface of the canal. Closes her eyes.

CHAPTER 9

MATTHEW – Day One

Matthew has been driving around Maidstead in the dark. Street by street. Round and round in circles. *Nothing.* It's close to midnight. He's now about ten minutes from home when a panic sweeps through him so sudden and so overwhelming that he's shocked to feel not just light-headed but unsafe. His eyes blur. His heart pounds. He is used to stress and is accustomed to managing fear in his job, but this throws him so badly, especially the blurred vision, that he's afraid he may lose control of the car.

He screeches into a lay-by, a lorry roaring past him, as the car comes to an emergency stop throwing his body forward, his heart pounding ever faster. He leans back in his seat and closes his eyes to find Amelie in her pink rabbit slippers carrying a puzzle in a box, staring at him.

Daddy, will you help me? It's too hard . . .

He feels sweaty but is paradoxically shivering too. He tries to remember the day with the puzzle. Ah yes. Sally at the Rayburn stove, sorting out a casserole for the slow oven for supper. He was on the way to work. Too busy. *We'll do the puzzle tonight, honey. Daddy's got to go to work.* Guilt now melds with the panic pounding through his body. He opens his eyes and tries to slow his breathing but can't seem to get any air into his lungs.

He tries to find the picture of Amelie again but she's gone. He presses the button for the electric window but the cold night draught makes no difference. In the end, he gets out of the car and stands, leaning with both hands pressed against the window frame, his head bowed, hoping that stretching out his chest might help with whatever this is.

It doesn't.

For a few minutes, he just stands, huffing and puffing. He feels both terrified and ridiculous. He's still feeling light-headed and has no choice but to wait until his breathing at last starts to steady. He waits some more until his heart rate slows also before standing up straighter.

He's disoriented. Embarrassed. Afraid. He closes his eyes but there is only darkness. Amelie still gone. He feels a punch in his chest. His heart?

Is he having a heart attack? Is that it? Or some kind of panic attack? Possibly. He's not sure because he's never had a panic attack before. Didn't think he was the type.

He is worried it will happen again, possibly with other people around. And what good is he to Amelie like this?

He remembers advice to breathe into a paper bag but who has a paper bag on hand? He decides it was maybe a bad idea to stand up and gets back into the car, leaving the window open.

Suddenly and most shockingly, he's crying. At first, he is just conscious of tears on his cheeks. A surprise because Matthew does not ever remember crying. He did not even cry when Amelie was born.

Next, his shoulders are rolling and he's not just crying but sobbing like a child, his whole body shaking. This goes on for quite

51

a time and he has absolutely no choice but to wait for the rush of emotion to pass.

When at last the crying stops, he closes his eyes tight, disorientated still as he wipes his face with the palms of both hands. He looks at the clock on the dashboard. Very nearly day two. Sally will be expecting him. Needs him. But she can't see him like this. It will frighten her. No one must see him like this, not because he's afraid to look weak but because he's afraid to *be* weak when his daughter and his wife both need him to be strong.

What he really wants to do is to drive to Cornwall right this minute and hunt down Dawn Meadows. He wants to search her house and any outbuildings and find out if she has some other property or lock-up. He wants forensic teams crawling all over her whole family. He wants to look her in the face and shout at her. *Where is my daughter?* The problem is he knows that he can't do this without betraying Mel's trust, even blowing the whole inquiry. Mel says she's on it. She's a good friend and the best cop he knows. And in any case, he's already tried to find Dawn Meadows on social media and through all the usual search channels and he's drawn a complete blank. Mel will have better resources. She may already know where she is and have sent someone to do the initial interview and check. He'll ask her directly tomorrow when they do the update on the ground search and the dive.

Matthew closes his eyes again, thinking of the dive. A range of different scenarios play in his head – possibilities that don't involve Dawn Meadows. Amelie slipping into the water. Amelie being pushed into the water. But Amelie can swim so wouldn't she be OK if she fell in? Next, he thinks of how cold water can be. How quickly someone can be overwhelmed by the cold. He thinks of muscles freezing. Water being swallowed – the thought so unbearable that his pulse quickens again.

He puts his seat belt back on and checks his face in the mirror, wiping his eyes with his sleeve. He needs to pull himself together and get home to Sally. Be there for her. To help her through this awful first night.

He picks up his phone to text Sally, warning he'll be home later than he said. Next, he pulls out of the lay-by, again checking the clock on the dashboard. Two minutes to midnight.

The problem is he knows too much.

Matthew knows that if Amelie has been taken by Dawn Meadows, there is a chance – just a chance – that they can find her and save her before Dawn panics and does something terrible. But if Amelie, God forbid, has been taken by a random predator who means real harm then the stats are terrible.

The majority of random predators who are inclined to kill do so within the first two hours.

Matthew hears a terrible noise escape involuntarily. Something like a howl. Something that echoes around the car and sounds as if it's coming from another body, not his own. He listens to the echo and understands the panic attack. It's this very thought he's been trying to suppress.

This terrible fear that it's already too late.

CHAPTER 10

MELANIE – DAY TWO

When her phone rings, she awakes to complete disorientation.

Melanie instinctively reaches left but there's no bedside table. She opens her eyes to unfamiliar shadows and it finally dawns where she is. She's put the seat cushions from two chairs on the floor to make a rough bed in the side office of CID. She reaches down to the floor for her phone and sits up, her back protesting. It's cold. The heating's off.

'We've found something, Mel.' It's Ed's voice, the dive team supervisor.

Melanie feels a wave of shock. The phone says 4.10 a.m. She'd expected the dive to *rule out* the water.

'A body?' The words make her stomach flip.

'I'm afraid so,' says Ed. 'It's in what seems to be a shopping trolley in a deeper part of the canal. But we don't have any details yet. I'm sorting the recovery right now. I thought you'd want to know straight away.'

'Thank you. I'll come straight down.'

'Be warned, these things are tricky and we need to proceed carefully. I'm putting a second diver in right now to do an extra assessment before we move forward on the recovery.'

'In a shopping trolley, you say?'

'The diver says it seems that way but the visibility's terrible down there. This is all from fingertip searching. He was right at the end of his permitted dive time so I had to pull him out. The only thing he can say for sure is it's a body. Long hair. Ponytail. He had to come back up before he could do a proper assessment.'

'OK. I'm heading down to you. Update me when I arrive.'

Melanie ends the call and pulls up straighter to try to ease the pain in her back. A shopping trolley?

For a terrible moment she envisages Amelie larking about. Riding in the trolley? Maybe playing with some other kids. A prank going wrong? The scene plays out in her head. The horror of the trolley rolling into the canal. But it somehow seems so unlikely. Not like Amelie at all. She's a sensible girl. Mature for her age.

She looks at her phone and thinks of Matthew. She wants to know if Amelie was wearing her hair in a ponytail when she disappeared but she daren't ask. Daren't ring. Matthew will want to know why she's asking.

Will guess.

CHAPTER 11

SALLY – DAY TWO

Sally's staring at the ceiling, longing for dawn. For light. For the phone to ring. *We've found her. She's OK . . .*

In this darkness she keeps replaying every moment in Freda's Fashions. Amelie's face. The bad feeling between them over the dress. *We don't have time. Put it back . . .*

She turns her head to see that Matthew has his eyes closed but she knows he's not asleep either. She can tell from the way he's lying. Matthew does this weird thing when he's asleep. He puts his finger against his nose as if to open his airways better. Maybe it's to try to stop himself snoring. Whatever, he's not doing that now. He's still dressed – sweatpants and a T-shirt, pretending to be asleep to try to encourage her to rest.

'Shall I make tea?' She sits up as she speaks. Sally's still dressed too. Leggings and a jumper. They climbed into bed in their clothes at about 2 a.m. as if being dressed would make the phone call more likely. The need to rush to the car to pick Amelie up.

Matthew turns his head. 'No, no. I'll get it. You stay here.'

They hold each other's gaze and she's not surprised that he doesn't urge her again to rest. What's the point? He's said it over and over, as has the family liaison officer, but they all know there can be no rest until they find Amelie. Sally fears there's going to be a lot of lying down and pretending to sleep.

She reaches to turn on the bedside lamp and watches as Matthew rolls from the bed and slowly leaves the room. She watches the way he moves, sluggish and unfamiliar. It makes tears prick her eyes, step after leaden step, like spooling forward decades to see Matthew move as he will as an old man.

She waits as he clicks the door closed and then she stares at the ceiling. The family liaison officer is due back at breakfast time. How long? Sally checks the time on her phone. 4.30 a.m.

She didn't tell Matthew but earlier she googled the role of a family liaison officer and was horrified to see that they are normally assigned when someone is dead. She'd wanted to scream. To tell Molly to get out of her house. That Amelie is . . . not . . . dead. But she found another article that explained they're sometimes assigned in cases of abduction or kidnapping and that made her think other dark thoughts. So they do believe that Amelie has been taken? By Dawn Meadows? Or someone else.

Sally shuffles up to a sitting position and pulls an extra pillow behind her back. It's cool in the room, the heating off, and she pulls up the duvet. She's thinking about the first time she saw Matthew all those years ago. The horrible ups and downs when they first met.

Her friend Beth had hired him to help them find an old school friend, Carol. They'd lost touch over a traumatic event in their childhood when they were at boarding school together. Matthew helped them not only to find Carol but to put it all right. Their secret. Their trauma.

Sally had bought this cottage, along with three more in a terrace, from an inheritance and redundancy pay-off. The properties were pretty much uninhabitable, but Matthew helped her with the renovations. She was surprised how handy he was. Anything bar electrics. Turns out his dad was a builder and he'd often helped. So Matthew did some of the work himself and helped her find good tradesmen for the rest.

They clicked instantly and fell in love very quickly too, and then there was this horrible time when he inexplicably pulled away. Suddenly told her it was over.

She fell to bits. It was Beth who challenged him. Made him come clean over why.

The boy who died . . .

In the end and very reluctantly, he shared it all with her. How he'd decided not to become a parent after the shock and the shame of Dawn Meadows shouting and cursing him outside the inquest. He felt guilty. To *blame*. That he didn't deserve parenthood after Jacob Meadows' death.

Sally listened and they talked and talked. And eventually over time he changed his mind. Or rather she changed his mind for him.

Sally sniffs and closes her eyes. She remembers the look of fear on Matthew's face when she told him she was pregnant. How he would worry about her as her belly swelled. *It's going to be all right, Matthew. We're allowed to be happy.*

She wonders now how she could have been so naive. Is this her fault? It was terrible what happened to Matthew when he was in the police, but no one felt that boy's death was his fault, apart from the grieving mother, and she, poor woman, could be forgiven for madness in the moment.

But she's had nightmares ever since the anonymous letters started. As Amelie's grown, she's had more and more dreams, worrying that she miscalculated over Dawn Meadows. Was wrong to dismiss any risk. Imagining and dreaming of this very thing happening . . .

At last Matthew appears, carrying two mugs. 'I've put the heating on. Freezing downstairs.'

'Is it all my fault?' She is staring, unblinking. 'Persuading you we'd be all right. To have a family. That Dawn Meadows was just temporarily mad with grief. That it would pass. I know they said those horrid letters weren't from her. But what if they *were*?'

He doesn't answer.

'Do you really think this is Dawn Meadows?'

CHAPTER 12

MELANIE – Day Two

In the car, Melanie's rehearsing in her head how to say it. She won't let anyone else tell them.

In college they were trained how to share bad news. To be kind and careful but also to be direct. Spit it out. Don't use euphemisms that will confuse people.

I'm very sorry to tell you that Amelie's been found. It's bad news. The worst. I'm afraid she's dead.

The rehearsal, the grim words echoing in her head, are too much. Melanie feels terrible shame for, in this moment, losing hope. She presses hard on the accelerator. It's nearly 5 a.m. and there's no traffic. She needs to know.

Is it Amelie?

She thinks of how little Ed was able to share from the dive. *A ponytail.* Did Amelie still have long hair the last time she saw her? Her dark hair is long in the photo Sally shared with them for the inquiry. The same photo Melanie was planning to use at the press conference later. But sometimes kids that age get their hair cut. Want a bob. Deep down she's hoping that Amelie has had her hair cut. Clutching at straws. But Matthew would have mentioned a change in hairstyle, wouldn't he? She made the right call, not to contact Matthew yet.

But a part of her wants to call her husband. For his support and to share this with him first, including the guilt over allowing herself to think the worst. But talking to Tom would be every kind of wrong. If the body in the canal is Amelie, Matthew and Sally must be the first to know. Also she thinks of the hour. Tom and George are still fast asleep in their Airbnb with family in the New Forest. Without her.

She pulls herself back to the inquiry. Back into professional gear. A shopping trolley? Was this disposal of a body after a crime? A wave of nausea hits her. But why a shopping trolley? Is that why the bag was placed over the CCTV camera in advance? A premeditated crime?

She needs to speak to Ed again. She's already messaged the coroner's office but needs more details to press for a pathologist on site pronto. She wants the works. Forensics crawling all over this. No stone unturned. Ed has texted that he's getting a tent on site to conceal the body from any media that may get wind while they wait for 'the team', but it will be getting light soon. They won't be able to keep this under wraps for long. The early dog walkers will be out before you know it.

And then, as if reading her mind, the phone's ringing, linking immediately to the hands-free media system. It's Ed.

CHAPTER 13

MATTHEW – Day Two

Matthew did a terrible thing when he fell in love with Sally.

He's sitting on Amelie's bed as he thinks of this. Amelie's double bed with its pink-striped duvet and fairy lights around the headboard. They bought the double bed only recently. Amelie's idea. More room for a friend for sleepovers. More room for a snuggle at story time. But in truth it was all about more room for the growing jungle of soft toys that Amelie so loves.

Matthew looks across to the cork board with pictures of Amelie in her ballet outfits. Big smile. Big frothy pink tutu. *You have to turn your feet out like this, Daddy. It's hard. You can't point them forwards.*

He closes his eyes.

His mind drifts and he thinks again of the terrible thing he did when he fell in love with Sally. Back when he was new to PI work, struggling to adjust after leaving the force.

He'd turned down counselling over the boy's death on the railway line. He couldn't see how talking would change anything. He'd been exonerated of any blame and praised for his courage in trying to get the boy off the live rail. But that hadn't changed how he felt.

Deep down, Matthew has always blamed himself, just as the mother at the inquest did. Why didn't he remember there was a railway line? Anticipate what the child might do in his blind panic?

When he fell in love with Sally, so fast and so unexpectedly, he experienced his own mad panic. He discovered that she'd come out of a bad marriage; that her ex had cheated on her. He also found out that she'd lost a baby in the traumatic mix of the separation and still longed very much to be a mother.

It all felt too much.

He didn't feel he deserved to become a parent himself, so he decided he was not the man to make Sally happy. That she deserved better.

And so Matthew did something stupid. And terrible. And cowardly.

He broke up with her by text.

Matthew squeezes his eyes tighter at the shame of it, smoothing his hand across Amelie's duvet and lying down on the bed. It was Sally's friend Beth who called out his terrible behaviour. Beth who had booked him in the first place to try to find their estranged friend Carol. Beth who then mistakenly assumed he was a man with commitment phobia. She stormed round to his office, fuming on Sally's behalf.

Matthew remembers so vividly how hard he tried to make Beth leave. He didn't want to tell her the truth about the boy who stole the cigarettes. He remembers reaching out to keep his hand on the middle drawer of the desk. The drawer in which he still kept a file of all the newspaper cuttings from what happened.

He held the wooden handle to the drawer tighter and tighter but there was this terrible stand-off. Beth simply refused to leave so in the end he gave in. Opened the bloody drawer and threw the file of cuttings across the desk. He told Beth about the pledge he'd made. He was not cut out to be any kind of family man. Not deserving of that particular kind of happiness.

Beth's face was completely white as she read the cuttings. And then she began pacing the room, gabbling that he must go to Sally and tell her. And that if he didn't do that, she would tell Sally herself. *They all say it wasn't your fault. The inquest. The inquiry. They said you were very brave, that you risked your own safety. You need to talk to Sally about this. She'll understand. She'll sympathise. Help you . . .*

'The boy was twelve, Beth.'

◆ ◆ ◆

Matthew suddenly hears through the wall the water running in the en suite bathroom next door to Amelie's bedroom. He hadn't realised it could be heard this clearly through the wall. Amelie's never mentioned it. Maybe she likes the comfort of hearing them padding about in their bathroom late at night. Early in the morning?

He urged Sally to take a shower in the hope it might comfort her. The warmth of the water.

He thinks of her in the shower and thinks of her face that night after Beth called at his office. It was quite late when he finally found Sally in the garden of this very house. The row of thatched cottages she'd bought on such a whim after she lost her job. He really didn't want to tell her what he'd done – the boy's death – but he couldn't bear the thought of it coming from Beth either.

Sally was sitting at a garden table, drinking red wine in the dark. Just the distant light from the kitchen and moonlight catching her bracelet as she lifted her glass.

She warned him that she was on her third. She sounded angry and told him to leave her alone, but seeing her eyes, he felt even more ashamed of how badly he'd handled it all.

Over the next few hours, after he had told her everything, Matthew knew his life would never be the same. And that fear was perhaps always going to be a part of it. Somehow, he unpicked all his promises and pledges and slowly slid into this whole new and dangerous space where he dared to let himself believe what Sally was saying.

You are allowed to be happy, Matthew. You can't punish yourself your whole life for something that was not your fault. That's ridiculous.

He was in this weird state for a long time after that – flipping between exhilaration and blind fear.

Matthew turns again to the ballet pictures. Sally has been obsessing about Amelie's new ballet shoes. Something about sewing on fresh ribbons . . .

A long and terrible sigh leaves his body. He feels so tired. A zombie-like state as if his brain cannot send instructions to his limbs fast enough. Slowly he lifts his head to take in the row of toys on the shelf above Amelie's desk. Pink Bear, so named for obvious reasons. Bought on a zoo trip, he can't remember where. Penny – a favourite doll with curly auburn hair.

I wish my hair was curly like yours, Daddy. Will you ask Mummy if I can use the tongs? She won't let me use her tongs. I'll be careful, I promise.

He glances to the side, to all the cushions on the bed, and realises Sally must still have Bunny, the pink rabbit, with her. He pictures Amelie in her white pyjamas with pink hearts, knees pulled up and hugging the bunny to her chest, chattering away before a bedtime story.

Thinking of her is unbearable and yet paradoxically all he wants to do. He needs to be thinking of her every second to keep the connection. To hold on to all the details of her. The strange freckle on her earlobe that Amelie says is the sign she's old enough to get her ears pierced.

It's to show the person where to put the hole, Daddy.

No way. You're too young for pierced ears. Not yet.

He needs to think of her constantly, however much it hurts. To be sending out his love and his determination like a beam in all directions to *find* her. Speak to her. *We're coming, Amelie.*

Matthew takes out his phone from his pocket. He wants to call Mel to see if there's any news, but he sees the time. Just past 5 a.m. If there's no good news soon, he's going to have to talk to Sally about the press conference.

He's suddenly aware of a new silence. The soft noise from the shower next door has gone. He waits until Sally appears in the doorway. His stomach flips.

'What is it?' She's trying to read his face. Sally can always read his face. 'Is there bad news?'

'No, no. There's no news. But there is something I need to tell you. Talk to you about.'

Sally looks wary and sits on the bed.

He doesn't want to say it. He thinks again of her out there in the garden on her third glass of wine all those years ago. Hurting. Why is he always hurting her when he loves her?

'Mel wants to hold a press conference today. And she thinks it would get better coverage if . . .' He breaks off, taking in Sally's exhausted face.

'Go on.'

'She would like one of us to be at the press conference.'

Sally frowns. 'What? In front of cameras?'

'Yes. There will be cameras there.'

'So do you feel up to that?'

66

Matthew closes his eyes and lets out a huff of air. Of course, she thinks it will be *him*. That he wouldn't ask her. Shouldn't ask her.

'They don't want it to be me. Just in case Dawn Meadows is somehow involved. They think it would make things worse.' He watches her eyes widen, the awful truth sinking in.

'They want *me*?' Sally stands up. She starts casting her head about just as she did in the car park. 'No, no, no. I can't do that. You know I can't do that.'

'It's OK. It's OK. I told them it would be too much for you. Sit down again. Don't worry. I'll ring Mel.'

'So why did you ask? Why did you even ask me?' Sally starts pacing. Matthew is terrified this will trigger another bad episode. Emotional overload. Like in the car park. But Sally keeps pacing and frowning and finally turns to stare right at him.

'So are you saying it would help? Do they think it would *really* help? Is that why you asked?'

Matthew can hardly bear this.

'Would it help? Tell me the truth.'

'You don't have to do it, Sally—'

'Be straight with me. *Please.*'

'Yes. It will probably get more coverage if you're there.' He hates himself for saying it. Wishes he could row back and unsay all of it.

Slowly Sally sits back down, tears now wetting her cheeks, the bunny up to her nose. 'Then I don't have any choice, do I?' Her eyes are wide and she looks bewildered. As if imagining what it will be like. All the photographers. TV cameras. She glances away to Amelie's books on the shelf opposite and then back at Matthew.

'So you're really saying that you *need* me to do this. Is that what you're saying?'

CHAPTER 14

MELANIE – Day Two

As she parks her car, Melanie's thinking of everything she's learned about bodies in water.

There are so many variations. All the ifs and the buts. Ask Forensics and everything apparently '*depends*'. On the depth. The temperature. The kind of water. At sea, most bodies eventually surface, even those tied and weighted. Something to do with gases. Melanie turns her head and clamps her eyes shut.

She realises as she feels to take the key from the ignition that she hasn't dealt with a body in a canal before. Ed says the water wasn't especially deep in the area behind the shops. What does that mean for what's been found? And silt. How does silt impact evidence?

She wants to hurry and yet for a moment cannot move. Melanie remembers watching a television programme once where cavers were looking for the remains of an abducted girl. They discovered a bag hidden deep in a cave and found that for a while they simply could not bear to open it. She understands now. Wanting to know and at the same time dreading the confirmation.

Suddenly there's a tap on the driver window and Melanie starts. Ed's staring through the glass. He steps back as she gets out.

'I was just about to ring you again. I've been looking out for the car.'

'Do we know who it is?' Melanie's voice cracks.

'No. But it's not Amelie.'

Melanie clamps her eyes tight again. Hand to chest.

'You OK?' Ed's tone is gentle.

'Just need a minute.' Melanie coughs. Lets the wave of relief course through her. *Not Amelie.*

She breathes in and out, opening her eyes again. She reaches out to put her hand on the top of the car door to steady herself. Finally, she finds her professional gear again, embarrassed for Ed to see this. She shuts the car door and fires the lock. 'Sorry. It's just difficult when it's—'

'Sure. We all understand.'

'So what do we have, Ed?'

'Adult male. We only confirmed that when the second diver went in. Ponytail threw us. And being wedged in the shopping trolley made it difficult to assess size that first dive. We have the body out now and we've got a tent up. Definitely an adult male. But no ID that we can find.'

'OK. Right.' A pause. 'I'm waiting to confirm a team on site. What can I share?'

'Well, like I say, he was in a shopping trolley. On its side and in a bundle. Blankets and the like. That's what kept the body underwater. But not tied. The rats have had a go.'

Melanie grimaces.

'Sorry, boss. Just preparing you.'

'OK. Any guess how long in the water?'

'You know how tricky water is, but I'd say not that long. Couple of weeks maybe? Pathologist may have other ideas.'

'OK. Thanks, Ed. And has the team finished checking the rest of the canal?'

'Yes, we have. No other bodies. Amelie's not in that canal.'

'Good. Thank God.' Melanie starts marching alongside Ed, back towards the dive team van. As they turn the bend, bringing the towpath into sight, Melanie sees a bright light moving on the opposite bank.

'That's the bad news.' Ed is following her gaze as he speaks. 'Local TV crew. They turned up about five minutes ago. Still setting up their gear.'

'Terrific. All we need.' Melanie's mind starts racing. The media are going to presume from the evidence tent that it's Amelie. Put out something damaging. Something speculative that Matthew and Sally might see. She glances around, realising that no amount of police cordons can fix this, given the location. Cordons are already stopping access to this tow path and the other side too, but she can see more clearly in this early light that there's a housing estate further back on the opposite side of the canal. The land slopes upwards. It's probably possible to see the dive team's activity from some of the upstairs windows in the distance. Early risers will have seen the tent go up. Worst-case scenario it will be on social media very soon.

'We tried our best to get it all done in the dark, Melanie.'

'I know and I appreciate that. I'll ring the press office. Figure out how we're going to handle this.' Melanie tries to calm her voice.

Truth is, she's thrown. There are big decisions to be made now. And quickly. This new crime, if it is a crime – a murder? – needs full attention. Respect and manpower. But it's a curveball she could do without.

The force is already stretched. They barely have the resources to search for Amelie and now they have a possible murder victim in the canal. Right behind the very shop where Amelie was last seen. Is that a coincidence?

Melanie goes over the facts again, narrowing her eyes. So was the man in the canal murdered or was it a bizarre accident? And does it have anything to do with Amelie? It doesn't feel that it does – this man most probably died before Amelie disappeared. But what about the bag over the CCTV camera? The coincidence of the geography?

Quite frankly, she has no clue what's going on. Only one thing's clear. It's too late for the man in the shopping trolley.

Her priority remains Amelie. She has to assume the little girl is still alive.

But it's day two.

The clock is ticking.

CHAPTER 15

SALLY – DAY TWO

Sally is sitting on a green sofa in an office next to the press room. Through the wall, she can hear the rumble of conversation and occasional metallic clunks as if chairs or equipment are being moved.

'You don't have to do this.' Matthew takes her left hand, her right still clutching Amelie's rabbit. 'I've told you. Right until the last moment, you can change your mind. Isn't that right, Melanie?'

Melanie forces a small smile but she doesn't say anything.

Sally meets her gaze and understands. Yes – she's been assured she can bail but the bottom line is they need her to do this. They need the publicity and they need the media on their side. They don't want Matthew up there on the microphone in case Dawn Meadows really is involved. In case seeing Matthew upsets her even more. Or upsets whoever else might have their Amelie.

This public appeal cannot be about the police. Or grudges. Or anything linked to the force. This needs to be about Amelie and Amelie alone. A little girl. An *innocent* little girl.

'Should I take the rabbit in or—?'

'Whatever you're comfortable with, Sally.' Melanie's voice is almost a whisper. 'You want me to go over the format with you again?'

'Yes please.' Sally realises Melanie has been over this twice already but she's struggling to hold information in her brain. It's the not sleeping.

'Up on the platform there will be me and you and the head of the police communications unit. Lisa. You met her earlier over coffee.'

'Right. Yes. Lisa.'

'I will speak first and do an update on the inquiry. Explain we now have two live investigations. I'll recap all we know about Amelie's disappearance. Our appeal for witnesses and photos. Anyone who might have taken selfies or photos in Freda's Fashions and the surrounding area. And then I'll do an update on the body of the man we found in the canal. After all of that, I'll say that you have something you wish to say yourself.' Melanie pauses. 'You have your piece of paper?'

Sally is suddenly panic stricken. She looks down at the sofa. Feels about. No paper. 'I don't know. I don't remember.' She went through it all earlier with Matthew. Wrote it down. The right things to say about their beautiful girl. Not too much. Not too little. But where the hell did she put it?

'It's OK. It's OK. It's in your pocket. Remember? Your jacket pocket.' Matthew's eyes are wide as he speaks.

Sally feels in her pocket and sure enough there it is. The single sheet of A4 paper printed off at home earlier and folded ever so carefully into four. She opens it out slowly and reads it silently.

All we want is for our beautiful girl to be home with us. She has a ballet exam coming up and she needs to practise for that. She has new shoes – pink satin – and I've sewn on the ribbons for her. Put the shoes ready on her bed.

Amelie is the sweetest little girl. She's like a ray of sunshine in the world and without her, our life is very dark right now. Please. Please help us to get her home. If you know anything or saw anything at all, however small or however inconsequential it may seem to you, please contact the police. And if anyone watching this knows where Amelie is, I'm asking you as a mother. Begging you as a mother. Please send her home to me.

Suddenly the door opens just a little and Lisa, the tall communications woman with a short pixie cut, leans into the room. 'How are you all doing? No hurry but we're ready if you are?'

Melanie looks at Sally, eyebrows high, and everyone waits.

'Like I said before – if it's too much.' Matthew's voice breaks as he speaks.

'It's fine. I'm nearly ready.'

'Matthew will watch on the screen in here. Like we agreed. Is that OK, Sally? I'll be with you with the media the whole time. Right next to you. We won't allow questions. Not to you directly. After you've read out what you want to say, Lisa will lead you out and I'll take questions after you've left the room. You can watch that with Matthew back in here.'

Sally nods. 'Sure. Just one minute, please.' She feels in her pocket again to source the wrapped biscuit. Pink foil. She unpeels the biscuit – chocolate coating with shortbread and caramel – and takes tiny bites, chewing slowly. It's a small biscuit but seems to stick in her throat. Takes an age.

'The sugar,' Matthew says, glancing at Melanie. 'We thought it would be a good idea. A sugar hit before she goes through.' He's watching Sally as she chews, eyes heavy with worry.

'Yes. Good thinking.' Melanie smiles and waits until Sally finally clears her throat and sips from the water on the table next to the sofa. 'There's more water where we'll be sitting. Ready?'

Sally takes a deep breath. 'Ready.' She stands as Matthew steps forward to hug her close, kissing her forehead and squeezing her free hand. 'This is so brave, Sally. I'll be watching. Right here, waiting for you.'

Lisa leads the way with Melanie walking alongside Sally, who clutches the pink rabbit ever more tightly as they enter the press room.

Sally has seen this kind of thing on the news and Matthew warned her it would seem quite noisy. And chaotic. The photographers and the TV crews. She thought she had understood all of this but still the clicking of all the cameras is a shock. It doesn't stop. A constant roll of clicking as they take up their seats. She was shown the room earlier but it's so different now with all these people. Every seat taken and some people standing at the back. It's much brighter too with the glare from lights alongside the TV cameras.

At last they're all seated and Melanie follows her plan, thanking everyone for attending, introducing herself, Sally and Lisa and then moving on to the update. She explains there are now two inquiries. Amelie's disappearance and the body in the canal. There's no evidence to link them but they're appealing today for information for both investigations. Sally finds that it's difficult to listen. There is still so much clicking, some of the photographers moving to get pictures from different angles.

She glances down at her sheet of paper, practising the words in her head. Melanie's voice seems distant for a while and then there is a pause. Sally senses everyone looking at her. Melanie and Lisa too.

'I was just explaining that you have something you want to say.' Melanie's voice is gentle and encouraging, obviously repeating herself.

'Oh yes. Right.' Back in the room now. 'Yes, I do.' Sally clears her throat and reads carefully from her paper. 'All we want is for our beautiful girl to be home with us . . .' As she talks, she thinks of the pain on Matthew's face as he watched her stitching the ribbons to the new ballet shoes in the early hours.

Why are you doing that now? There's no need to do that now . . .

At last she finishes reading out her statement. There's a lot more clicking and Sally clears her throat, refolding the paper ever so carefully and waiting for Melanie's cue to be led from the room, but suddenly there's a man standing in the third row.

'So do you think this may have anything to do with your husband's work? The coverage *recently of his return to the force?*'

'*Please.*' Melanie's tone is firm. 'We'll open the floor to questions in a moment. But Amelie's mother needs a break. I'm sure you understand. Lisa?'

Lisa stands and moves along the platform to wait for Sally to stand also before steering her from the room. Sally feels flustered, conscious that the TV cameras are moving, the lenses following her, but tries very hard to walk slowly. Worried about tripping.

She manages to fight back the tears until she is in the small office next door. Where she collapses into Matthew's arms.

'Bloody media.' He holds her tight. '*Bastards.*'

CHAPTER 16

MELANIE – Day Two

They let the questions run over – nearly fifteen minutes. Melanie is keen to get back to see Sally and Matthew; to thank Sally in particular for being so brave. But soon after they share the graphic with the dedicated phone number for the Amelie inquiry and the body in the canal mystery, one of her sergeants appears in the room.

Sam, an experienced detective in his forties who's heading up the push to find the Meadows, walks up on to their small stage and whispers in her ear.

'He's phoned in.'

'Who?'

'Adam Meadows, Dawn's husband, has just phoned in.'

Melanie tries to keep the shock from her face, aware that she's being filmed. All efforts to find the Meadows have so far drawn a frustrating blank. The couple moved years back and failed to update their driving licences. No offences. No benefits and no pensions. Nothing on the system to help trace them.

'OK. Well, again – can I thank you all for coming. And thank everyone for helping with this inquiry.' Melanie is standing as she speaks. Lisa stands too, taking the cue. Sam leads the way to the door, Melanie and Lisa close behind.

'Right, so what exactly did Adam Meadows say?' asks Melanie in the corridor.

'Simon took the call. He said that he's been expecting contact from us and would rather get it over with.'

'And Dawn?'

'He says he and his wife split up a long time ago and he has nothing to hide. He doesn't know where Dawn is these days but is certain she has nothing to do with Amelie's disappearance.'

'Well, he would say that, wouldn't he?' Melanie narrows her eyes.

'Interesting that he phoned in, though.'

'Maybe he was expecting us to put out their names at the press conference. Where is he living now?'

'Rugby,' Sam says. 'Long drive.'

'Right. We leave immediately and I'd like you to come with me.'

'No problem.'

'And we've got local police booked to search his home meantime?'

'Yes. All in hand. The super's handling the warrant application, so we can get straight on the road. Just in case he's tricky about a full search.'

'Good.'

'As soon as that comes through, the Rugby team's briefed to check everything. House. Outbuildings and to look for any work premises. Lock-ups and so on. Adam was a builder, though we don't know if he's still working.'

'Excellent.' Melanie's impressed with Sam. So much is in motion already. She wonders if he had plans for this evening and feels a pang, thinking of Tom and George. Her own little family on holiday without her.

She checks her watch, eager to get going, but first she has to see Sally. She marches along the corridor to open the door to the neighbouring suite where Sally and Matthew are waiting.

'Sorry about that question, Sally.'

'Oh, that's all right.'

'You did great.'

'Really?'

'Absolutely. You really helped us. Helped Amelie. We're getting lots of calls already. Also offers to assist with the ground search, so it couldn't have gone better.'

'Any leads?' Matthew is pinching his bottom lip with his fingers.

'Early days. But listen, I've got to go. Get myself up to speed with the team as the calls come in.'

'Has something happened?' Matthew looks suspicious.

'No. Just important I'm with the team. I'll ring you if we get anything solid.' Melanie would love to tell him that Adam Meadows has come crawling out of the woodwork, but she daren't. She knows Matthew too well. He'll get in his own car and try to find him, whatever promises he's made not to interfere.

Five minutes later she's in her car, Sam alongside.

'So were local police thrilled to handle the initial search for us?'

She knows how stretched all forces are – most struggling to handle their own caseload, let alone help out other forces.

'Actually very helpful,' says Sam. 'I guess when it's a kid, every-one parks the politics. They have my details for the update and Mr Meadows will be told you're on the way; that you also want a word.'

'Good.'

Melanie smooths her hair back from her eyes as she indicates to turn right, nearing the slip road to the dual carriageway. The team had discussed whether to mention the Meadows in the first press conference. A difficult call, but Melanie decided, without any real evidence, that it would be wrong to suggest them as key suspects to the media. It was also legally tricky and could put the focus of the appeal in the wrong direction and stop someone phoning in with some other important lead. Also, it could be a dangerous trigger for the Meadows if they *were* involved. So this call from Adam Meadows is a gift, solving her immediate problem. The urgent need to count them in or count them out.

Melanie's mind is whirring, wondering how long it will take to search Adam's home. How soon they might get a call. If he's still a builder, it could be trickier as he might have access to a number of properties. They'll need to be thorough. She has also left instructions for her team to update her hourly on all the calls from the public received after Sally's appeal. It's going to be busy.

'Best news is I brought snacks,' Sam says suddenly, opening his backpack. 'Quality sandwiches and chocolate biscuits.'

'I'm sorry. I don't allow eating in my car.' Melanie keeps a straight face and watches Sam's horror. She concentrates on the road for a while, enjoying his misery. He's tall and wiry. Probably has hollow legs. High metabolism like her husband Tom who always has a snack in his pocket. Finally she breaks and shares a small smile. 'Sorry, Sam. Joking. Couldn't resist it.'

Sam lets out a huff of relief. 'Grief! Got me there. Without snacks, I am a monster. Was warned you're not one for meal breaks.'

'Whoever told you that?' Melanie's smile broadens. She's well aware the team has clocked her sleeping bag in the office.

'Chicken and bacon with mayo or tuna salad?'

'You choose.' Melanie glances at the sat nav.

Three and a half hours. The search warrant should come through quickly, given it's a missing child.

Melanie starts to make a plan in her head for when she meets Adam Meadows face to face. What to say, what not to say. She feels the familiar shot of adrenaline. A child's life is in danger. She can't afford to get this one wrong.

CHAPTER 17

MATTHEW – DAY TWO

Back at home, Matthew checks his watch for the umpteenth time. Seven minutes to the main evening news. Six. Five. He glances across the room to Sally, who's sitting, legs crossed, with her right foot flicking up and down.

They're in the kitchen extension, both with iPads in hand, scrolling to check all the news updates online since the press conference. The amount of coverage is good but it's still harrowing and utterly surreal to see Amelie's smiling face on so many news sites, her bright blue eyes looking straight at the camera. Not just the local papers but national papers too. And although they know that this is the best way to get their little girl back safely, the reality of it is still a shock, even to Matthew, who knows more than Sally how these things usually play out.

'Will it make the national news, do you think?' Sally seems to feel his gaze but doesn't lift her head as she speaks, eyes still fixed on her iPad as she continues to scroll.

'Yes, I think it will. Which is good from Mel's point of view and ours. The more people who are helping the better.'

'So you really think this might help find her?' Sally has looked up now, her face drawn. Eyes exhausted, Amelie's pink rabbit alongside her on the sofa while Matthew is sitting on a wooden chair at the dining table.

'We have to hope so. We have to stay positive, Sal. For Amelie. You were very brave up there and a lot of this coverage is thanks to you. You heard Mel say how many calls were coming in.'

'Yes. But I was a bit surprised she disappeared so sharpish. Has she texted since?' Sally looks wary as if trying to read his face as he answers.

'No, but I expected that.' This isn't entirely true and he feels himself colour. Fact is, Matthew was equally surprised by Mel's hasty exit but he's trying to work through the range of positive explanations. She said she'd text an update but there's been not a whisper. 'She'll be working through all the calls. Sifting through the information and prioritising what they need to act on first.'

'Act on?'

'Investigate. It's just how it works after an appeal.'

'Right.'

The silence is interrupted by Sal's phone ringing, which startles them both, eyes wide. They react to all texts or calls like this now. Mouths dry. Hearts pounding.

Sally stares at the screen of the phone on the sofa.

'Is it Mel?' Matthew can't help himself.

She shakes her head. 'No. It's *Carol*.'

Sal's expression is one of apprehension as she takes the call. Carol is the old school friend Matthew helped her find all those years ago when they first met. Carol lives in one of the adjoining cottages but is on an extended break in France. They haven't seen her in over a month.

Is it true, my darling? I've just seen it on the BBC website. Can't believe it . . .

Sally has the volume up high and Matthew can hear Carol's voice, all alarm, bleeding into the room.

'Yes, I'm afraid it is.' Sally starts to cry and has to clench her eyes tight and clear her throat before she can continue. 'We can't believe it either. Matthew's here with me.'

Oh, Jeez. I'm sending you all my love and I'm going to come back home to be with you. Soon as I can get a flight . . .

'No, no. There's no point doing that. We're busy with the police and everything. There's going to be an appeal on the news tonight. We're hoping it will make the national news. Get more people helping.'

So who else is with you? Beth's in New Zealand still, isn't she? Does she know?

Matthew watches Sal's face in the long pause. He's torn. Beth and Carol are Sal's closest friends but both have been away travelling lately. Sal could do with more support. Sal's mum moved into a nursing home six months back. She has a heart condition and dementia and they've agreed not to tell her about Amelie yet, worried about the effect of stress on her health. The staff have been warned to keep her away from the news tonight.

'It's OK,' says Sally. 'I have this family liaison woman. She's a bit – I don't know. She means well. And it means I'm never alone.'

Right. It's decided. I'm getting a flight first thing in the morning. No arguments. I'll get there as soon as I can, darling.

Sal starts to sob, reaching into her pocket for a tissue.

'Thank you,' she manages.

They'll find her. Stay strong, my darling. They'll find her.

'OK. I'm going to have to go now. We need to watch the news.'

OK. I'll message tomorrow when I land. A pause. *All my love to you both. I'm thinking of you constantly and wishing I was there already.*

'OK. We'll see you tomorrow.'

Sally ends the call and puts the mobile back on the sofa alongside her before Matthew has any chance to share his misgivings. No time now to work out what to say; what to do about Carol. He uses the remote to turn on the television, quickly adjusting the volume. Too low at first.

He moves to sit next to Sally on the sofa, transferring her phone to the side table to make room. The first story is flooding, which has killed more than fifty people abroad. And then the second story . . .

Sally gasps as Amelie's face is full frame on the television. *Police are appealing for help to find an eight-year-old girl who vanished while shopping with her mother.*

Matthew reaches for his wife's hand and they sit in silence through the coverage, including a live link, on the flooding story. The misery on-screen is terrible and Matthew feels uncomfortable that he can feel only agitation. No emotional bandwidth left to connect with this other tragedy. He finds he is tapping his hand on the arm of the sofa until at last the newsreader turns to the story of the missing little girl.

There is a picture of a smiling Amelie behind the newsreader. A quick summary of the story and then a full report with pictures and clips from the news conferences and several more photographs of Amelie. The one they first gave police and then more snaps that Sally chose later for the appeal, including a favourite of Amelie in her ballet outfit, dancing.

Matthew can see a tear rolling down Sally's cheek and can hear her strained breaths. He squeezes her hand a little tighter as the reporter's voiceover suddenly mentions his name. They now show *his* picture and the narrative references his work history – leaving the force after a 'tragic case which involved the death of a child' and then the recent coverage of his decision to *rejoin* the force and work again alongside his colleague DI Melanie Sanders who is now heading the inquiry to find Amelie. There is now a piece to camera, the male reporter in a dark navy coat in the pouring rain outside the police station. Black umbrella.

Police are not commenting on whether past cases may be at issue with this inquiry. Or whether reaction to Matthew Hill's decision to rejoin the force is in any way a possible line of inquiry . . .

Matthew feels the blood drain from his face and there's suddenly a strange tingling in both his arms. The reporter continues to summarise details of Matthew's career, the pitter-patter of rain on the umbrella increasing so that he has to raise his voice.

'Why are they saying this? I don't understand.' Sally's tone is genuinely incredulous. She turns to look at him briefly and then moves her gaze straight back to the television, frowning. 'This isn't helpful. Surely this isn't helpful?'

The report then returns to shots of the news conference. A close-up of Sally holding Amelie's rabbit. A clip of her speaking and then shots of her slowly leaving the room. The voiceover repeats the appeal for information of any kind and there is a graphic with Amelie's picture alongside the dedicated phone number.

'That's good. It's good they're repeating the appeal with the phone number again.' Matthew tries to keep his tone positive for Sally but his heart is still racing. Mel will be as upset as he is; she'd hoped by keeping him away from the press conference that his background wouldn't be mentioned. The only relief is the reporter didn't detail the threats that were made at the inquest. Lawyers would have vetoed that, he suspects. Libel risk.

'It's not good, is it?' Sally repeats. 'It's not good that they mentioned you rejoining the force as potentially relevant? Showed your picture. What if Dawn Meadows is watching?'

CHAPTER 18

MELANIE – Day Two

Melanie sits very still a moment before closing the news app on her phone. Alongside her, Sam shifts in his seat.

'It's great they kept the graphic on-screen so long. With the phone number.' Sam's still looking at his own phone, trying to spin it. Lift her spirits.

'Yeah – but why the hell did they mention Matthew rejoining the force? Everything we don't need.' Melanie badly needs to discount Dawn Meadows from the inquiry. But what if her gut is wrong and she *is* involved? That press conference will not have helped. Might have wound her up.

'You reckon the husband will have seen it? The coverage?' Sam glances at the shiny green front door several houses down. Adam Meadows' place is only just within sight, given the bend in the road. They had to park up close by to catch the news, having been held up by an accident on the motorway. Even putting out a plea to traffic police locally for support hadn't helped. A lorry had jack-knifed, and the priority was getting the fire brigade through.

'Of course he will have been watching. Right. Before we go in, there's something I need to share.' Melanie feels her stomach tense.

It's a risk showing Sam the most recent anonymous letter. He'll wonder why it's not up on the incident room board, but she has no choice. She spools through her phone and holds up the screenshot. 'This is an additional anonymous letter that came in to me after the media stories about Matthew Hill joining my new team.'

She watches Sam reading the letter on-screen.

> Matthew Hill is a child killer. You take him back on your team and you will all be sorry.

'Jeez. That's a bit stronger than the other letters. How come it's not on the digital file?' Sam turns to her, his expression wary. He's bright and Melanie trusts him, but she needs to be careful.

'Forensics found nothing again. Probably posted in Dorset. But no prints. It was put aside as more of the same. Nasty but probably harmless. You know how much hate mail we get.' Melanie feels herself colouring. 'Point is, I don't want this getting out to the media so I'm keeping the details of this letter tight for the moment. I don't want it leaked and splashed all over the front pages.'

Sam frowns. 'But we need to put it to Dawn Meadows. We need to—'

'Of course. Which is why I'm showing you. I'm going to talk round it to Adam Meadows but I don't want to give him the words. I want to spook him. And I want something up our sleeve to trip Dawn up when we find her. You OK with that?'

'Sure.'

'Also Matthew Hill hasn't seen this letter yet.' Melanie is speaking very fast, trying to cover her discomfort. 'And I don't want it leaked to him either. With the state he's in. So just between the two of us for now. Yes?'

'OK, boss.' Sam still sounds wary.

'So let's do this. Let's look this Adam Meadows in the eye and see what we think.' Melanie removes the key from the ignition and springs from the car so quickly that Sam only just has time to shut his own door before she fires the lock.

Adam Meadows' property is impressive and once she's standing in front of the green door, Melanie realises it's not what she expected. A large, double-fronted property with bay windows, smart shutters and carefully manicured box trees in large pots on either side of the door. Adam's construction business must be doing OK. All the same, she'll get the team to check his finances.

As Melanie rings the doorbell, she thinks of the update from the local force. The search found nothing in the property and Adam Meadows was apparently calm under initial questioning. The local team sent the draft statement through. His story is that he and Dawn split up years back. They have no contact and he has absolutely no idea where she is. He only phoned in *to get this all over with*.

Melanie gets out her badge as they hear footsteps on the stairs inside. Adam Meadows, when he finally answers the door, is older than she expected. Melanie holds up her badge, quickly doing the sums in her head. He'd be fifties but looks sixties.

'DI Melanie Sanders. Are you Adam Meadows?'

'I am.'

'I understand you were told we'd be calling. Can we come in?'

'If you must. I've had hours of it. Your bloody search teams. What did you expect? That they were going to find that little girl hidden away here?' He scoffs as he swings the door wider. '*Seriously?*'

Melanie walks into the hallway, followed by Sam. They wait at the entrance to the sitting room. 'In here OK?' Melanie asks but Adam Meadows just shrugs his shoulders.

The sitting room is large with a black wood burner and a curved open-sided basket stacked with logs alongside. Two large matching sofas in deep burgundy are set around a rustic coffee table. All very tasteful. Expensive looking.

'May we sit?' Melanie tilts her head.

'Please yourself. But forgive me if I don't offer drinks. Like I say, I've had quite enough of all this today. Just want to get this over with.'

'So – remind me again why you phoned in, Mr Meadows?'. Melanie sits on one of the sofas. She immediately regrets the decision. The sofa's lower than she expected. Adam Meadows remains standing.

'I saw it online about the girl missing. It mentioned her dad. Matthew Hill. And I guessed you'd start pointing fingers at Dawn, so I thought I'd nip all that in the bud. As I say, I just want to get this over with.'

'And why exactly did you think we might point fingers, as you put it?'

His head twitches and he finally sits. 'Let's not play games, DI Sanders. We both know why you've driven here.'

Melanie pauses, taking in his expression. She can't quite make out his mood. Anger or just exasperation? His face is strained but difficult to read. There is clearly a lot going on underneath as if there is some internal struggle, but that could be hurt rather than guilt.

She decides to wait. Alongside her Sam does the same, both of them just staring at their interviewee. It takes a while but at last he speaks.

'Matthew Hill stole my life, DI Sanders.' Adam Meadows is staring at her, unblinking. 'First, I lost my boy. Jacob. And then I lost my wife. I have my faith now. That sustains me – but pardon me for not being a fan of the police.'

'I'm sorry for the loss of your son. A terrible tragedy. But you knew we would need to do a search, Mr Meadows. After all the threats your wife made. And the letters which were sent.'

90

'My wife never sent those letters. You never proved they had anything to do with her.' He pauses. 'Look. My wife was ill with grief. She didn't know what she was saying back then. And me?' He looks away to the bay window and then back. 'My life unravelled because of Matthew Hill. But, like I say, I have my faith now.' He glances to a small crucifix above a bookcase in the corner of the room. 'I don't wish anyone any harm. Certainly not a child. Quite enough sadness already, thank you very much.'

Melanie can feel Sam turning his head towards her as she watches Adam Meadows who's still staring at the crucifix.

'I hear from your initial statement that you and Dawn split up a couple of years after your son died.'

'That's right. She couldn't get past it. Couldn't find a new purpose. Other than anger.'

'At Matthew Hill.'

'Yes. At Matthew Hill. At me. The world. Everything.'

'Why at you?'

'Because I was with her every day, I guess. And I didn't handle it brilliantly myself at first. There was a bit too much drinking.' He turns to look back at Melanie. 'I'm not proud of that.'

'And the drinking. How bad did that get?' Melanie tilts her head.

'No violence if that's what you're implying. I'd never hurt anyone, least of all someone I loved. But I did withdraw into myself, which must have been hard for Dawn.' He pauses. 'I'm told it's not unusual. Couples breaking up after the loss of a child.'

'Again. I'm very sorry for your loss.' Melanie looks once more at the photograph of Jacob Meadows on the mantelpiece. A big smile. His school tie all askew. All at once she's thinking of her son George. Unbearable thoughts that she tries to push away. But next there's the crushing thought of Sally and Matthew. The weight of what might lie ahead for them.

Melanie clears her throat and sits up straighter. 'Can you tell us more about the break-up?'

'I went to my doctor about the drinking. Got help. And through the counselling, I got back into church. Used to go as a kid. Found it comforting. The thought of an afterlife. For Jacob, I mean.'

'And Dawn?'

'She was very anti. Very bitter. It was hard for her to believe in anything. We ended up arguing about that as well.'

'About your renewed faith?'

'Yes. It wound her up.'

'Wound her up how?'

'She felt there couldn't be a God who would let a child die the way Jacob died.' Adam Meadows closes his eyes and a deep frown distorts his face. 'I tried to explain that's not how God works. But it just caused more fights.' He opens his eyes.

'So she was still angry and bitter when you parted?'

'I guess you could say that.'

'So it's perfectly possible that she did send those nasty letters. May even have sent some *more* letters? She may have stayed more angry at Matthew Hill than you realised. Maybe that anger spiralled after you parted. Every time he's been in the news—'

'I get where you're going with this but I'm telling you, you're wrong.' He takes a deep breath. 'Dawn wouldn't have anything to do with this. With the girl being taken. The divorce was sad. I felt bad about it but I needed peace. I couldn't stand the fighting. I just wanted calm. I couldn't help Dawn and in the end we just couldn't be around each other. We split things fifty-fifty. Dawn made it plain she didn't want to stay in touch. No point. Too painful, she said.'

'We need to speak to your wife urgently. There's no trace of her on social media. Do you not have any mutual contacts? Mutual friends? Her relatives? Can you think of anywhere she might be?'

'No. I told you. We've had no contact.' He's looking once more towards the window. 'She had a sister in New Zealand. She said she might go there but I don't know if she did. They had a falling-out in the past. Typical sisters. I have no idea if it was just talk – moving to New Zealand.'

'You have a name and an address for her sister?'

'Anne Peters. Christchurch. But I don't have an address.'

Melanie watches Sam writing in his notebook. 'Anyone else?'

Adam shakes his head then looks at the floor before taking a deep breath.

'Look. My wife lost all hope after Jacob died. She lost faith in life itself. But she didn't mean those threats she made. She was eaten up with sorrow. I tried to help her get past it, to accept what happened to Jacob as a horrible accident. But she just couldn't do that.' A pause. 'She ended up on antidepressants. She was like a totally different person. But she wouldn't hurt anyone. She didn't take that little girl.'

'You seem very sure of that. How can you be so certain?'

'Because all that anger came from loving her child so much. You can't love one child that much and want to hurt another. You just can't. You're wasting your time if you think Dawn had anything to do with this.'

Melanie continues to ask questions, taking in Adam's slightly robotic replies, all the while Sam making the official notes. After about fifteen minutes, she asks about his building company.

'Any current projects? Working on any sites?'

'No. Fully retired now. As I say, Dawn and I split things fifty-fifty. We sold our house together and I bought this one. It was a wreck. I didn't do much to it while I was still working. But once I wound the business down, I put all my time into this place.' He glances around. 'Doing up this house was my last project. I told all this to the local police earlier.'

Melanie hands over her card. 'Well, we'll stay in touch, Mr Meadows. And if you think of anything. Or if you hear from Dawn—'

'I won't hear from Dawn.'

'She might see it on the news too?'

He shrugs. 'If she does it will simply stir very sad memories, as it did for me. That's all. She won't ring me.'

'And yet you phoned us.' Again Melanie watches him really closely for his reaction.

'Just being a good citizen. Getting it over with rather than waiting for you lot to bash my door down,' he says. 'I'm regretting it now though because you're not listening, are you? You're determined to bark up the wrong tree.' He pauses to smooth imagined crumbs from the knee of his jeans. 'It's very sad this little girl is missing. Very sad. But it has absolutely nothing to do with us.'

CHAPTER 19

SALLY – DAY TWO

'So why the hell didn't you say something while she was on the phone?' Sally's staring at Matthew, hardly able to take in what he's implying. 'You're seriously saying the police will see Carol as a *suspect*?'

'No. I'm not saying that. What I'm saying is that they will want to question her to eliminate her from the inquiry, which will be upsetting for everyone, especially for Carol. I'm just preparing you. Warning you.' Matthew pauses. 'You're right. I should have warned her when she called but the press conference was just about to come up on the news—'

'I don't believe this.' Sally's head is spinning as she tries to take this in properly. Matthew has turned away as if watching something in the garden. 'No. Please. I need you to look at me.'

Slowly he turns back, his expression strained. Sally looks straight into his eyes. 'Tell me the truth. Do you think Carol could be involved?'

'No, I don't think that personally.' He holds her gaze. 'But you must see that Mel will have to be told of the history. What happened.' He thinks of the baby. Of it all over the news all those years ago, just like now. 'Otherwise, I will lose her trust. This is protocol, Sal. We can't not tell Mel.'

'Protocol?! You point the finger at one of my best friends, who has been to hell and back, and you call that protocol?'

'Please, Sal. I'm not pointing the finger. I'm just being straight with you. Let's not do this, not now—'

They both fall silent. Both still standing. Matthew keeps facing her but looking at the ground, his eyes closed, and so finally Sally takes out her phone. 'Right. I'm calling her. Telling her not to come. I'm not having her put through all that. No way.'

She tries to dial but the call won't connect. *Damn.* 'Looks like she's switched the phone off. Sal checks her watch. 'Maybe she's already at the airport. Has put it into flight mode. So what do we do?'

Matthew looks up and opens his eyes. 'I'm so sorry, Sally. But there are procedures. Rules. It's tricky for me.'

'But why? We both know that Carol has nothing to do with any of this. So why can't we just keep quiet? Spare her the trauma.'

'We can't do that.'

'Why not?'

There is this terrible pause in which Matthew scrapes his hand through his hair. His tic. The signal that he's totally exasperated.

Sally finds that she's on the verge of crying again and she's now the one to turn away. It's too much. Thinking of Amelie. *Where are you?* And now on top of that horror, she has the worry of what Carol may be put through just for trying to be a good friend.

For a terrible moment Sally travels back to that hotel room all those years ago. The moment in which she and Beth found out the truth about their friend Carol. She remembers the complete and overwhelming shock of it all.

She can picture the baby in the cot. The disbelief. But most of all she remembers her fear. How brave Beth was and how terrified she felt herself.

Call security. Call the police . . .

She turns back to look again at her husband, remembering his part in their history with Carol – how much he helped them – and she realises the worst thing of all.

That he's absolutely right.

She should have thought this through the moment Carol rang; she should have made some excuse. Spared her.

It doesn't matter that in her heart she knows that Carol would never harm a fly. The police will see it differently. *Mel* will see it differently.

She should have told Carol *not* to come.

CHAPTER 20

MELANIE – Day Two

'You want me to take a turn at the driving?' Mel is spooling through her phone while also checking the time. It will be late when they get back to Devon but she has a lot more to catch up on with the team. Several have volunteered to stay on. The offer to drive is merely polite and Sam will know this.

'No. You carry on. I'm happy to drive.'

'Correct answer.' Mel is still looking at her phone as she speaks but from the corner of her eye catches Sam smiling. 'I'm going to check in with Ali.'

'Fine. But do you mind if we do a drive-through? I'm hungry.' Sam is checking his watch before glancing at the sat nav.

'You really do have hollow legs, don't you? How the hell do you stay so slim?' Melanie has found in the last few years that she can't eat the way she used to. She's not fond of the gym and has surprised herself by trying a sequence of faddy diets. Low carb. Low fat. Low food . . .

'Metabolism, guv.'

'Melanie. Call me Melanie.'

'Sorry. Lucky genes. So a drive-through's OK? Within the next half hour?'

'Sure. But park up and eat fast. I don't want to watch you eat and drive. No offence.'

'No problem.' A pause. 'And by the way, would you mind awfully if I just call you guv or boss? It's just—' Sam takes a deep breath. 'I don't know. Maybe I shouldn't say this but . . . no, forget it. I shouldn't say it.'

'Boss is fine if you prefer. But not guv.'

'Thanks, boss.' He's smiling again.

Melanie speed-dials the incident room and it's Alison, a DS, who picks up. 'Hi, Alison. Melanie Sanders here. We're heading back from Rugby. Please share that I'm grateful for the team putting in the extra hours. No need for everyone to stay but has anything else come in since my last call?'

'Actually I was just about to phone you, ma'am.'

'Boss. Please call me boss.' Again she catches Sam grinning alongside.

'Sorry, boss. It's just we have an incident developing. Only just escalating. I've bumped to the super here and he's called in the press office. They were about to phone you.'

'OK. So what's happening?' Melanie bites into her bottom lip.

'Vigilantes. Out on the Park Estate. There's a crowd, a dozen or so with more joining them, outside the house of one of the men on the sex offenders' list. Word on social media is someone has a petrol bomb.'

'Oh great. So who is it? And is he home?'

'I'm sending you all the details right now.'

'Are uniforms there? Anyone in imminent danger?'

'We've got him out. Someone was tipped off about trouble brewing so we took him to a safe address earlier. One of his relatives. The house on the Park Estate is empty. It was searched when we were checking all the local suspects day one. But the crowd don't believe the team on the ground. Uniforms and the fire brigade are on site. The super's heading out to make a statement as the media are apparently turning up.'

'Terrific.' Mel narrows her eyes, aware of the sarcasm in her tone. A complete nightmare that the superintendent is having to handle this. It should be her. She doesn't regret travelling to do the Adam Meadows interview herself but given it's led them nowhere yet, she's frustrated to be so far from HQ. 'What mood's the super in?'

'Raging, ma'am. Sorry – boss. He had some big dinner he's had to cancel.'

'Perfect. So fill me in. What do we know? Has there been a leak? How did the guy's name get out?'

As soon as Amelie went missing Melanie had ordered immediate checks on the six local men on the sex offenders' register. They all came back with alibis. Four checked out immediately with CCTV and/or reliable witnesses. Two needed further inquiries, so their homes were searched. The guy on the Park Estate on the outskirts of Maidstead was one of them but had since been cleared of suspicion. He'd belatedly admitted he was at an AA meeting when Amelie disappeared. Six witnesses. It checked out.

All the names from the register were highly confidential and Melanie had ordered her team to be careful there were no leaks.

'Seems the locals on the Park Estate have known for a while that he's on the register. They saw officers turning up to do a search, put two and two and two together and made five. Decided to post all over social media that he must have Amelie.'

'Excellent.' Melanie shakes her head. A body in a shopping trolley and now the complication of vigilantes when all she wants is to work on finding Amelie. She'd been through the files of all those on the sex offenders' list herself. Some had been done for flashing, which Melanie had always taken more seriously than some others on the force. One on the list had previous for approaching children outside their schools. But so far there was no evidence to link any of them on the list with Amelie's disappearance.

'I'll send you some of the social media links. Blown up really fast. That's why the super and press officer are heading out. To try to calm it all down.'

'Look. I'm so sorry I'm not there but you keep me informed. Yes? Any more news on the ID of the body in the shopping trolley?'

'Not yet but we've had a good few calls on that too so we're checking everything out. The super said he's going to call you for an update on everything.'

Mel closes her eyes. *I bet he is.* 'Thank you.'

CHAPTER 21

MATTHEW – DAY TWO

'Sally. You seen this?' Matthew is at the kitchen island, waiting for the espresso machine to reach temperature. The television is across the large, open-plan space with the sound down.

There's no response. Sally's supposed to be lying down but he knows that she's trying to phone Carol again on the quiet. 'Sally. You need to come and see this.' Matthew raises his voice as he moves across the room, frustrated that he can't find the remote to turn up the volume.

He tries under the cushions on the sofa. Under some newspapers carrying coverage of the press conference about Amelie's disappearance. He glances from surface to surface, all the while taking in the mute shots of a crowd, some carrying banners, outside a terrace. Finally he moves the fruit bowl on the coffee table to spy the remote on a pile of parish magazines behind it.

As he turns up the volume, he recognises the place. The Park Estate. Not a good locale. The scrolling headline says *Demonstration over the search for missing Amelie Hill.*

'Reports are coming in of a demonstration linked to the search for Amelie Hill . . .' The news presenter puts her hand to her earpiece as if taking instructions. 'These are live pictures just coming in now.'

He's turning up the volume as Sally comes into the room to stand alongside him. 'What's going on? Have they found something? Have they found her?'

'No. I mean, I don't know. I assume no. Mel would have rung.'

They listen to the newsreader explain that demonstrators are demanding that a house be searched for Amelie. The home of a man who is apparently listed on the sex offenders' list. There are banners. 'PAEDO'. And 'WHERE IS AMELIE'?

There is suddenly quite a lot of shouting as uniformed officers try to disperse the crowd.

'What's happening, Matthew? Could he have Amelie in there? This man they're talking about. Is that what this is?'

'I don't think so, but I need to speak to Mel.' Matthew feels his stomach clench. He wonders how the man's name got out. 'Mel told me all the names on the sex offenders' register had been checked. Discounted one by one. Alibis sound. I don't know what this is but it's not good. This is local people getting wound up.'

'But police sometimes make mistakes. You know that. What if they're wrong? What if they didn't check properly? What if she is in there?' Sally has walked closer to the TV, her hand up to her mouth. 'Ring Melanie. See what's going on. Oh – good grief. What if she's in there? In that house—'

'Hey there, Sally. I don't think she's there, love.' Matthew pulls Sally into a hug but she pulls away quickly to look back at the television. 'Let me try to find out what's going on.'

Matthew dials but the number goes to answerphone just as the news coverage cuts to a reporter live at the Park Estate who is now with a senior police officer. Matthew recognises him as a superintendent. He doesn't remember the name and wonders where the hell Mel is.

The reporter thrusts his microphone right under the officer's chin. 'Is this address a new lead? What can you tell us? And what is your comment on this demonstration?'

'This is not a lead, this is dangerous activity which needs to stop,' the superintendent says as his name is confirmed on-screen. 'We understand how upsetting it is that Amelie has not yet been found but I can assure you we have the best team doing everything possible to find her. There is no lead here. No evidence pointing here. We cannot have people taking matters into their own hands. This crowd needs to go home and leave the search for Amelie to us.'

'You must be aware there are rumours on social media. A name's been shared. People are angry. Worried.'

'I'm not going to comment on what is being inappropriately shared on social media,' he says. 'All I can say is there is no suspect here and this protest appears, in essence, to be harassment. And I am warning that if there is any illegal activity online or in person here, we will take action and bring charges very swiftly. This is a serious police investigation and this isn't helping. People need to trust us. We are grateful for the search support we've had so far and for all the calls into the incident room but this behaviour here tonight is totally out of line. Unhelpful. And I am warning that people need to go home and to leave the inquiry to the police. Or we will be making arrests.'

Matthew dials and put his mobile to his ear as the news cuts away to more live shots of the Park Estate which appear to show at least two people struggling with police, apparently resisting arrest.

At last she picks up. 'Mel. I've been wondering what's happening. Why you haven't phoned. Answered my messages. We're watching the local news—'

'Yeah. Me too on my phone. A right pickle.'

'So what the hell's going on? Why aren't you there? Did the super overrule you?'

'Look. I'm sorry I haven't phoned but it's been manic. I'm actually travelling back from talking to Adam Meadows.' There's a pause as Matthew takes this in. A punch to his gut.

'You've found the Meadows? Where? Why didn't you tell me? And what do you have? Any firm lead? What's Dawn saying?'

'We've done searches and found nothing. We haven't found Dawn, only the husband. Turns out they split up years back. They don't have contact any more according to Adam. I have my team chasing the information he gave us to try to track down Dawn as soon as we can.'

'He could be lying.'

'And you think I haven't considered that?' Her tone's changed and Matt checks himself.

'Sorry. Sorry. I'm a bit all over the place.'

'No problem. Look. I'm sorry you found out watching the news, I didn't have time to warn you. Word is the local community already knew the name of the guy out at the Park Estate. They've been gagging for an excuse to target him. Amelie's disappearance has been the petrol on a bonfire the locals were already building. We're trying to calm it all down before things turn even nastier.'

'So they all definitely have alibis. The names on the sex offenders' list.'

'All thoroughly checked, Matt. Like I told you before. Alibis checked. And homes searched just for good measure. There's no lead from the local list but we're also running an ANPR check on any number plates that cross-ref with other forces.'

'Good. Good.' Even as he speaks, Matthew realises that he will have caused offence questioning all this. Mel is good. She will have followed all the normal procedures. And then some.

'I'm sorry,' he says. 'I didn't mean to doubt you. We're just going quietly mad here.'

'I understand. I can't imagine how it must feel. And for the record, I didn't tell you about the Adam Meadows interview because I was afraid you'd try to beat me to him. Do something stupid.'

Matthew closes his eyes tight and realises she's right. That's exactly what he would have done. Tried his utmost to get the address and question Adam himself.

At last he opens his eyes and looks back at the TV where the crowd is finally dispersing as two men are loaded into a police van.

'Looks like they're breaking it up.'

'Yeah. The super's about to ring me. Word is he missed a dinner to cover for me. So I'm looking forward to that conversation.'

There's a long pause. Matthew watches the news programme cut back to the presenter and move on to another story. He presses the mute button.

'We're going to find her, Matthew. I'm doing everything I can, I promise you.'

He doesn't answer, not because he doesn't believe her but because it is every kind of hell, knowing as much as he knows. *Too much.* The statistics. The ticking clock. The question booming in his head. He believes that Mel will find his daughter but won't say the subtext out loud. Will it be in time. *Alive? Will you find her alive, Mel?*

Instead he says, 'Can we meet again, Mel? Talk through where we are. The details.'

She doesn't answer.

'Please, Mel.'

'Depends if the FLO can cover. We can't have Sally on her own.' A pause. 'What time does Carol say she's landing tomorrow?'

'You know about *Carol*?' Matthew is shaken. He was both planning and dreading to tell her face to face. That's why he wants to meet.

'Yes. Sally messaged me. You know we're going to have to check that Carol really has been in France. And if so, precisely how long? If it turns out she's on a flight back, as she's told Sally, we'll be picking her up at the airport. You do know that?'

CHAPTER 22

SALLY – Day Two

Sally is sitting on the end of the bed, staring at the framed Whistler postcard on the dressing table.

It's getting late and she's drained. She feels a shiver but can't work out if she's cold or just afraid. Fear is her default setting now; she can't remember what it was to feel normal in her skin. She glances first to the hook on the back of the door and then to the chair beside the wardrobe but there's no dressing gown. She tries to think but can't remember where she left it. Finally, she stands and paces to the chair to put a cardigan over her T-shirt. She waits a moment but finds that she doesn't feel any warmer. Just feels as she has since Amelie disappeared. Out of place in this space. In the world.

She just stands there until there's a noise downstairs. The scraping of a chair. Some clicks. Matthew moving around. She pauses until it's quiet, then sits once more on the bed to take in the picture on the dresser again.

It's a postcard of a Whistler painting called *Three Figures: Pink and Grey* which she, Carol and Beth saw in the gift shop on a gallery visit when they were at boarding school together. She's always felt this sweep of warmth when she looks at it. A happy memory. An emblem of a friendship still dear to her. But the postcard brings no warmth or comfort today. Today it makes her think of Carol being met by police at the airport and the worry of what might happen next. Matthew has warned that no way will the police just take Carol's word that she was abroad when Amelie went missing. They're going to check every detail.

Sally reaches out to take the frame into her hand and stares at it unblinking until her eyes start to water. At the gallery shop all those years ago, they became almost giddy when they first came across the picture.

They had this thing where Beth hated the grey blankets she'd been sent to school with (it was before the popularity of duvets) and Carol had swooped in to cheer her up by sharing her soft, pink blankets. They mixed them up – grey blankets underneath and the soft pink blankets on the top. So the Whistler, with the grey and pink colour scheme, seemed painted for them especially. Three young women with everything ahead of them.

In a youthful surge of joy, they bought three copies of the postcard and promised to always keep them close. Sally has kept hers on show ever since. Beth uses hers still as a bookmark – always in her handbag. As for Carol? Sally realises that she does not know where Carol keeps her Whistler or even if she still has it.

Sally stands again, the frame now pressed against her chest. How she wishes she could go back in time and undo it all. That youthful but terrible mistake they made.

The truth is she can only think of Carol as gentle. Damaged – yes – but kind to the core.

Though Matthew is right and that's not how Mel will see it.

They have a daughter missing. And a dear friend who will now be misunderstood and questioned by the police.

Again.

CHAPTER 23
MELANIE – DAY TWO

It's nearly midnight before Melanie is alone again on the makeshift bed in the office. She dials her husband's number and feels the complex mix of longing and guilt and love, all churned together with exhaustion.

'Hey.'

'Hey.' Tom's voice is quiet also.

'I'm sorry I couldn't talk longer earlier.' She'd managed a quick call to say goodnight to George while Sam was eating his burger but, thanks to her nagging, he ate quickly – positively wolfed it down – so there was very little time to speak to Tom. Too little.

'It's OK.'

'No, it's not. I was with a colleague so I couldn't—'

'Yeah. I guessed. No problem. So how's it going? Have you told Matthew about the letter? Is that all going to be OK for you?'

She fights the sudden and rare urge to cry, squeezing her eyes tight then moving her phone from her left ear to her right. 'I'm having to keep the letter quiet for now to avoid a leak to the press.' This isn't strictly true but she can't bear Tom's disapproval. Not tonight.

'But I've confided in a sergeant. And we'll put it to Dawn. Just as soon as we can find her.'

Melanie takes in a long breath. 'The truth is I've made no real progress *at all*. Nothing concrete.' A pause. 'I don't feel I have anything much to go on, Tom.'

'Oh, darling. I'm so sorry. So – what can I do? You want me to abort? Come back with George. Be nearby?'

'No, no. Don't do that. It's still full on. I wouldn't have time to see you much. It's crazy here.'

'So you really don't have any leads? I saw the hassle on TV. The vigilantes doing their thing.'

'Yeah. We could so do without all that. Two arrests. In court tomorrow. I've bumped that to someone else on the team. But the suits aren't happy I wasn't there to handle it all myself.'

'You in a hotel? It's late.'

She pauses and glances around. For a beat she considers lying. 'No. I'm camping in the office.'

'Oh, Mel. Are you at least eating? Getting some sleep?'

'I'm eating enough. And sleeping enough. It's just the ticking clock.' She doesn't need to say it. It's very nearly Thursday. Day three. At 4 p.m. it will be forty-eight hours since Amelie went missing. She had originally said she would give the investigation two days. Regrets saying that now.

'So you need to stay on there? See it through?'

'Could you bear it? I've got the super on my shoulder. The media all over us.'

'I understand.' A pause. 'So are you still hopeful, Mel? Finding her?'

'I don't know. I have to be honest and say that statistically, it's getting less likely we'll find her . . .' She can't bring herself to say the word. *Alive.* 'But it's not impossible so I'm not giving up on that. I just don't have anything *strong*. No real evidence.'

'So talk to me.'

'OK. So, as I said, we haven't found Dawn Meadows yet though we've now interviewed her husband as you know. And so we're chasing his lawyer who handled the divorce to try to find Dawn's lawyer, hoping they have an address. Also a sister in New Zealand and doing the usual bank and phone checks. I'm really hoping something will come from all that tomorrow. But I have this really unexpected new line.'

'OK. So what's that?'

'You know Sally's friend Carol?'

'The Carol we met at theirs, you mean?'

'Yes.' Carol lives in one of the neighbouring cottages to Sally. They've had supper a few times. Barbeques. Coastal walks. 'Well, it turns out she has a record that I didn't know about.'

'What kind of record?' His tone mirrors her own surprise. Carol is so nice. Ordinary. Gentle and unassuming. The last person you'd expect to have a police record.

'She took a baby once, Tom.'

'You are *kidding* me.'

'I wish. It was a good few years back and she was unwell, apparently. With a controlling and violent partner. She spiralled and it happened out of the blue. Not premediated. But she was given a custodial sentence. Suspended.'

'And Sally and Matthew *knew* this? Never said anything?'

'I've spoken to them very briefly. Not in detail yet. As I say, it was a long time ago. When Sally and Matt met. I've called up the files and it was a very sad case. Out of character. Carol was unable to have children herself. Psych reports said she was very ill. But the bottom line is she took a child. A baby in a pushchair from an airport. Not for very long and the child was unharmed. But it was abduction all the same.'

'And you think—'

112

'I don't know what to think. She claims she was in France when Amelie went missing but we're still to confirm that. She's supposed to be on a late flight home from Paris to Bristol but it had technical problems so she's now flying early tomorrow. Cameras at the airport in Paris show her clearly alone at the moment. She's been put up in a hotel and we've checked in with security there and CCTV. No child. No Amelie. She's definitely alone tonight. So we're going to let her travel, check in with the airline to keep the situation monitored. Then we'll pick her up when she lands and drive her down for interview.'

'Will you do the interview yourself?'

'Yes. They'll bring her straight here soon as she lands.'

'I'm surprised they didn't arrest her in France.'

'We'd need more than a previous offence to arrest her and get a search warrant. As I say, the CCTV shows her alone for now. Technically she was in France when Amelie disappeared so that's a potential alibi. Unless she's lying or she took Amelie to France but that all seems unlikely. Would need a false passport.' She's thinking aloud. Her brain's so tired. 'I have to assume she could be lying until I figure this out. To be honest, I just don't know what to make of this. It's very unexpected. And it's going to add a layer of stress for Sally and Matthew too. Her being a friend, I mean.'

'You really are overloaded. Look, darling. You need to at least try to get some sleep. Let your brain rest.'

'Yeah.'

'OK. Get off to bed. I love you.'

'You too. And I'm so sorry I'm not with you for the holiday.'

He doesn't answer and she thinks again of the new letter and how Matthew will react when she finally tells him. Also Sally. Her brain's swimming with what is really behind Amelie's disappearance. Dawn? Carol? Matthew's job? 'Hang on. Before you go, can I ask you something?'

'Anything.'

Melanie closes her eyes and conjures the terrible looks Sally exchanges with Matthew when they don't realise she's watching. Something so hollowed out and so beyond pain that it's uncomfortable to witness.

She's also thinking how conflicted Sally was over Matthew's plan to join her team. *It's not that I don't admire what you all do. It's just so bloody dangerous.*

'Be honest. Do you hate me being a police officer?'

CHAPTER 24

MATTHEW – Day Three

When Matthew finally returns home, the FLO, Molly, is sitting in the kitchen alone, a single lamp lighting the room.

'I'm sorry I was longer than I said.' He's been driving the streets again. More than two hours this time. He said he'd be back for midnight but it's well past 1 a.m. It's not even that he expects to find Amelie this way, circling Maidstead over and over. He knows there are volunteer groups out looking now as well as the police. Facebook groups organising rotas and checks of parks and meadows and backstreets and bins. And all the unthinkable. But driving around makes him feel that he is at least doing *something*. That he just might spot some small thing; some tiny suspicious thing that could help. And in any case, it's so hard to stay at home . . .

'It's OK,' Molly says. 'But I'll get off now if that's all right with you. Sally's upstairs but she's not sleeping. I just checked on her.'

'Thank you. Sure you don't want to stay over?'

'No. I'll grab a few hours at home.'

'Of course.'

Molly picks up her coat and bag and Matthew sees her to the door. Thanks her again.

Back in the kitchen cum diner, he slumps on to the sofa by the doors to the garden, not bothering to put on more lights. Feels more comfortable with the dark. He checks his watch. Thursday now. Day three. Amelie has been missing for thirty-four hours and fifteen minutes.

The maths is eating into him like a tumour. His insides feel permanently tight as if there isn't enough room for his organs anymore. Everything sort of pressing together. Yes. Just as if there is a tumour.

He remembers that when Amelie was born, he used to worry about what would happen to her if one of them died young – him or Sal? Car accident or cancer? Life was suddenly serious; everything else seemed trivial. It no longer mattered whether his dodgy knee could manage the tougher runs skiing. Winter holidays were a thing of the past. It was suddenly all about survival. Keeping this little life safe. Keeping themselves safe.

And he'd failed at all of it. Amelie *gone*.

Matthew checks his phone. The last message from Melanie says she expects to interview Carol early. Uniformed police are driving Carol from Bristol Airport to the station in Maidstead where Mel has her incident room. All such a mess.

There's no way Matthew believes Carol is involved with Amelie's disappearance but he knows that Melanie will have to play it completely straight. Do it all properly. And it will be unpleasant. Questions that will offend Carol. Hurt Sally too.

All those years ago, when Carol had her 'breakdown' and took the baby, it was such a dreadful shock. Matthew, who had simply been brought in as a PI to find her, obviously didn't know Carol at all. He just wore his professional hat and was appalled first and foremost for the mother whose child was missing. Yes, he sympathised with Sally too. His feelings for her were growing fast. But he was piggy in the middle.

Sally, naively, had imagined that the police would be sympathetic when they found out the truth of Carol's life. Her controlling and violent partner; that awful life that Carol had hidden from everyone. The reason she had withdrawn from her friendship with Sally. But Matthew had tried to make Sally see how differently it would all be seen by others. All the sympathy would rightly be with the mother of the child – missing for several hours.

Carol will be charged, Sally. Imagine what it's been like for the mother of the child she took . . .

But Carol is ill, Matthew. Surely they will take that into consideration?

In the end, the judge did consider Carol's situation as mitigation. But just as Matthew predicted, she was still given a custodial sentence, albeit suspended. Sally had been numb with shock.

Matthew feels a long sigh leaving his body. Shoulders slumping. He thinks of the most horrible irony. That Sally is now the mother of the missing child. Finally and so cruelly getting to feel what that mother had felt all those years ago. With Carol right in the middle of the two nightmares.

Sally was right. He should have spoken up as soon as Carol phoned from France. He should have warned her to stay away for her own sake but mostly for Sally's. To spare his poor wife this extra stress. Why didn't he do that?

Matthew scrapes his fingers through his hair and closes his eyes. He's tired from the lack of sleep and all the driving. Is he losing it? His judgement? That powerful instinct that has served him so well right up until now.

CHAPTER 25

MELANIE – DAY THREE

Seven thirty a.m. and the message comes in that Carol will be at the station within half an hour.

Melanie's already at her desk, checking through the latest updates from calls to the incident room and the various inquiries being made by her team. She's set the next briefing with her team for nine thirty after she's interviewed Carol.

Her eyes are glued to her screen, so she's surprised when a hand appears to place a takeaway coffee cup on her desk. A good brand.

'Cappuccino, boss? Went to the good place. Got them to pop in an extra shot.'

She turns her head to see Sam standing just behind her desk. 'Thank you. You're early.'

'I'm hoping to hear from Adam Meadows' solicitor first thing. See if he is in touch with Dawn's solicitor who might have an address. He knows it's urgent. I'm hoping to have the latest before your briefing.'

'Excellent. Though I doubt the solicitor will be in before nine.'

'Actually, the message from his secretary said he's due in early. Prepping for a family court appearance. Hoping to ring me beforehand.'

'Great.' Melanie flips the small plastic insert on the coffee cup. She sips. 'Crikey. Delicious. Perfect temperature.'

'I did mention you were *particular*.' He grins. She smiles back. They had talked on the drive about the best places for coffee. Getting the temperature just right. Not too hot to burn the flavour. Not too cold. For a moment Melanie thinks of all the conversations with Matthew over coffee and feels a strange little pull inside and suddenly feels just desperately sad. She sips again.

'Right,' she says. 'As you're here early – do you want to assist on the Carol interview? I'm going to go rogue and lead. But I'd like you there. I have met Carol, so I'm declaring that I know her. I don't see it as compromising. I've only met her at a couple of social events. She's not a friend. But to be sure we go by the book I'd like your input. And your take.'

'Sure. I'll chase the solicitor before she gets here.'

Forty minutes later Melanie is sitting alongside Sam with Carol, who looks incredibly tired, across the Formica table. Carol's wearing jeans and a smart red jumper. Stylish. Her navy bag looks designer too. But the bags under her eyes say she didn't sleep on the drive. Nerves? Or guilt?

'Thank you so much for agreeing to this. Just a chat.' Melanie has Carol's record report in front of her and she clocks Carol trying to read the paperwork upside down. Melanie lifts up the cardboard folder, opens and reads some more, then puts it back on the desk, this time closed.

It summarises what she already knows. That Matthew had been hired by Sally and mutual friend, Beth, to trace their estranged friend Carol for a school reunion at their old boarding school. It was nearly a decade ago. The school was closing down and Sal and Beth saw it as a last chance to get their little besties' trio back together. Matthew helped find Carol and at the last minute she turned up at the hotel with a baby in tow. Claimed an adoption had just gone through and she was on top of the world. It was in the middle of the night that Carol's violent partner turned up and the horrible truth came out.

That there was no adoption. Carol had, in a moment of madness, snatched the baby from the airport . . .

'I expect you've guessed why we needed to speak to you.' Melanie looks up from the file and watches Carol closely as she lets this sink in. She then waits. Her usual tactic.

Carol lets out a huff of air, looks away to the corner of the room, and finally back at the closed file on the desk.

'It's what happened all those years ago. When I was very poorly. Yes?'

'Yes, Carol. I didn't know anything about that. But you must see that with Amelie Hill missing, we have to ask everyone questions. And with this case on your files, the abduction of a child—'

'Look. I was very unwell back then. Not myself at all. And I've regretted what I did every single day since. But I'm better now. I would never do anything like that again. I love Sally. And I love Amelie too. I'm in shock about her going missing. I just want to get home to Sally so I can support her.'

'Yes. Of course. So tell me, where have you been the past few days? We just need to verify everything. Tick all the boxes, as I say.'

'You want an alibi?' Carol looks genuinely shocked. 'But I was in France. That *is* my alibi.'

'Sure. Sure. But I have to check the timeline. When did you leave for France?'

'Three weeks back.'

'OK. We'll need the flight details. Your full schedule since, especially Tuesday when Amelie went missing. You understand, yes?' Melanie pauses. 'So were you with anyone who can vouch for you? Confirm you were in France. Your schedule?'

'You don't believe me?'

'It's not that. It's just procedure. This is how it works, Carol. Every alibi has to be checked. So – can you tell us if you were with anyone?'

'Yes. I was with a friend called Emily. She's younger. I took her under my wing when she was a teenager and we've stayed good friends. Like an unofficial godparent, if you like. We've been sight-seeing this past week. We did some museums together. I have tick-ets and pictures I can show you.'

'Great. So if you could write down your schedule. What you were doing the time that Amelie went missing. Share Emily's num-ber. Show us your pictures and where you were staying. We can check all that very quickly and let you get back home to Sally. Tell you what. I'll leave you to go through all that with my colleague here. I need to get ready for a briefing.'

'Right. Good. I'll do that.'

Melanie stands and turns. She stares at the door a moment then turns back deliberately. 'So you don't have children yourself? Am I remembering that right?' She feels this question land on Carol like a slap. Feels momentarily bad for the hurt now showing on Carol's face but only because this is Sally's friend. Melanie needs to observe Carol's reaction. She could be lying about France.

'No. I can't have children. It's always been a source of sadness to me. It's why I got ill. And made that terrible mistake over the baby. But I've had counselling. And a lot of time to come to terms with

121

my life.' She turns to look at the wall which has an empty cork-board attached. 'I'm still sad about it. That I'll never be a mother. But I *have* come to terms with it. I'm not ill anymore. And like I say, I would never do anything again to upset or hurt a family.' She pauses again and turns back to look at Melanie directly. 'I was ill when that happened all those years ago. A different person.'

'Right. Yes. I understand. Thank you.' Melanie forces a small smile. She announces that she's leaving the room for the tape and tells Sam that she will leave him to finish up. Take the schedule of Carol's movements and any tickets on her phone.

Back in the office, Alison, the DS from the incident room, is waiting by the door. 'OK. Two biggies. I have a teenager downstairs who says he has information on the body in the trolley. And I have a message for Sam from a solicitor. He says it's urgent. So shall I interrupt the interview or wait until he's finished?'

'No. Don't interrupt. Share it with me. I'm across it.'

Alison hands over a note with a summary of the message. Melanie feels a rush of cold move through her. Then adrenaline.

'And what about the teenager?'

Melanie can hardly think straight, eyes narrowing.

The message makes no sense.

'You want me to talk to the teenager? It's just he's asking for you.'

'No. No. I'll go down and talk to him.' Melanie is still scanning the note, her mind now working at a hundred miles an hour. The message from the solicitor says he's handled all the Meadows' business affairs for years. He's confused. Wants an urgent phone call.

He says there was no divorce. There's been no division of the business or personal equity.

As far as he's aware Adam and Dawn Meadows are still very much married.

PART TWO

PART TWO

CHAPTER 26

OLIVIA

I stare out of the train window on the way back to Oxford in a daze. Hard to figure out how I really feel. Sort of confused and disappointed. But also ashamed.

I was so sure Matthew Hill was going to be my breakthrough. My solution. And now?

Now all hope's gone. Poof. *Nothing.*

As I tilt my head, the folly up on the hill comes into view. It means I'm nearly home and I get this really strong muscular pull in my stomach. At first I think it's nerves but it's not. Something nicer. Warmer. I used to walk up there with Mum when I was little. Staring at the folly, I'm surprised to remember for just a moment *exactly* what that felt like. Holding my mother's hand. Staring up into her face.

I haven't been out here for ages and it shocks me that the sight of the folly can do this. Trigger such a strong sensation. Like time travel. It's such a nice feeling – warm and unexpected – that I try really hard to hold on to it, but all too soon the folly has passed out of view. It means there's just five, maybe ten, minutes of the journey now. I squeeze my fingers with my thumb, trying to hold on to my mother's hand but the memory is gone. She's gone. All the warmth is gone with her and I feel a sudden tremor of panic.

I've missed Chloe so much. We've never been apart this long. I was supposed to return yesterday but a stupid landslip cancelled all the trains. I was in an absolute panic and tried to find a bus. I phoned my friend who's looking after Chloe but she said she was having the time of her life. *Perfectly OK, hun. She can stay another night, no problem.* Funny how parents always assume the worst and then the kids surprise us.

Whatever. Trains all fine today but I'm worried now about how my father will be when I get home. I don't travel by rail often so I'm nervous about missing my stop. When exactly I should get up. Take my case down from the rack? Is it too soon?

I glance around the carriage to see if anyone else is moving and press my hand on to my stomach to try to steady my nerves.

The truth is I have no idea what to do next. I don't mean the luggage; I mean about finding Mum. Where to turn now. I want to feel sorry for Matthew Hill. And I do. I saw it all on the news in the Premier Inn. Shook me right up – the real reason he bolted from our meeting.

I was in shock when he threw me out of his office. Had no idea what was going on. I remember watching his car. I wanted to run along the pavement, stand in front of it. Try to stop him. Make him explain. *Listen to me.*

I kept thinking about it all, stuck in the hotel for a second night. I just couldn't believe it. Matthew Hill's poor wife's face in that news conference. But here's the shameful bit. I don't just feel sorry for them. I feel sorry for *me* too. And yes. Angry too. Bloody furious actually.

I watch the trees whizzing by – the blur of green making me feel almost dizzy. I take out my phone to call up Google. Search the latest.

As I watch the wheel whirring, searching, I think how cruel it's been. Of all the people I hoped would help me, I had to pick the one person whose life was about to blow up. His kid gone. Who could believe it?

It's as if the universe is laughing at me. *Ha, ha, Olivia. Thought you were so clever, didn't you? Thought you'd found someone to help. Well, guess what?*

I finally get a stronger signal. The page loads but there's nothing fresh on the news website. Just more appeals for witnesses. The number to ring for the incident room.

I think again of his wife – Sally Hill – at the press conference. I stared at her face on the TV screen when the camera zoomed in – all pale and close to tears – and I remember thinking it would break me into a million pieces if anything happened to Chloe. I don't think I could survive that. So – yeah. I feel really sorry for them, I do. But I also feel – I don't know – as if the whole universe is against me. Sending me a signal that this is how my life is and I just need to accept it and stop dreaming. And that makes me really, really angry. Which I suppose is why I feel ashamed.

Matthew Hill said he would try to find someone else to help me. I assume he meant another private detective, but that's not going to happen now, is it?

First thing this morning, after breakfast in the hotel, I was thinking of dialling his number and leaving a message. Ask him to recommend another detective. Just a name. Or a link to a website. Someone else, anyone else who might help us. Me and Chloe. But I bottled it, because I realised, what kind of person troubles a parent when their kid's missing?

I phoned Alicia again instead. She's my friend. The best. The one looking after Chloe for me. Her first sleepover for little Suzie's birthday. To be honest, I was worried that Chloe might get scared and want to come home, especially with the train delays. She's only five and my dad wasn't keen on her going. Says she's too young and kids grow up too quickly these days, but like I say, Alicia says the girls are having the time of their lives. She sent me pictures.

Goodness. Alicia's partner must be doing well. She's really splashed out. Got those sleepover tents with fairy lights and everything in pink. Unbelievable. Chloe was wearing a fairy costume – wings, the lot – and didn't even want to come to the phone for another FaceTime this morning. The family have a dog and a new kitten which I suspect is a big factor. Chloe was so happy – just shouted across the room. *Hello, Mummy. See you soon.* Upshot is they've asked if I will pick her up a bit later today than we said, so the girls can play for a bit longer. They're going to have a picnic lunch inside their tents.

Wait. The train announcer says we're nearly there. I check my watch. Feel another flutter of nerves. The journey's gone so much more quickly than I expected. I feel the panic over the luggage again and decide to go for it. I put on my coat quickly and get everything lined up on the spare seat next to me – suitcase and backpack. And then I get worried about negotiating the aisle, so I move through to the little area by the door, to make sure I can get out first.

I stare at the little button to open the door. And I can't help it. I had expected to feel hopeful on this journey. I'd expected, after all the planning and the saving and the worrying, to have finally got things under way to find my mum. Instead, I've wasted so much money on the train fare and having to extend the hotel stay – and achieved precisely nothing.

So, yeah – I'm angry. Savings dwindling and right back at square one.

It feels weird getting off the train. Fresh air on my face again. Windier than I expected. On the walk from the station back to the house, I try to get my head back into the right gear. Trying to decide who to channel today.

Little Women? Yes. Always Jo.

I do this a lot. Climb into a book when I don't like what's going on in the real world. Look out on the world through the eyes of a character I love. When I was younger, I used to learn their lines. Whole chunks from favourite books . . .

That child lives in a world of her own. That's what my mum used to say when she heard me chanting. I can hear her voice now. Teasing but smiling too. I used to have this favourite reading place – a window seat with deep-red velvet curtains and cushion. It felt a bit like being on a tiny stage. Learning my lines.

Dad's so different. A numbers man. Teaches maths. I think it winds him up that I gave up maths after the GCSE and am obsessed with novels instead. I try to explain that I need them. My stories. My escape. I've always found it difficult to fit in. I don't know why. Never had many real friends. To me, books feel kinder and easier than the real world.

I'm a little out of breath from walking so fast from the station and as I reach the doorstep, I pause. I take in the bright red paint. The shiny brass knocker and the number four alongside. All so familiar, but I can't find my key for a minute. I frown and try a different pocket in my bag. There it is. Deep breath, Olivia. Key in the door. Today I am going to be Jo. Strong and brave. He's going to be very mad I've been away so long. He'll know I've lied to him. So – yes. I'm going to need to channel Jo. Ride this out.

I open the door with the key, chin up, but Dad's already standing there, which throws me. He normally waits in the kitchen.

'Where the hell have you been all this time? Give me your phone.' He has his hand out.

'Sorry?'

'Give . . . me . . . your . . . phone.'

I do as he says but am confused. I can hear *Frozen* playing on the TV through in the sitting room, which is all wrong. Chloe isn't supposed to be home yet. So – he's picked her up early without telling me? Without Alicia telling me? Did Chloe suddenly get homesick after my phone call this morning? So why didn't Alicia text me?

I can feel panic bubbling as I hand him my phone and march through to the sitting room to sort out what's going on here. Make sure that Chloe is OK.

The TV is up loud. She's sitting on the floor, back to me with her eyes glued to the telly, but adrenaline shoots through me. Because it suddenly feels as if I'm in a dream. That the picture can't be real.

Because in this picture Chloe is too big. And she has the wrong hair. Brown, not blonde.

I freeze, trying to work out what this picture means but she hears me and turns. And cold suddenly shoots through my whole body because I cannot compute what I'm seeing. It's not Chloe. My Chloe.

It's the girl from the news last night . . .

'Amelie. Is it Amelie?' I can see the terrible fear in her eyes. Wide and wary as she nods. 'It's OK, Amelie. I'm Olivia.' I try very hard to calm my voice for her and fake a small smile, but it feels as if my whole body is crumbling. Yes. As if the skeleton, the bones within me are all *crumbling*, giving way so that I worry they will no longer hold up the flesh. That I will crash to the ground.

'Hello, Olivia,' she says. Her eyes soften just a little but her shoulders are tense and it's clear she's still both confused and *very* afraid. 'Can I go home now? Is Mummy better?'

CHAPTER 27

SALLY – DAY THREE

As Carol walks into the room, Sally feels as if a lever's being pulled. Water gushing. The roar of a Tube train finally pulling into the station.

Somehow Sally is on her knees. Then sitting on the floor. Slumped forward, her shoulders heaving with the sobbing.

'It's OK. I'm here.' Carol's voice, low and gentle, her arms gripping Sally tight.

'I'll leave you.' The voice of the family liaison officer who opened the door to Carol. Even her voice is trembling.

'Oh my darling. I'm so sorry. So very sorry.' Carol is sitting on the floor alongside Sally, smoothing her hair now as she speaks. 'I would have come sooner. I wish I'd found out sooner.'

It takes Sally a long time to work through the sobbing. Her body eventually exhausted by it. Her breath huffing as if she's climbed a steep hill.

'Let's get you on the sofa.'

She feels Carol's arms supporting her. Guiding her. She's afraid of collapsing again but Carol is slow and steady and finally she is sitting on the couch by the sliding doors on to the garden.

'I'll make tea.'

Sally doesn't answer. Can't. Shocked by how the sight of Carol, dear Carol, has somehow made it all real. Not some terrible dream from which she will wake up. Amelie really gone.

She hears the kettle. Carol is using the Aga kettle, not the electric. Knows this kitchen, unlike the policewoman. There is the clinking of metal on china. The fridge door. All the while Sally just stares out on the garden. A windy day. Amelie's swing is moving slightly and she finds that she can't bear to look at it.

Sally moves her gaze to the far end of the garden where the branches of the trees lining the back wall are swaying. For some reason it makes her think of Amelie dancing. The shoes up on her bed for a ballet exam she may never now take. Anything and everything leading her thoughts to her daughter. The tears come again . . .

'It's OK. Here's your tea. I've put sugar in. Sip it slowly.'

Carol's hand is again stroking her hair.

'I'm sorry.' Sally's voice breaks up as she speaks.

'Don't be silly. There is nothing for you to be sorry about. I'm here now.'

For a long time they just sit, sipping their drinks, Carol smoothing her hair. Sally crying. Stopping for a bit. And then crying again.

'I think it's only just hitting me. That this is all real, Carol.' She clears her throat. Sniffs.

'It must be very hard, darling. The shock. I really don't know what to say.'

Finally, Sally turns and tilts her head. 'Was it horrible? At the police station? Did they ask a lot of questions? Matthew warned me they would have to—'

'It was fine. I'm fine. Never mind about me. Let's worry about you. I take it you're not sleeping?'

Sally shakes her head.

132

'Eating?'

Again, Sally shakes her head.

'Do you think you could manage a piece of toast?' A pause. 'For me. Could you eat a piece of toast for me, Sally? Just one.'

Finally, Sally nods. 'OK. One piece.'

Carol stands and walks across to the blue breadbin on the kitchen counter. The clink of the lid. Rustling of the bread packaging. Then finally the click of the toaster.

Sally is remembering that back in boarding school together she had chicken pox once. Was put in isolation. Couldn't eat and lost a lot of weight. The nuns were all very worried, wondering if she should be sent home to recover.

It was Carol who was the first person allowed to visit. She'd already had chicken pox.

Toast. Look, Sally. I've brought you toast. Just one piece. Come on. You can manage one piece for me? Yes? Otherwise they're going to send you home . . . and you'll miss the end-of-term party.

'They don't seem to have any real leads, Carol.' Again Sally sniffs as she speaks. 'It's nearly two full days and as far as I can tell, they don't have any proper leads at all. We thought it might be a woman who threatened Matthew once. But now we don't know. We just don't know.'

CHAPTER 28

MELANIE – Day Three

Sitting opposite the teenager, Melanie's mind is in overdrive. The boy, or young man, says he knows something about the body in the trolley. But *what*?

It's hard juggling two inquiries now and her priority is Amelie. She's already assigned Sam to try to get to the bottom of the Meadows' true situation. Where is Dawn? Why did Adam insist they were divorced when they're not? Did another lawyer handle things?

Richard, another detective on the team, suddenly appears at the door with tea. He'll sit in on this chat. Observe.

'So – what is it that you have to share, Zak?' Melanie looks down at her note to check she has the name right. At the front counter, Zak had said he would only speak to her. The woman on the telly. The one leading the investigation. He's eighteen and says he doesn't want anyone to sit in.

'Is this like formal, then?' Zak stares at the box that is used for recording interviews. Melanie notices his hand is trembling. He's wearing the teenage uniform of black T-shirt and dark jeans which are ridiculously tight. Short, dark, cord jacket with a fur lining.

'Because if this is formal, I need some kind of amnesty.'

'Amnesty?' Melanie can't help her tone of voice. 'This is a murder investigation. And a missing girl inquiry. It's a very serious situation. Why would you need an amnesty?' She pauses, aware that she should control her irritation. 'If you have anything to share, you have a duty to share it, Zak.'

His face changes. Fear. Something else. He looks as if he might cry. More a boy than a young man suddenly.

Melanie regroups, glancing at the sergeant. 'OK. So it's good that you've come in, Zak. If you can help us – if you have information that will help our inquiry, then we're very grateful. That will reflect well for you. But you do need to talk to me. Tell me what you know. Why you're here.'

'The guy in the shopping trolley.' Zak's head jerks. His expression all anxiety.

'Sip your tea, Zak. Take it slowly. What do you know about the body found in the shopping trolley?'

Zak glances to the corner of the room, frowning. He closes his eyes. Melanie waits. And then at last . . .

'I was there. When it happened.' Zak opens his eyes and turns back to look her in the face.

Melanie turns again to her sergeant and then back to Zak. 'OK. Good. You've done the right thing, coming here. The hard thing. So take it slowly and tell us everything that happened. So you were there at the canal when the man and the shopping trolley went into the water. Is that right, Zak?'

'Yes.'

'So tell us exactly what happened.'

'I tried to stop them.' Zak rolls his lips tightly together. 'I did try to stop them.'

'Stop who, Zak?' Melanie can feel a punch of adrenaline. She puts her left hand into her lap so she can clench it unseen. Needs

Zak to stay calm. Not change his mind. Demand a lawyer. He's eighteen. She can press on if he keeps going. Stays calm. 'You've done the right thing, coming in, Zak. You've done the hard bit. Making the right decision. Take it slowly.'

Silence. A pause which feels too long. Melanie has been in this spot so many times and has learned that it can go either way. Zak looks fragile.

'In your own time, Zak.'

Again the teenager looks away to the corner of the room as he starts talking again. 'We'd been drinking. Quite a bit. Lager and cider mostly. Cheap stuff. To celebrate finishing our mocks.'

'Who's we?'

'Me and three friends from school. Milburn House.'

Melanie exchanges another glance with the sergeant. Milburn House is a private school on the outskirts of Maidstead. High fees. And known for high jinks. Police were involved last summer when pupils celebrating the end of A levels had trashed the ballroom of a local hotel. It was all over the local press. Several hotels saying they were sick of posh boys who didn't know how to behave.

'Go on.' Melanie watches as Zak closes his eyes again before taking a deep breath.

'We were a bit drunk and Ben said it would be a laugh to go see the trolley guy by the canal.'

'What do you mean, trolley guy?'

'He was homeless. Often in the same spot, sort of begging. Kept his sleeping bag and bits and bobs in a shopping trolley. Sometimes he slept under the bridge further down the canal. Sometimes nearer the shops. He was often drunk. Funny. Shouting about politics and the monarchy. We took him alcohol sometimes. Ben thought it was hilarious. Winding him up. Talking politics and stuff.'

'So what happened this time?'

'He was already drunk. Pretty much out cold when we got there. Ben was disappointed, so he said – why not get him in the trolley and take him for a ride. Wake him up.'

Melanie feels a terrible wave of realisation.

'I didn't think it was a good idea. I said we should just leave it.' Zak is now staring at Melanie, his eyes wide. 'I didn't help them.'

'OK. I'm going to need the names, Zak. Ben's surname and the full names of the other boys. Who was with you?'

Zak's lip trembles. She waits.

'We have to have the names.'

'Ben Delaville. Tom Broadmoor and Harry Clifton. We were in the same A level group for History. We'd just done some mock exams. For retakes.'

'So what happened?'

'Tom and Harry and Ben got the guy in the trolley. It was difficult. They wanted me to help lift him but – I promise – I said no. Then they pushed him up and down a bit. Just for a laugh, I think. So then they started to let go of the trolley. Letting it freewheel on the slope.' A pause. 'They did that twice, pushing him back up the slope of the canal path.'

'He didn't wake up?'

'No. He was out cold. From the booze. I think that's why they pushed it faster. To try to wake him up.'

'Tell us exactly how he ended up in the water.'

'It wasn't deliberate.' Zak is ghostly pale as he finishes. 'I don't think any of us realised how deep the canal was alongside the path. They pushed him down the slope a third time. The trolley suddenly veered quite fast to the right. And into the water. We all thought it would just get stuck. That the water would come up to the middle of the trolley or something. But it went right under. I thought he would come up. I really thought he would come up. Float or something. But he didn't.'

'And you didn't call anyone? Try to help him?'

'No.' Zak begins to cry. 'I realise we should have done. I keep having dreams about it. But we were just too scared. Ben and Harry started to shout that we needed to run. Tom said the same. And I did the wrong thing.' Tears on his cheeks now. 'I ran.'

'OK. So we're going to need to write this all up in a proper statement, Zak.'

'Am I going to be prosecuted?'

'You should have come to us before, Zak. You know that. But it's good that you've done the right thing now. I can't say what will happen. You're an adult but I suggest we call your parents. Get them here. Have you told them you're here? Have you told them what happened?' Zak shakes his head, his lip still trembling. 'We need the exact time and date this happened.'

'It was about 11 p.m., maybe 11.30 p.m. on the sixteenth. We'd been celebrating the end of exams and so I checked on my phone.'

Three weeks before Amelie went missing from the shop nearby. So the death in the trolley is not connected. Just as Melanie always assumed. A horrible and nasty prank gone tragically wrong.

'There's something else.' Zak's eyes are wide again. 'About the girl.'

'The girl? You mean Amelie Hill?' Melanie feels a jolt.

'I saw her.'

Melanie leans forward. Not understanding.

'I started to go back to the canal. A couple of times a week. To check if anything had surfaced. I felt so terrible. I didn't know what to do. I couldn't sleep. Harry and Ben said we should just stay away. Lie low. Say nothing. But I was dreading the water level dropping. Or his body floating up . . .' He breaks off and sniffs. 'Anyway. A few days ago, I was there, checking the water from further down the canal path on the other side. I knew that there was a plastic bag still over the only camera on the path so I knew I wouldn't be filmed. I only went when it was really quiet. When there was no one about. And on Tuesday I saw this girl, just outside the back door to a shop.'

Melanie can hardly believe what she's hearing.

'And you're sure it was Amelie Hill? Not someone else?'

'Yeah. I saw her picture from the press conference on the telly. That's why I realised I had to say something. Come forward. About all of it.'

'OK. So tell us everything you saw.'

'The girl, Amelie, she was just standing and she seemed to be talking to someone.'

'Talking to who, Zak? This is really important. You need to describe the person she was talking to. Everything you can remember.' Melanie sits up straighter. She feels herself lean in closer to the table.

'I'm really sorry but I'm afraid I couldn't see. From the angle, the corner of the building that juts out was hiding whoever she was talking to.'

Melanie tuts. Squeezes her eyes shut as she lets out a huff of air. She feels her left hand clench into a ball, her nails driving into her palm.

'I legged it then, so I didn't see what happened. Where she went.'

'So how long did you watch her?'

'Just a few seconds. I was worried she would see me. Or someone else would see me down by the canal.' A pause. 'But the thing is – and I don't know if it's important – but she wasn't wearing what you said in the press conference.'

'What do you mean?'

'All the appeals said she was wearing jeans and a pink hoodie. But she was carrying those over her arm.' Zak looks as puzzled as Melanie feels.

Melanie frowns. 'So what was she wearing?'

'A green dress. She was wearing a green dress.'

CHAPTER 29

OLIVIA – Day Three

In the car now, I am sitting in the back with Chloe beside me and Amelie next to her, leaning her head against the tinted window. I have no idea where my father is taking us. I wanted at least one of us to sit in the front where the windows have normal glass: where we might be seen more easily. But my father wouldn't allow that.

We picked up Chloe earlier and I'd hoped to raise the alarm with Alicia somehow but Dad parked around the corner and went to the door alone. Locked the car doors on us. He's told Alicia I've lost my phone. Gone back to the railway station looking for it.

I've told Alicia you'll be in touch after half-term . . .

It's all so mad and happened so quickly, I've been frightened for Chloe and haven't figured out how to safely get help. All I've been able to do is try to calm Amelie. She looks exhausted as well as terrified. My dad put her in Chloe's room at night while I was away apparently. She says she's been given sandwiches and pizza but she clearly hasn't slept much.

Back at the house – all four of us – he made me pack up things really quickly. He was devious. Unplugged the landline and carried Chloe piggyback with his pocketknife in his palm. The knife closed but the shiny red casing clearly and deliberately visible to me. *Chloe stays with Grandad while you pack a bag and get in the car.* Like some horrible threat in case I ran to a neighbour or called out for help. I wish now that I *had* tried harder to raise the alarm straight away but it was all such a shock. I was so scared for the girls and just trying to cover up my fear and keep them calm. And now it's too late. We're off again. No idea where.

'Why's Amelie crying?' Chloe is whispering, her face all worry.

'She's just missing her mummy. But she'll be back with her soon.'

Amelie turns her head as I speak and her eyes glance between the back of my father's head and my face, frowning. She tried to talk to me some more before we left the house for the second time but my father closed it down.

Your mother is still ill, Amelie. We are looking after you as a favour and you need to stop asking questions. You understand?

'Now. You probably need the toilet soon, Chloe? Yes. Shall we make a stop? Get you comfy?' I try to keep my tone upbeat. My job to keep my father calm and these girls calm too.

'No. I'm fine, Mummy. Grandad said to go before we left.'

'What about you, Amelie? Do you need to stop for the toilet?' It's all I can think of. The car's child locks are on again. I keep thinking about that at traffic lights. I can't figure out how to get us all away from him safely. A service station or the toilets at a garage are my best hope to find someone to help us.

'I'm fine.'

'Well, I'm going to need the toilet soon. Can we stop soon?'

'I'm sure you can hold it,' says my father. 'It's not far. Goodness, if the young ones can manage, you can manage.'

He catches my eye through the driver's mirror and I try to find a fake smile to appease him. I have no idea quite how to play this. When he's had a bad turn in the past, I have always just kept my head down, spent time with Chloe and waited for it to pass. I had thought it was some kind of depression. Overprotective of me. Controlling and uncomfortable, yes – and it's become *so much* worse lately. It's the reason I've been so desperate to try to find my mother. But I had never imagined him capable of something like this.

This shocking. This bad. Taking someone else's child.

I look at Amelie and my heart breaks for the fear on her face. I still don't understand how my dad did this. *Or why.* I catch Chloe glancing again at Amelie, who is wiping her tears with her hand. Chloe in response takes hold of my hand and I squeeze hers to try to reassure her.

I close my eyes briefly and think. Think. *Think.*

My best hope is that the police will find us. Stop us. Yes. Put an end to this madness. The police must have CCTV of Amelie being taken by now surely? Maybe they already have my dad's number plate? I just need to keep the girls calm and wait this out for someone to spot the car.

'OK. So how about we play a game?' Again I try to make my tone cheerful. 'You're bound to be missing your family, Amelie. But it's going to be OK. And the time will pass faster if we keep ourselves busy. Now – when I was little we used to play a game where you had to count how many red cars. How about we do that? And when we get to twenty, I have sweets to share.' I reach into my pocket to check they are still there. I had so little time to grab things. My father made us leave in such a hurry.

'When will I see Mummy and Daddy?' Amelie's eyes are desperate. 'It's been ages.'

'Enough questions.' My father's voice. 'You just play the game with Olivia and Chloe and I'll let you know when your mother is better.'

I still haven't figured out all that he's told Amelie. There hasn't been time and I've been wary of frightening her even more with too many questions. But my father's story is clearly pure nonsense. What was he even doing in Devon? How did he get her away from Maidstead and into the car? To our house in Oxford. And – why?

Why? Why? Why?

I'm longing for more time alone with her so I can try to figure out exactly what's gone on. I glance again at the door. Remember the child lock. There's nothing I can do while we're travelling at speed.

It's just getting dark now and I notice my father has used only minor roads. I assume that's to avoid motorway cameras. Damn. But there will be cameras on A roads as well, surely? Dashboard cameras in cars. Surely someone will see us. Report us. Share the number plate. I just need to stay calm. Keep my father calm so that he doesn't make matters worse. And try to keep Chloe and Amelie calm too.

'I can't see the colour of the cars. It's getting dark.' Chloe is pouting as she speaks.

'OK. Well, look out the side and watch the cars as they pass closely. You could wave if you like.' I don't know how well we can be seen through the tinted glass in the back but it's worth a try.

'No waving.' My father's voice is firm. 'Maybe the car colour game is not such a good idea.'

'Oh, I think it will be fun for the girls. Pass the time—'

'I said NO! You stop the game right now,' he bellows suddenly, the colour of the back of his neck turning red. His head twitches and both girls burst into tears. Proper crying.

'It's OK. It's OK.' I reach out to squeeze first Chloe's shoulder and then Amelie's. I fish in my pocket for tissues for them and keep shushing and trying to soothe them. 'It's going to be OK.' But my heart is pounding out of my chest and I have no idea how I am

143

going to conceal the fact that I am every bit as frightened now as they are.

'Let's just be quiet and it will be fine,' I whisper.

Amelie blows her nose in the tissue and turns to me. I try so hard to find some small reassurance in my expression for her but it's no good. She is clearly terrified, her eyes pleading with me for help.

CHAPTER 30

MATTHEW – Day Three

'Good of you to meet me, Mel. We're going mad.' Matthew finishes his coffee. He arrived at the café first, the only one near enough to the police station to give them some privacy. But Mel has turned down coffee. Keeps checking her watch and phone.

'I'm sorry but I'm *really* stretched. I'll come out to the house later this evening – see you both together – but I've only got minutes.'

'Understood. So where are we?'

Matthew leans in and tries to read her face. Melanie has been in regular touch but mostly by phone and sometimes through the family liaison officer, which he's found frustrating. Unlike her.

'OK, so I'm sorry I've been a bit distant but I needed to be careful – professional – while I ruled out Carol.'

'And you *have* ruled her out?'

'Yes. We've spoken to her friend in France and also had confirmation of their museum visits on CCTV. They tally with the time Amelie disappeared. I'm sorry I had to wait for that. But you know how it is.'

'Sure. So we're OK – you and me?'

'Of course we're OK.' She rests her hand on his arm. 'I'm just sorry I don't have anything concrete for you yet.'

He fights his response. The panic. The images in his head that stop him sleeping. He turns momentarily to the window. Dark outside. Can't bear the thought of another night, a third night, without Amelie. For a second, he thinks of the statistics. How few survive an abduction for this long . . .

'So – what's the update?'

'Adam Meadows is lying to us. Says he and Dawn are divorced. His lawyer says they're not. We're chasing her bank details. Last known car. The usual. Nothing's come up yet but we're throwing everything at it, Matt. I've got some good people working late tonight. I've also spoken to her sister in New Zealand. No contact in years. They weren't close. But she confirmed Dawn and Adam fell apart and talked about a split after losing the boy. She has no idea where she might be. I have the team chasing every possible avenue to find her.'

'So no travel. Nothing from passport or tax office.'

'Not so far. She's still on the company accounts. A director of the building firm. Receiving dividends into a personal bank account. We're trying to trace her through that.'

'Anything else?'

'A boy, a teenager, has just come forward about the body in the trolley. Between us, it looks like a nasty prank gone wrong. He felt bad about it, returned to the canal several times to see if the body had surfaced. On one visit, he saw Amelie outside the shop. At the back of Freda's Fashions near the canal. She was wearing a green dress, not her pink hoodie. Must be the dress she had her eye on. She was talking to someone but the witness couldn't see who. And the CCTV was out of action, as you know.'

146

Matthew feels a terrible wave of dread pass through him. He imagines it. Dawn Meadows talking to Amelie. He holds Mel's gaze.

'You think it was Dawn she was talking to?'

'I don't know. The witness ran off. Only watched for a few seconds and it was a bad angle. As I say, he couldn't see who it was. But it confirms that's where Amelie disappeared. From the rear of the shop. So I have the team going over all the camera footage near the canal again. As you know, there are two car parks within close walking distance. We've been through all the CCTV but I'm getting them to check it all again with the updated information that she was in a green dress. Not in her pink hoodie and jeans.'

'Good. That's good. This could make a difference.' He pauses, frowning. 'So she was in green. Right. Not pink.'

'Yes. And if we get anything – *anything* at all, I'll ring you, Matt.' This time Mel pauses. She takes a long, slow breath. 'How is Sally holding up?'

'Bad. She's not sleeping. Obviously. But it's good she at least has Carol with her now. We've been liaising with the home looking after Sally's mum. They had to call us because her mother saw something on the news. It was a mistake. They were supposed to keep her away from the television. It's been horrible. Sally's not well enough to visit her mother but they spoke on the phone. All very distressing. And the worse thing? With the illness, the dementia – her mum overnight has forgotten already apparently. Has started asking for Sally again. And it's so very hard for Sally, all that. Not knowing what to do for the best.'

'I can't begin to imagine.'

'So what can I do, Mel? Is there something I can do? Help with?'

'It's probably best you're with Sally. With all this stuff breaking on the guy in the shopping trolley, it's manic. They're just kids.

147

Eighteen. We've got them in custody, all lawyered up, so I need to get back and oversee the interviews. Almost certain we'll charge them tonight and do a press update before the late news. It's crazy busy.'

'OK. I get that. And I said I'd go back later to be with Sally, but can't I help go through that CCTV again? If anyone can spot Amelie, even a glimpse, it's me. And with this new update on what she was really wearing . . .'

A pause.

'Please, Mel. If you have people working late, I can work alongside them. Speed things up.'

'Officially – I can't have you on the team. Not properly. And certainly not asking questions. You know that.' She leans in as if checking he fully understand this. Her difficult position.

'I get that. I promise I won't meddle.'

'OK. If you want to help the officer going through the car park footage again, I can arrange that in a side room. Say it's our best shot to try to spot Amelie. But you will be there as the parent, not an investigator. OK?' She checks her watch as he nods. 'Good. I need to get back now but if you follow – say in half an hour, I'll put that in place for you. Ask for me at the front desk.'

'Thank you. I just need to be doing something. *Anything to get things moving.*' And then he clocks a change in Mel's expression, the light in her eyes suddenly different. 'Sorry. I do know you're doing everything you can, Mel.' He means it but struggles to get his tone right.

Melanie just nods very fast. And so he fears that – *yes* – he got the tone wrong, making things worse between them and realising in this moment as their eyes stay locked that she's hurting badly too. Dark circles. Skin dull.

The world – *his* world, this petrifying new world in which Amelie is still gone – weighing so very heavily on her shoulders too.

CHAPTER 31

OLIVIA – DAY THREE

'Right. So make yourselves at home. We'll be here for a bit.' My father is standing by the door and locks it from the inside. It's dark and he uses the torch on his phone at first, then pulls two camping lights from his rucksack and switches one on.

I glance around the caravan. It's old. Dirty and neglected. Remote too – at the end of a bumpy and windy track. We haven't been here in years. I had no idea my father still had it. That it was still here even.

Chloe moves closer, eyes full of fear and confusion. She clings to me as Amelie stands alongside us, head bowed and silently crying. The horror of our new situation and the weight on my shoulders suddenly feels crushing. Dry mouth. Pulse increasing.

The lights look battery powered and I'm immediately worried how quickly the batteries will drain.

'It's OK, girls.' I try to keep my tone calm. Cough to clear my throat. I can't let them see how afraid I am. 'This is going to be fine. Like a little adventure.' I reach out to take Amelie's hand to find it's clammy. Trembling. I give it a squeeze, all the while my father watching so closely.

'So, the girls are probably hungry,' I say. 'So what were you thinking we do about food? Maybe a shop? We could all go to a supermarket together. Get some supplies? Food. And some cleaning things. Maybe torches and batteries too?'

I smile at my father to play along as if this is a little holiday, scanning the caravan and trying to remember the last time I was here. As a small girl. My mother standing at the little sink and cooker, making food. When was that? Ten years ago? No. More.

I need to somehow coax my father into a calmer place. Unpick this madness. I'm hoping if we take Amelie to the shops someone will recognise us and this hell will be over. 'We could get sandwiches for tonight and some things for breakfast. Maybe some bacon?' Dad loves bacon sandwiches. And shops will have CCTV. 'There must be somewhere with twenty-four-hour opening.'

'You're not going anywhere,' he says firmly. 'Not tonight. You need to sleep. Get to bed.' He glances around the caravan as I try again to remember the layout. There's a door to a tiny bedroom. Yes. I remember my parents took that little room. Just a bed with a few fitted cupboards above on one side. One high and tiny, narrow window. It's coming back to me now; I had to sleep in the sitting area, the bench converted to a bed.

'When am I going home?' Amelie's voice is shaking, tears pouring down her face.

'It's OK, Amelie.' I squeeze her hand again and pull Chloe close into my side. 'I used to come here for adventures when I was a little girl. And we always went home afterwards. It's on a farm, this place. And it's near a lovely wood. We could maybe go for—'

'Stop it, Olivia. Just stop it. Not another word, OK?' He looks around the caravan. 'I'll go and get some supplies. But you need to stay here and make the beds ready. And first we need to give thanks. All together.'

150

He looks at us in expectation. Amelie turns to me with panic in her eyes, but Chloe is already on her knees, hands together in prayer. Ready. Practised. She has done this a hundred times before. It's one of Grandad's rules.

The floor is filthy but I kneel too and stretch out with my hand to touch Amelie. 'It's OK,' I say. 'This is just a family thing.'

Amelie looks even more terrified but, to my relief, follows our lead. Puts her hands together. 'We don't go to church,' she says. 'I don't know what to do.'

'Everyone should go to church,' my father barks. 'And we wonder why the world is the way it is. Teenagers having babies. Girls running away to London.' He stares daggers at me, eyes blazing, and then raises his hands, palms upwards like a priest.

'Dear Lord. We beg forgiveness for our sins and thank you for your patience. For our health and for this place. And for all that you give us. We are so grateful.'

'We are so grateful,' Chloe and I chant together. My father glares at Amelie.

'We are so grateful,' she says in a little voice full of fear. Relief courses through me. *Clever girl.*

'We rejoice in our father in heaven, and we honour our true and familial father on Earth.' Still his hands are cupped upwards. Chloe has her head bowed, well used to this. Amelie's hands are trembling as she holds them together in prayer. She has stopped crying but her eyes are terrified and confused.

'You can all take the bedroom. There are sleeping bags and blankets in the drawer under the bed. I won't be gone long.'

No one moves.

'I said you can take the girls into the bedroom, Olivia.'

As we all stand slowly, I glance at the bedroom door to see there's a bolt on the outside at the top. A heavy metal bolt with a padlock. I remember again that the window in the bedroom is tiny.

No way even Chloe could squeeze through. 'But they might need the toilet while you're out,' I say. 'And I think they're hungry now. How long will you be? Why don't we come with you—'

'*No*, Olivia,' he bellows. 'You go to the toilet now. All of you. Chloe first.' He reaches out his hand and Chloe takes it as he guides her to the tiny toilet cubicle. 'You be a good girl for Grandad.'

Chloe steps inside the cubicle but then stops. 'It stinks. And there's no light. I don't like it.' My father moves forward and pushes her inside, holding the door ajar for her. I can't bear to watch. Chloe's getting really scared.

'It's OK. Grandad won't shut the door fully,' I say. 'It's like camping, Chloe. Only it's better than a tent because we have a roof and won't get wet.'

We wait. I watch my father holding the door ajar and wonder if he has my phone in one of his pockets or if he left it at the house. How the hell am I going to get help for us? Pull him back from whatever this madness is?

After Chloe, Amelie is encouraged to use the toilet. At first she refuses but I press her, worried about how long we'll be trapped in the bedroom. Will he actually lock us in? I tell her I will guard the door if she's embarrassed. Several minutes pass with her inside.

'You OK in there, Amelie?'

'Yes. Fine. It's just hard to see.'

The noise of the flush as my heart starts to race. I need the toilet myself but don't want to leave the girls with my father. Not with him in this weird state. He has been up and down over the years but nothing as bad as this. I close my eyes briefly, thinking suddenly of what happened in the cellar recently and realising that I am at fault; that I should have seen this coming . . .

I take a breath. I have no idea how long he will be gone to get food. Or if he will even come back. I have no choice but to use the toilet until I work out what's going to happen next. I'm assuming the bolt means he *is* going to lock us in the bedroom and so I'm already trying to figure out a plan to escape. Caravan walls can't be that solid, can they? I frown, wondering which window might break most easily, the one in the bedroom or the bigger one in this part of the caravan?

'Here,' I say finally, taking a small book from my backpack and handing it to Amelie. 'Will you read this to Chloe while I use the toilet? Can you do that for me? She loves this book and I'll be really quick.' I widen my eyes, pleading with Amelie to cooperate.

How I wish now I'd had more time to pack before we left. There were just minutes to get a backpack ready. My father insisted we leave immediately. I grabbed a few books and juice cartons and wipes. Unbeknown to my father, I also have a packet of biscuits and three tiny boxes of raisins. It was all I could manage as he hurried us out of the house. I realise now I should have been more methodical. Thought of a torch. What if he's gone for ages? Abandons us? What if I can't break out of the bedroom?

'Sure. I can read to her,' Amelie says. 'I'm a good reader.'

'Good girl.' I watch them sit together on the bench close to the battery light. Then I use the toilet as quickly as I can. Chloe was right. The flush works – must have some kind of battery back-up – but it still stinks.

When I emerge, my father's holding a large bottle of water, presumably from his own backpack. In his other hand he has a big bar of soap.

'Right. We need to do our cleansing now. Before I go out.'

'Yes, of course,' I say. 'Girls. Come here so we can all wash our hands.'

There's a tiny red plastic bowl in the caravan's stainless steel mini sink. My father pours some of the water into the bowl and I go first to show Amelie what to do.

'I wash my hands in the name of the Lord,' I say. 'To cleanse my flesh and to cleanse my soul.'

Amelie again looks as terrified as she is confused.

I help Chloe next, coaxing her to repeat the words in her small voice. 'I wash my hands in the name of the Lord. To cleanse my flesh and to cleanse my soul.'

I dry her little hands on a grubby old tea towel by the sink.

'And you,' my father barks, nodding his head towards Amelie, who steps up to the bowl. I move closer to help her. 'Say it after me. I wash my hands in the name of the Lord.'

'I wash my hands in the name of the Lord.'

'To cleanse my flesh and to cleanse my soul.'

Tears are once more rolling down Amelie's cheeks, her bottom lip trembling as she pauses to take a deep breath before finally continuing, 'To cleanse my flesh and to cleanse my soul.'

My father then opens the bedroom door. 'Inside.' He holds out one of the lights and flicks the switch on the other.

'No. Please. There's no need to lock us in,' I try, taking the light all the same. 'We can wait for you out here.'

'You do as I say, Olivia. *Right now!*' His tone is furious once more. He grabs my arm and shoves me roughly into the bedroom. Both terrified girls follow, clinging to me and crying again. So that as he slams the door and bolts it from the outside, I hold them tight, trying again to soothe them but fearing that by challenging my father, I am simply making things worse.

CHAPTER 32

MELANIE – Day Three

There's good progress by the time Melanie gets back to the station. All three boys from Milburn House School, the ones named by Zak, are in custody, ready for interviews. All lawyered up. Zak's also in custody. All the parents are in reception, causing a commotion.

Given all three boys have had their eighteenth birthday, they're being treated as adults. It's late but Melanie wants these interviews done tonight – ideally all three suspects simultaneously but there are only two interview rooms free, so she picks Ben Delaville and Tom Broadmoor to go first. From Zak's statement, these two had seemed to take the lead.

Melanie takes up her post in the small adjoining office with both cameras from the interview rooms up on-screen in front of her. She's warned Sam and Richard, the two sergeants leading the interviews, that she will oversee and intervene if information from one interview needs to be relayed urgently to the other.

She feels a surge of adrenaline as both sergeants start the tapes and run through the usual information and cautions.

At first both Ben and Tom try the silent treatment. 'No comment' to every question, glancing occasionally at their lawyers.

The same scene in stereo. But both sergeants are thankfully experienced. Melanie knows from her own early days in CID that silent interviews are the most stressful. She got lucky and a senior officer referred her for additional training based on emerging research. She's ensured her team have had similar additional training to overcome the stress when 'no comment' is the defendant's strategy.

Sam, the sergeant who accompanied her to Rugby, is the first to let this additional training click into play. 'You should know that this silent treatment is fine by me.'

Ben Delaville glances again at his lawyer.

'The thing is we know what happened,' Sam continues. 'Of course, I'd prefer to hear it from you too. But if you don't want to cooperate, that's your decision. We don't need you to tell us.'

Ben's expression becomes more alarmed, the colour draining from his face.

'You see, we have a full account of what happened by the canal from your friend Zak.' Sam pauses. 'You stay silent, which is your right, then you should know that I'm happy to go with Zak's account of what happened, to corroborate with Forensics and refer all this to the prosecutors. Makes things a lot cleaner and quicker from my point of view. Might even get home for some late supper. Quite fancy picking up a curry.'

Ben's eyes widen and he shifts in his seat.

'So, according to Zak, you were one of the ringleaders in the prank which led to a shopping trolley containing a homeless man going into the canal at the rear of the Maidstead High Street shops. We understand that you and Tom Broadmoor and Harry Clifton put the man in the trolley, pushed him up and down a bit and then did absolutely nothing to help him when the trolley rolled into the water. Where he drowned. Is that right? Feel free to say no comment but I should warn you that isn't a good look from where I'm sitting. I'm not the one who makes the final decision, but I'd say that's manslaughter. Or murder.'

'It wasn't my idea.' Ben is leaning forward. His solicitor puts his hand on his arm.

'As we discussed earlier. You don't have to say anything.' The solicitor's tone is firm, but Ben remains agitated.

'So you were the ringleader, Ben. Yes?' Sam blanks the solicitor and stares at Ben.

'No. Absolutely not. I said it was a bad idea. I never wanted to be involved. It was the others . . .'

On the second screen, the same blame game is being conducted with the finger pointing in a different direction.

'No way was it my idea. I kept telling the others to leave him alone,' Tom says as his lawyer also leans forward to remind him that he is *not obliged to say anything at all.*

Melanie takes a deep breath. This is not going to take as long as she feared. She checks her watch – nearly 10 p.m. – and decides she will just let these two interviews run, given both suspects are talking now, and will then oversee the interview with Harry Clifton and a final update with Zak, this time with his lawyer involved.

Melanie glances again from screen to screen, taking in how young the suspects are. Boys more than men. She thinks of all their parents in reception.

It's a relief to see this unexpected manslaughter – or murder – case resolving as it will allow her to refocus all her attention and all resources on the search for Amelie. But she also feels angry. And above all desperately sad for the poor homeless man in the trolley. But also for those mothers and fathers in reception whose lives will never be the same.

She's about to organise new instructions to be taken into the two interview suites when a message comes up on her viewing screen: Matthew Hill is waiting in reception. A deep breath.

Melanie heads straight downstairs, sorts the security clearance with reception and makes Matthew, under protest, wear his visitor's badge, before leading him up to the incident suite, where she's arranged viewing of the car park security footage in a side office.

There are three staff still on duty in the main office, waiting to mop up after the interviews, and she watches Matthew thank them all for working so hard, so late, to find Amelie, their expressions becoming solemn. Melanie doesn't need to make introductions. The whole team knows who he is.

The ex-cop, the father in the position no one wants *ever* to be in.

It is in the side room as they wait for the detective to fetch fresh coffees for the viewing session that Matthew brings up the subject she's been most dreading.

'So. Have you been thinking about the stats? Going into our third night, I mean.' Matthew is looking at the floor as he speaks.

Melanie is grateful she is already seated and closes her eyes. She's been thinking of little else. Not many abductions end well. And statistically very few after this amount of time.

'Some do survive this long and we can't give up hope. We have to keep going, believing we will find her well.' She tries to make her tone neutral. Not over-the-top positive because he would see through that. Truth is, she's becoming desperate herself, knowing the statistics too well. But it's her job as his friend to stop him falling into that black hole.

'I can't discuss this with Sally. You know I can't. But it's eating me up, Mel. I need to ring her. Tell her about the green dress. But should I be preparing her for the worst? Is that where we are? Am I wrong to be trotting out all the optimistic stuff? Have we reached the point where I should be preparing her—'

'If it were George, I would hang on to hope until hard evidence told me otherwise. Any parent would. And should.' She says this very quickly. Means it. Meets his gaze eye to eye.

His face changes.

'Look,' she continues. 'We both know the stats aren't good. But we keep going, Matt. We keep going until we find her. And we hang on to hope because what else is there to do?'

CHAPTER 33

SALLY – Day Three

Sally's shaking as she puts down the phone. She had been standing when Matt phoned from the police station but she finds her legs are suddenly unstable. She goes to sit. Instead collapses on the sofa, just staring ahead of herself.

'What is it?' Carol is immediately alongside her, watched by Molly, the family liaison officer, who checks her own phone across the kitchen, imagining a key update. Bad news?

'Is it a breakthrough?' Carol's voice again.

'No.' Sally doesn't know how to say it. Absorb it. Process it. 'Not really. I don't know.'

'So, what, darling?' Carol strokes her hair.

'It's something I don't understand.' Sally narrows her eyes, trying to picture it. 'It's just they think Amelie was wearing something different when she disappeared. A green dress. Not her pink hoodie and jeans.' Sally breaks off, sobs suddenly choking her as Carol sits closer, pulling her into a hug.

'You want me to stay a bit longer? It's no problem.' Molly had been just about to leave, a late end to her shift, but places her coat which was over her arm on to a chair.

'No. It's fine,' Sally says, fumbling for a tissue from her pocket. Trying to compose herself. She's very conscious that Molly is a mother too. Has her own family. 'I have Carol. We can manage. You go.'

'You sure?' Molly looks uncertain what to do.

'Really. It's OK. We'll see you tomorrow. I've got this,' Carol adds.

Sally keeps her eyes closed as they exchange goodbyes and she hears Molly picking up all her things, her footsteps to the door and then the click of it closing.

Only after Molly is gone do the tears come fully. A horrible wave of sobbing. Carol says nothing for a time, just sits alongside her.

'You tell me when you're ready. I'm here. No pressure,' Carol says finally. 'You want a drink?'

Sally shakes her head. So tired of cups of tea. She reaches into her pocket, looking for a new tissue but can't find one. Carol immediately rescues her by darting across to the kitchen counter to grab a tissue box which she then moves to the coffee table in front of Sally. She blows her nose, firing the tissue into the bin in the corner. Missing. Then grabbing yet another fresh tissue to pat her eyes.

'I should have let her buy the dress.' Sally turns to look directly at Carol. 'Why the bloody hell, didn't I do that?'

'Hey. Hey. Now then, none of this happened because you didn't let her buy the dress. You know that.'

'Do I? If she was wearing the green dress, she must have gone back inside while I was on the phone because she was cross with me. Do you have any idea what this means? Oh Jeez.' She bows her head. Closes her eyes. 'This means she was cross with me. That this happened because I—'

'Now then. I'm going to be really straight with you. You can't let yourself do this. Amelie wouldn't want this. Everyone gets busy and everyone has to say no to some things when they're in a hurry. You had a birthday party to get to, you told me.'

'Yeah, but I took the phone call, didn't I? They say I was on the phone to Laura much longer than I realised.'

Sally keeps very still, fighting tears. Carol tries to squeeze her shoulder but this time Sally wriggles free. Puts up her hand. Needs not to be touched. It doesn't help. Makes it worse. In her head Sally is picturing Amelie in the changing room of Freda's Fashions. Then for some reason heading through the rear door near the canal.

Why would Amelie do that? What made her do that?

And why, oh why, didn't I just buy her the sodding green dress?

CHAPTER 34

OLIVIA – Day Three

I lie very still, staring at the curved ceiling of the tiny caravan bedroom. It's just past 11 p.m. To my surprise and relief both Chloe and Amelie have at last fallen asleep alongside me on the small double bed. Chloe has her head in the crook of my arm. It's uncomfortable, my whole arm numb. I'm dreading pins and needles but am worried even the tiniest movement will wake them both. Amelie cried herself to sleep. She's missing her parents. She knows our situation is not right, despite all my reassurances, and is increasingly afraid.

I turn my head very carefully to the left to take in the high, narrow window and curse the fact it's too small to climb through, even if I could smash off the padlock my father has put on it. When did he come back to this caravan and add all these awful locks and bolts? I feel a chill sweep through me. *So – was that just for security? Or did he plan this?*

Soon after I heard his car pull away, I tried with all my might to force the bedroom door and then the window but they simply wouldn't budge; the padlocks are much stronger than I expected. Worse – both Chloe and Amelie became hysterical as they watched me. They couldn't understand why I was saying everything was going to be all right, while desperately trying to break out.

It's OK. It's OK. We're fine in here. We'll be OK. I was just worried one of us might need the toilet again before he gets back.

To try to calm them, I read from the storybook Amelie had been reading to Chloe. The tale's a bit young for Amelie but she didn't seem to mind. And I shared the juice and a few of the biscuits. I told them that my father is obviously unwell at the moment. Overtired and overworked. He is a big man and I can see that when he shouts, it's very intimidating for the girls. I realise I need to stop triggering him, making him bellow at them. But I have told the girls he will not hurt them if we all stay calm. Do exactly as he asks.

We will be OK, girls. Tell Amelie. Has your grandad ever hurt you, Chloe?

No. Never.

There you go. We'll be fine. We just need to stay calm while he's feeling so unwell. You let me do all the talking. And we do as he says. OK?

OK.

For myself I won't sleep. Daren't. I have the light on its dimmest setting to spare the batteries and am listening out for my father's return, trying to decide what I will do if he doesn't come back. I glance again around the tiny room, looking for anything I might use to try harder to force the window and the door in the morning if he stays away long enough. There are small fitted cupboards above the bed on one side and I wonder if I could force one of the doors off, then use it as some kind of lever or battering ram on the main door? Yes. That might do it.

I let out a long sigh. I'll tell the girls when they wake that I need to force our way out of the room to use the toilet. That they mustn't be scared. Must stay back while I try again to get us out of the bedroom.

I turn my head once more to stare at the girls, wrapped up tight in their sleeping bags. It's surprisingly cold, as if we're sleeping outside in a tent, not inside a caravan. There's condensation building up on the inside of the tiny, narrow window with its wretched security.

Their breathing's steady. Deeply asleep. Probably pure exhaustion from the worry and the fear. I begin to feel more concerned now about the cold and so I chance the small movement of carefully reaching down with my free arm to the tiny strip of floor between the bed and the caravan wall to scoop up the one blanket I placed there earlier. We need it. Slowly and as quietly as possible, I spread the blanket over myself and the two girls in their sleeping bags as an extra layer, praying the cold will not wake them.

The movement makes Chloe stir. She rolls over on to her other side and I'm able to free the numb arm at last. I'm cold myself but will have to cope. We're all fully dressed so should be OK for this one night. I listen out for my father. If he does return, I'll try to negotiate – kid him that I am going along with this madness. Give him a list of things we need for our stay. Not just food and water but some more blankets. More batteries. Torches. I'm so worried our light will fail. That the girls will be terrified of the dark on top of everything else.

Finally, I close my eyes, not to sleep but to *think*.

Earlier when Chloe fell asleep first, Amelie whispered to me with more details about what happened. She's worried that her parents will be angry with her for sneaking back into the shop to try on a dress. I made her change back into her jeans and hoodie before we left the house but she made me bring the green dress in my rucksack. I've told her that no way will her parents be angry about it.

She said my father appeared at the back door of the shop when Amelie was looking at herself in the communal mirror and said her mother had been taken ill and she needed to come urgently. That there was an ambulance on its way. Amelie couldn't understand why this was at the back of the shop but she thought it might be to do with access for the ambulance. My father had a handkerchief and she thought he was going to make her blow her nose. But he put the handkerchief over her face and she felt dizzy and sick. Later she woke up on the back seat of the car and he was angry and impatient, saying that he had to look after her until her mother was better.

I'm still trying to work out what he was doing in Devon. My only thought is he must have followed me. Found out I was going to see Matthew Hill somehow. He is always saying I must never leave him. Which means it's my fault he came across poor Amelie. I squeeze my eyes tight and curse myself for being the trigger. My whole ridiculous plan to try to find my mother. I never imagined it might push him over the edge; drive him to do something this extreme. All I wanted was somewhere to take Chloe. A safer place for her. Why did I risk that? *Why?*

I breathe in and out slowly to steady myself and the answer comes in a flash of pictures as another long sigh leaves my body.

It was the cards. The birthday cards. I can picture them so vividly, tied in a bundle with a neat red ribbon in the trunk at the bottom of my bed back home. I think of all the times I've taken them out to read them secretly when my father was out. Those birthday cards from my mother were always so precious to me. Like a little beacon of hope. Yes. An invisible thread still linking us.

My mum has been sending me birthday cards and Christmas cards ever since she left. Which was when I was eight. Same age as

166

Amelie. My dad always gets really tense when the cards arrive and a couple of times he's tried to hide them from me. I think he's always been worried that one day she'll include an address and I'll go and live with her instead. I see now that I was right. That's been his big fear. Me leaving. Why he started to lie to me about the cards.

Once, on my twelfth birthday, he said there was no post for me. I checked through the pile of letters myself. Nothing. I thought she'd forgotten. I was so upset I went to my room and lay on my bed and cried. He came and stood outside my door and said he was sorry but she wasn't worth it. She met another man and chose him over me. He said he hated to see her upsetting me. *But what kind of mother leaves her own child.*

But later, I found the birthday card from my mum in the bin when I went to put the vegetable peelings in there. I couldn't believe it. He'd thrown it away. Lied. I can't describe how I felt. So angry that it actually frightened me. I felt like I wanted to explode. Hit him. Hurt him.

I took the card, all covered in tea stains and bits and bobs from the bin and I put it on the coffee table beside his empty mug and I just looked at him. I remember that his face was sort of fixed. As if he didn't know what to say.

Why did you put it in the bin? Why would you do that?

He didn't say anything for a long time and so I did something extreme. I picked up a glass paperweight from the dresser, a gift from his brother which I knew he loved. Really loved. And I dropped it on the floor. It smashed into a lot of pieces and in that moment I was really glad.

But here's the thing. He didn't get mad. He just told me in a very quiet voice to clear up the mess.

I was waiting for him to get mad and to shout at me because I badly wanted a fight. The religious rituals weren't so bad back then. Sometimes he had tablets in a brown container on the kitchen worktop and when he took the tablets he seemed a bit calmer. I wasn't yet truly frightened of him. I just thought our life was weird. Not dangerous. Weird. But he didn't even raise his voice over the smashed paperweight. He just told me to control myself and to clear up the mess. I wanted that fight SO badly. But he just told me to get the dustpan and brush and clear up the mess.

Later he said that he was sorry. That he put my mother's card in the bin because I was better off without my mother. That any mother who would leave her daughter wasn't worth thinking about. He said he knew that the cards upset me because they reminded me of her leaving, abandoning me, and he was trying to spare me the pain.

I open my eyes and stare again at the bolt on the caravan window. Even if I could somehow smash out the window, it looks way too narrow for even Chloe to squeeze through. And in any case what would little Chloe do out there on her own?

I narrow my eyes and start to picture where this caravan is. The approach road is nothing more than a dirt track. I remember from my childhood that the caravan was on the edge of farmland near a wood. Several miles from the nearest village. I remember before my mother left, my parents bringing me here a couple of times and calling in at the farmhouse about the arrangements. The caravan, as far as I remember, is more than a mile, maybe even two, from the farmhouse itself. And I realise it's too much to ask of such a little girl, even if Chloe could make it through that tiny window.

Fact is, we're stuck. Our only hope is that the police will by now have some CCTV pointing to my father and be looking for his car.

Beyond that? I honestly have no idea what to do.

CHAPTER 35

MATTHEW – Day Three

Matthew's eyes are getting tired. Spooling through the car park security tapes is essential but mind-numbing. Bad enough when you're feeling on form. Purgatory when this exhausted.

It's good to feel that he's at least helping in some small way but more than an hour of spooling so far and – nothing. Not a glimpse of any girl, let alone his beautiful Amelie. Some of the tapes are in colour but there's no flash of green dress. Nothing helpful at all.

For a horrible moment, Matthew wonders if Dawn, or whoever has Amelie, put her in the boot of their car. He takes a deep breath, leans back in his seat and closes his eyes to the imagined scenes of a struggle. Amelie terrified. Crying out for him and for Sally? No. That would have attracted attention, surely? According to the cameras that were working further along the canal path, it was very quiet. Hardly anyone about. But there were half a dozen or so cars in each of the two nearest car parks. Drivers parked nearby have been asked to come forward but only six have done so. They saw nothing. That's the puzzle. Why the hell didn't anyone *see* anything? It's so infuriating that the schoolboy who finally gave a statement over the shopping trolley death didn't see who Amelie was talking to. Equally infuriating that someone put that bag over the security camera near the shop.

'You OK? Fancy another coffee?' Jack, the detective alongside Matthew, reviewing footage on a second screen, suddenly leans back in his chair. He turns to share a small smile.

Matthew is grateful for the company. Jack must need the overtime to be here this late. They've said they'll keep going until midnight. Matthew won't be allowed to stay unsupervised. He nods to Jack over the coffee offer, then immediately regrets the decision as the detective stands, stretches and heads for the door. It will be appalling instant coffee. Cheap brand. He almost calls out to change his decision but stops himself as he watches the guy leave the room. He's remembering Amelie watching him use the espresso machine at home.

When will I be allowed to have coffee, Daddy?

Who cares what kind of coffee he gets. Matthew suddenly recalls that awful panic attack in the car and takes deep breaths to calm himself. Must not let the dark pictures and the dark imaginings take over his mind.

He stands and walks around the small room as if to stretch his legs but really to try to calm his thoughts. The problem is the overthinking. Involuntarily but compulsively raking over so many memories. The lovely ones are comforting, of course. Amelie out on her swing with her hair blowing in the wind. Amelie up on his shoulders on walks when she was smaller. But the problem is the difficult times are also creeping into his thoughts now; all the times he's got it *wrong* with Amelie. Impatient with her constant questions when she was a toddler. Tutting and teasing her over the Barbie collection and the weird plastic ponies with neon hair. The obsession with Disney, watching the same films over and over. *You can't want to watch it again, Amelie. You know the words . . . Hell's bells. Even Daddy knows all the words.* Oh – and the outfits. Nylon and sequins and garish fairy wands and crowns.

You can't wear your fairy costume to bed, Amelie.

Why not?

He's always adored his daughter. But he's tortured now by the memories of cross words. Irritation. And so many things that have baffled him about parenthood. And now he's wondering why didn't he just go with the flow more? Why did he ever tut. Or tease. Or wish for the years to pass more quickly. Willing Amelie past the terrible twos, for instance.

A click of the door. Matthew turns his head to see the detective walking back into the room, moving very carefully with two mugs of coffee, steam drifting from the surface. Matthew takes his drink with a smile, blows on the surface. He sips and it is every bit as terrible as he feared. 'Thank you.'

'You're welcome. Tough time for you.' A pause. 'So you and the boss used to work together?'

'Yes. We trained together, actually. A long time ago.'

'So was she always like this?'

'Sorry?'

'Sleeping bag in the office. Workaholic.'

'Driven, I think, is the word she uses.' Matthew didn't know Mel was staying on site.

They both smile. Matthew is thinking of their younger selves. Him and Mel back in uniform before they had any idea how their lives would work out. Both of them determined to earn transfers into CID. Neither of them imagining that he would end up outside the force. A private investigator.

He found it very tough at first. Civvy street. There weren't always good cases going. At first he turned down any work collecting evidence for divorces. But he soon had to climb down. Sometimes cash flow meant he had no choice. And then he had started working occasionally with Mel. Liaising quietly in the background. A sort of advisor. Sounding board on big cases. And then finally in recent months she persuaded him to rejoin the force. On the new team she's to rebuild in Cornwall. It was in the papers, some of them referencing back to the case that led to him leaving the force. Does that have anything to do with Amelie's abduction? Did Dawn Meadows see the coverage?

'You OK? Is the coffee OK?'

'Sorry. Mind wandering. The coffee's fine.'

'We will keep going until we find her. Whatever it takes.' The detective's expression is suddenly very serious and they both keep very still.

'Thank you.' Matthew has to clear his throat. 'I appreciate that. Right. Let's get back to it then.' Matthew sits down. Tries to find a small smile of encouragement. And gratitude. He starts to scroll and almost immediately sees it.

At first he thinks it's his imagination. Wanting to see something. But he rewinds and there it is again. The *tiniest* flash of green on the bottom left-hand corner of the screen. He rewinds a second time, freezing the shot as the green appears. Infuriatingly there's nothing much in shot or in focus. The frame shows a flash of what might be the back of a figure close to the camera. A man? Hard to be sure because it moves immediately out of shot and is out of focus. But there is definitely something green, something that could be green fabric just moving in and then immediately out of shot. Also what looks like a foot in a trainer. A white trainer with stars on it, just like Amelie's. Again – not quite in focus.

'What about this? Does that look like green material to you? Could that be a green dress? Someone wearing a green dress? And trainers. White trainers.'

The sergeant moves across to his screen and Matthew rewinds the sequence several times. The sergeant pulls a face. 'Hard to say.

Out of focus. I guess we can try to get it enhanced. But it could be a green dress. Just caught on the periphery of the camera.' The detective pauses. 'Almost swinging past, wouldn't you say? Like the foot. Moving quite fast across the camera?' A pause. 'As if someone' – he pauses – 'is being carried maybe?'

'Yes. I agree. I tell you what' – Matthew's mind is back into professional gear, adrenaline starting to pump – 'I doubt we're going to get much from the enhancement but let's zoom in and take the registrations of all the cars in the near vicinity of this. Check them all out. The owners. The drivers. We need to consider them all as witnesses. Or suspects. Worth a shot?'

'Always worth a shot.' The detective's expression is more animated and he takes out his notebook to start writing down the number plates as Matthew zooms and freezes each frame, calling out the letters and numbers from each of the nearby cars.

After a time the detective excuses himself to go to the toilet and, alone at last, Matthew plays the short sequence of green fabric flashing across the corner of the shot with the trainer with stars on. He watches it over and over and over. It's her. He's sure of it.

CHAPTER 36

OLIVIA – Day Four

I'm still lying awake, worrying and plotting, when there's a noise outside. I keep very still and listen. It's definitely a car drawing up. I wait. Finally, there's the sound of a car door being slammed, footsteps and then various metal and jangling sounds. The key opening the door? Sorting out the bolts he must have put on the caravan's main door as well?

He's definitely back. In the main area next door. I hear rustling. The click of cupboards. My stomach growls with new fear and dread. It's bad news that he hasn't abandoned us. I can't try to break out now. But his car may have been seen, which is good, and at least he will have supplies. I need to get breakfast into the girls. Keep their strength up while I figure out how to get us away from him.

I check my watch. Barely 6 a.m. My father's been gone for hours. Maybe he struggled to find a twenty-four-hour supermarket around here, out in the middle of nowhere?

I turn my head to see that Amelie has her eyes open, though Chloe is still asleep. I put my finger up to my mouth to hush Amelie and whisper.

'I'm going to try to talk to my father. You stay in here. OK?'

She just nods in reply and again I am amazed at her composure. She's a brave little girl. She fully understands that none of this is OK and has been terrified at times and yet somehow she's managing to hold it together.

I stand up very slowly, keen not to disturb Chloe, and tap lightly on the bedroom door.

'Hello?'

Nothing.

I tap again.

'What is it? What do you want?' My father sounds angry. Inside I feel another punch of fear and my hands are suddenly trembling. But I think of the girls and steel myself. They only have me and I have to do something. Try *something*.

'I need to talk to you.'

'Later.'

'*Please*. The girls are still sleeping. I can make you a coffee. Just the way you like it. We could have a chat. About the . . . situation.'

There's a long silence and then at last I hear the jingle of keys and he opens the door to let me out.

I try to find a small smile, wanting to keep him calm and praying he'll be in a more sensible frame of mind. But his eyes look wild and exhausted as if he hasn't slept at all. He's staring at me, unblinking. Testing me?

'Well?' he says. 'Out with it? Cat got your tongue?'

That's when I see it, leaning up against the front door. I feel my pulse increasing. I try not to look at it, or rather not to let him see me looking at it. I've always known that my father owned a shotgun. I've never liked the idea of it in the house with Chloe. But he said it was nothing for me to worry about; that as a boy he had been taught to shoot rabbits which caused havoc on his father's farm. He has a licence and belongs to a gun club. All official. At home it is kept in a secure cupboard and he only takes it out occasionally when he attends his club to keep up his target practice.

But now that same gun leaning against the caravan door is absolutely terrifying. Why has he brought the gun here? He must have put it in the boot while I was calming the girls.

Until very recently I never saw my father as someone who would hurt me very badly. A bully – yes. Controlling and mean – yes. Weird and unwell. Rough with me. But he was always saying I should never leave him. That he could not bear life without me. Stupidly I thought that drew a line in the sand. Now I see there is *no* line in the sand and have absolutely no idea where this could all end.

With him in this state, the gun in the room is *very bad*. I want to ask him straight – *why the gun? Is it loaded?* But the words stick in my throat. I'm worried it will trigger him. Make him panic. He's closer to the gun than I am. He's already taken a girl off the street – something I never imagined him capable of – and I have no idea what he might do next. I have to protect the girls. Get them away. I decide it's much too dangerous to challenge him openly over the gun and so instead, I try to steady my breathing and glance around the interior. No sign of any shopping bags.

My gaze lands on a drawer in the sink unit, wondering if there might be a knife inside. Do I have the strength and the nerve? To use a knife on him? *Should I? Could I?*

'So,' I say, fighting the pounding in my chest. 'Shall I make you a coffee? Have you put the milk in the fridge already?' There's a tiny fridge under one of the cupboards. I've been hoping he might arrange power. Switch it back on somehow? But when I open the fridge, the inside light doesn't come on and it smells terrible.

'There's no power,' he says, his voice flat.

I shut the fridge door and look around the kitchen. 'So did you get long-life milk then?' Still I'm glancing around the space, wondering if he's already put the cereal for the girls away in the overhead cupboards. After a moment, I reach for the drawer as if I'm just looking for a spoon. I pull it open quickly hoping to find a knife but he dives across to slam the drawer closed, deliberately trapping my hand.

'Ow!' The pain is surprisingly bad but he keeps his full pressure on the drawer, squeezing the wood tighter and tighter against my flesh. 'Please. You're really hurting me. I was just looking for a spoon.' I try to keep my voice down, not wanting to frighten the girls. But it's hard.

'Do you think I'm stupid, Olivia?' He pushes even harder on the drawer and I can't help it. Cry out in pain.

'What is it, Mummy? What's happening?' Chloe's voice from the bedroom.

'It's OK, darling,' I gasp, leaning forward with the pain.

'Be quiet in there,' my father barks.

And then finally, staring right into my eyes, he loosens his grasp on the drawer and I slowly release my hand, the fingers red and throbbing.

'No silliness, Olivia. And *no* coffee.' He is glaring at me as he speaks. 'I've got a new plan for us all now.'

I go cold, thrusting my sore hand into the crook of my arm and squeezing to try to calm the stinging, not letting my gaze move again to the shotgun.

He sinks down on to the banquette seating. 'I've been driving around, praying. Asking God for guidance.'

My hand is really hurting and I feel my heart rate increasing even more. A pounding in my ears too as if the blood is suddenly rushing around my veins too fast.

'You shouldn't have tried to leave me, Olivia,' he says, looking straight at me. 'I've always told you. You're my everything. You know that I can't go on without you. This is your doing. I have

177

done all this to protect you. To keep you safe. This all happened because—'

'I'm never going to leave you. I promise.'

He stares at me for a very long time and I feel almost giddy at the hardening in his expression. So much of what he says these days is pure madness. I feel so guilty. Should have realised sooner that something really bad might happen. The contradiction. Saying that he cannot bear for me to leave him. And yet seeming to *enjoy* hurting me. I feel sick suddenly, bile in my throat. I turn my head to glance back at the door to the little bedroom behind me, still shut, and decide to sit down on the banquette opposite him to hide how unsteady I feel.

What's coming next? How on Earth do I keep him calm? Keep him away from that *gun*? Away from the girls.

I have no phone. No iPad. No way of knowing what's going on in the world beyond this caravan, but Amelie's disappearance must still be headline news. They will be searching for her and appealing to the public to look for her too. I glance to his pocket and see that it's bulging with his iPhone. So he'll know exactly what's being said. I need him to run errands. Somewhere cameras might pick him up. And I need to get Amelie outside where someone might recognise her. One of the farmworkers?

'How about we have some breakfast and then a bit of exercise outside. Me and the girls. A little walk. Some fresh air.' All you can see from the caravan windows are the wood to one side and farming land to the other. Fields stretching as far as the eye can see. No sign of life. No sign of tractors or farm activity so far. But there must be *someone* out there and I have to somehow boost the chance of them noticing us.

'I've said it already. Do you really think I'm stupid, Olivia?'

'What?'

'Do you think I was born yesterday?'

178

'No, it's just that the girls are going to find it a lot more difficult if they're cooped up all the time. Chloe's so young. And Amelie—'

'I prayed while I was out. I asked for guidance about what to do.'

So this wasn't planned. He really doesn't know what to do next.

'Look. Here's an idea,' I say. 'We could leave Amelie here. Head off somewhere, you and me and Chloe. And then when we're somewhere safe – somewhere so far away that they'll never find us – we can call from a payphone, tell the police where they can find Amelie. And it will all be sorted. Over with. In the past. Nobody need ever know it was you.' My pulse is again pounding in my ears. My fingers are still throbbing. It feels so risky to even suggest this. But if he has no plan? Still I try not to look at the shotgun leaning against the door. I have to come up with options. Some straw he might grasp.

He thinks for a while, as if considering my idea, then sniffs. 'No,' he says finally. 'We're not doing that.'

'Can I use the toilet?' A voice behind us.

We both turn our heads to see Amelie standing in the doorway of the bedroom. She looks terrified. I pray that she doesn't notice the gun. But she does. Her eyes widen but she doesn't say anything.

Clever girl. Don't say anything. Please don't say anything.

She looks back at me and I raise my eyebrows, sharing as much reassurance in my expression as I dare.

'Go back to your room,' says my father.

'But I really need to go,' she says. 'I'm really very sorry to be any trouble.'

Good girl. Clever girl.

My father reconsiders. 'All right,' he says. 'But be quick. And then back into the bedroom with you.' His voice is clipped. Cross.

'Of course, thank you.' Amelie moves across the small space to use the toilet. We hear her emptying her bladder. The noise of the chemical flush. So it's still working. Good. She comes out and asks if she can wash her hands at the sink. My father nods and to my surprise, Amelie repeats the chant as she washes her hands.

'I wash my hands in the name of the Lord. To cleanse my flesh and to cleanse my soul.'

Clever girl.

'See,' I say, close to tears. Astonished again at how smart and brave she is. 'Amelie is a very good girl. The Lord will be pleased with her and will want her to be safe.'

Amelie looks at us both and then obediently goes back into the bedroom, shutting the door. There is mercifully no more noise from Chloe. Amelie must have warned her to be quiet.

'So this is my new plan.' My father leans forward and has dropped his voice to a whisper. 'The Lord is guiding me, Olivia. I *have* to listen to him. You know that.'

I have that horrible taste again in my mouth. Bile. It's clear to me that any voice he is hearing has *nothing* to do with God. I bark a cough trying to clear it, my heart still racing.

'He wants us to fast.'

'*Fast?*'

We've never fasted before. For all his religious rituals, we've never done that before. Not at Easter. Not even for Lent. No fasting, not ever.

'Yes. I should have seen that before now.' His voice is still very quiet. 'I drove around in the dark when I left and I realised it was too dangerous; there are cameras everywhere, Olivia. Garages. Shops. We can't risk the main roads. What if they know? That I have taken Amelie to save her. Just as I am saving you and Chloe.' He is shaking his head as he speaks, his eyes wild. 'No one must find us because they won't understand. They will *misunderstand.*'

I have no idea what to say. How to turn this situation around. He's right, I hope. They will be looking for us. Hopefully all of us. They will have picked up on cameras that he has taken Amelie and they will be looking for all of us right now. If I can just keep my father calm, they will surely find us before he panics. Reaches for that gun . . .

I tell myself they will have helicopters and a big search strategy. Drones in the sky? They will surely have his number plate by now. Or maybe someone up at the farmhouse has noticed my father's car parked in the field.

'And so I prayed. And the good Lord answered me.' My father's expression changes. 'We don't need supplies. We don't need to go anywhere. He wants us to *fast*. So that's what we're going to do. We are going to stay here. And fast. All of us.'

I glance at the kitchen tap. 'So just water. We just drink water?'

He shakes his head rapidly. 'No. Don't you see? That's the beauty of it. Nothing, Olivia. To be absolutely pure. To be cleansed. We don't eat and we don't drink. Nothing.' His own gaze now goes to the sink. 'This water is only safe for washing and the toilet anyway. The tank is dirty, Olivia.'

'But the girls.'

'They need to be *cleansed* too.'

I feel a wave of pure dread pass through me. I think of the single carton of juice left in my bag. The few biscuits and the one small box of raisins I brought with us. Wishing now I had been more careful to ration them and praying he won't search my bag. Why didn't I think more clearly back at the house? In the rush to leave, I was worried about how to entertain the girls without a phone or iPad. I brought paper and colouring pencils. A few books. Why the hell didn't I bring more to drink and eat? When he took my phone and my iPad, I was just panicking. He saw me packing chewing gum and confiscated that but he didn't notice me take the juice and the biscuits. Was too busy barking at Amelie to hurry up.

'It's decided.' He lifts his chin, his expression more determined now. 'No food and no water. It is God's will, Olivia.'

CHAPTER 37

MELANIE – Day Four

In her dream Melanie is in the middle of an interview when the familiar trill of her phone interrupts. *Sorry, sorry*. She tries to silence the phone but the bleeping continues.

Her eyes snap open in panic. It's dark. The bleeping continues: somebody's trying to FaceTime. It takes a moment to realise she's in the office in her sleeping bag, the phone on the floor alongside her glowing with each chirrup. Melanie stretches out her hand but cannot reach it. She sits up, eyes heavy with exhaustion and in no mood for a FaceTime with anyone until she sees who's calling. Tom.

Barely 6 a.m.

Oh my God. What's happened?

Melanie accepts the FaceTime to see her husband, grey and exhausted, full frame. He's in unfamiliar surroundings. The background doesn't look like the Airbnb. White with a flash of grey screen or some kind of curtain.

'Right. So the first thing to say is George is OK. It's all sorted. He's right here listening. He's had a little accident but he's OK. We're just out of X-ray and the plaster clinic. He's sore but he's going to be fine. George. Come here. Say hello to Mummy.'

A few seconds and George appears in shot, Tom gently lifting him on to his knee, and holding the phone further away so she can see them both on-screen. George is wearing a plaster cast on his right arm. No. Left arm. Mirror image.

For a beat, Melanie is filled with a mixture of both terror and anger. How could this happen? And why the hell didn't Tom ring the very moment it happened? But George is staring anxiously into the screen.

'Hey darling,' she says, trying to appear calm. 'It sounds as if you've been a brave boy. What happened?'

'I fell out of the bunk bed. I'm sorry. Daddy said I was to stay in the bottom bunk but I wanted to try the top one. I needed a wee and I missed the ladder with my foot.'

'Oh dear. So is it very sore, darling?'

'A bit. Are you cross?'

'No. Of course I'm not cross.'

'Right. So the drama's all over, Mummy,' says Tom, 'and the doctors say it's a clean and simple break. It'll mend just fine. George has been lucky. They saw him and treated him quickly. Another woman was telling me her nephew didn't get a cast straight away a couple of weeks back. Just given painkillers and sent home to wait for plaster clinic. So we've done well in the circumstances. He just needs to take it easy, don't you, buddy?'

George nods, eyes wide. Melanie wonders what drugs they've given him. He looks a little spaced.

'So why didn't you phone me straight away, Daddy?'

'I was worried you would get in the car exhausted and drive straight here.'

Melanie feels a punch to the gut. That's exactly what she would have done.

'I didn't want you driving when you're tired. I decided to get George to the hospital and find out what was what before calling you. In fact, it was all way better and quicker than I expected. We were in a zone where phones aren't allowed at first so I decided – and please don't be cross, Mummy – that it was better to just get it all sorted out and then FaceTime you once I really knew where we are. If it had been more serious, any tricky decision or anything like that, I would have rung before.'

Melanie feels winded. 'Right. So I'll get on to the chief inspector and the super. Sort cover. Get down there as soon as I can.'

'You can do that? Abandon the case?' Tom's expression is difficult to read. 'It's just we only have two more days here now. I was thinking let's see how today goes. If it's too tough for George, I'll bring him home early. If he manages, we'll come home as planned and see you then.'

Melanie notices that he doesn't mention the original plan of her giving this case two or three days max and joining them belatedly. That boat long since sailed.

'What do you think, George? Do you think you can manage, darling?'

'I want to see you, Mummy.'

'Yes, of course. And I want to see you too, darling boy. You've been very brave—'

'Right. So Daddy's calling this,' Tom interrupts. 'How about we have today here. You can show your cousins your plaster cast and get them all to sign it. And if you want to go home, we will drive home this afternoon. Mummy's very busy with work but she can at least see you at home. But if you want to stay at the holiday house until tomorrow, that's OK too. How about we let you decide, buddy.' Tom is looking at George, holding him close and then kissing him on the forehead.

Melanie feels overwhelmed. Every ounce of her being wanting to just throw clothes on. Get . . . in . . . the . . . car.

'Is that OK with Mummy? We let George decide when we come home early. Later today or tomorrow. So either way we will both see you very soon.'

Melanie just nods, unable to speak. She blows kisses and George blows kisses back.

'We're going to go now but I'll ring from the holiday house once George is settled back there and I bring everyone up to date.'

'I don't know what to say. I'm so sorry, Tom. I wish—'

'It's fine. He's been a very brave boy. We understand how busy you are. How important it is what you're doing. I'll ring you later when he's back with everyone.'

'Thank you. Love you both.'

'We love you too.'

Melanie watches them disappear but keeps staring at the phone as the FaceTime home page sits there. A part of her wants to call straight back. Do the right thing. Get on the road.

But how can she? Melanie starts to go over in her mind an imaginary handover to another SIO. Manslaughter charges have been brought against three of the boys over the homeless man's death. A decision's still pending on what Zak will be charged with. Matthew's breakthrough with the car park footage means five cars need to be traced. Their owners interviewed urgently. Adam Meadows is being brought down for interview. Dawn Meadows' bank details are due in this morning. There's more trouble from the vigilantes out on the Park Estate. They've had to find another safe house for the man on the sex offenders' register. The list goes on. And on . . . Trying to hand this over to another senior officer will be a nightmare. So much more, all the next steps and new strategy, is still swimming around in her head, not all of it on paper or computer.

Melanie realises that she's crying. Which is rare. She crosses her arms and clutches her body tight, rocking to and fro. How she wishes George were right here. On her lap so she could cuddle him tight, tight. She's never broken a bone. Doesn't know how much it will hurt.

Suddenly she's remembering all the conversations with Matthew about juggling work and family. Lately, while negotiating his return to the force to help her build a new team in Cornwall, it was his biggest worry. Doing right by Sally and Amelie. Melanie realises that up to this point, she has always found the juggling difficult. But doable. And only in this moment, does she fully understand why.

Tom.

She starts typing a text to him. This man, this beloved man who has shouldered so much over the years to let her pursue the career she loves. She writes several sentences before realising she's rambling. Borderline incoherent. She deletes it all. Tries again.

I do not deserve you. xx

CHAPTER 38

SALLY – Day Four

'Oh, good grief. Sally, Sally – what are you doing out here? You're soaked through.'

Sally turns her head to see Carol running from the patio towards her.

'Come on, honey. We need to get you inside. Get you dry. And warm.'

Sally lets Carol take her arm and help her from the swing. She wasn't swinging, just sitting with her feet firmly planted on the ground. Hadn't even noticed she was wet.

'It wasn't raining when I came out.' She casts her head about. Feels so disorientated. Remembers only that she was staring at the swing. Found it unbearable to see it there. Empty. Still. And so she went out to sit on it so that she might feel closer to Amelie. And also so she wouldn't have to look at it. Out there. *Empty*.

'Quickly, love,' Carol says, looping her arm and striding back towards the open door to the kitchen cum diner. 'Let's get you upstairs and out of these wet things.'

And now suddenly Sally realises that she *is* cold. She sees the water dripping from her clothes on to the wooden floor as they make their way through the room. Up the stairs.

'That's it.' Carol's voice is all alarm. 'I should never have left you. I thought you were sleeping.'

Sally remembers now. Carol said she was taking a bath before breakfast. Sally was in her bedroom, fully dressed as always, lying on the top of the covers. She got up and went over to the window. She stared and stared at the swing. Got upset. Went downstairs . . .

Carol is pulling Sally's hoodie over her head. 'I'll start running the shower. Get it warm. We need to get you warm as quickly as we can. Strip off everything. Leave it on the floor and I'll fetch your dry robe.' Carol moves over to the shower cubicle in the corner and reaches in to switch it on, feeling the spray of water with her hand. 'That's it. That's a good temperature. You get stripped off and get in. Yes?'

Sally takes off the rest of her clothes and moves across to the shower. She's not embarrassed. They were in boarding school together. She steps into the warm spray and only now realises just how cold she was.

'That's it. Get warm, lovely. I'll get your robe. And a cup of tea too.' Carol scoops up the wet clothes from the floor and leaves the room.

◆ ◆ ◆

A while later they are back downstairs together, sitting at the breakfast bar. Sally has her hair wrapped in a towel. Her clean robe on which Carol warmed on the radiator.

'You feeling better? Warmer?'

Sally nods but then frowns. 'Warmer. Yes.' She needs to qualify that she doesn't feel better; can't imagine when she will ever feel *better.*

'Shall I dry your hair so you can try to go back to bed? Have some more sleep?'

'No. I don't like to sleep. It feels so wrong. You know – when she's out there.'

'I get that but she needs you to be strong. And rested. And so do the police. How about one of the tablets the doctor left? Or just half a tablet?'

Sally shakes her head. The truth is whenever she's slept even a little bit, she's woken disorientated and drenched with guilt, feeling worse not better. Also – she's terribly afraid of what she'll find in her dreams.

Anxiety dreams about Amelie started a good while back, *long* before she disappeared. Sally confided in both Carol and their mutual friend Beth. It was when the anonymous letters started when Matthew was in the papers.

Sally's friends tried to distract her. Play it all down. Their thinking – that the police never proved who sent the letters. And all parents worry as their children get bigger. Now Sally is wishing she'd not allowed herself to be reassured. Fobbed off? Listened more to her gut.

'You remember when I told you that I'd started to have dreams. A few years back. Worrying about something happening to Amelie?'

'Honey, I don't think it helps to talk about that now.'

'Was I wrong from the very beginning, Carol? To talk him into all this. Marriage and parenthood. Was it selfish of me? Naive of me? Did I start getting those bad dreams because deep down I knew that? Especially when those letters started. That I was wrong to talk him into all this when he knew he had that threat hanging over him. Hanging over us.'

'No, darling.' Carol sighs. 'It wasn't selfish. All mothers worry about their children. But we can't have a world in which the police can't have families, for heaven's sake. Anyway. No one knows what's really happened yet. We don't know for sure it's this Dawn woman so there's no point blaming yourself. When no one's to blame. Even if it is her. Matthew did nothing wrong. And you did nothing wrong. You're terrific parents.'

'Doesn't feel like it—'

'Hey. Hey. You need to *stop* this, Sal. Going over it all. You're just going to make yourself ill. And like I said, Amelie needs you to be strong.'

'But the thing is, I thought I was angry with Matthew deep down. For doing the job that he does. But I think I'm really mostly angry with myself. Pushing him to have a child with me when—'

'Sshhh now. This is not the way, Sally. You can't have good people blaming themselves when bad people do bad things.' Another pause.

'I've been googling other cases.' Sally closes her eyes tight.

'What do you mean, darling?'

'Cases where children are taken and survive.'

Carol doesn't reply at first and Sally opens her eyes and turns her head to the garden again. The empty swing.

'I found a case of a girl who was taken and found after ten years. The parents were so thrilled. But then they found out what she'd been through. Crashed down to Earth with the shock of it. Turns out she was not the same as the girl who was taken. So damaged. And I find myself feeling so terrified—'

'They are going to find her. Amelie is strong and you are strong. And this is going to be OK.'

'Is it?' As Sally speaks her phone buzzes in her pocket. It's a long text from Matthew. She skims through it quickly. He's on his way and will be home in fifteen minutes maximum. He says he caught a glimpse of a green dress on the CCTV. The police have been trying to trace a number of drivers who may have seen something in the car park near where Amelie disappeared. They've just found two of the drivers and team members have gone out to interview them.

Don't build your hopes up but it could be important.

Sally straightens her back.

'What is it?'

'Some news from the investigation. They've traced a couple of potential witnesses overnight. Drivers who were at the car park near the High Street.'

'You mean someone who may have seen what happened? When she disappeared.' Carol sits up too.

'I don't know.' Sally doesn't understand. 'It's something to do with the green dress. The dress I wouldn't let her buy.'

CHAPTER 39

OLIVIA – Day Four

We're locked back in the bedroom again. Chloe's doing some colouring on the bed. Amelie is just lying beside her with her eyes shut. Both girls are trying to be brave but they're hungry and thirsty. I'm worried about Amelie in particular. She's missing her family more and more. I'm nervous about how much she overheard earlier. And she's obviously so much more aware than Chloe of just how bad our situation is.

My father's gone out again. No idea where or why. He's locked the front door and taken the shotgun. He says he won't be long and I heard the car pull away. He warned me it was my job to make sure the girls behave.

Nothing silly. There will be consequences if you get silly.

I feel I'm letting the girls down so badly because I just can't decide what to do. A part of me feels I should try to break down the door and get them far away from here right now. But the gun has changed everything. What if he turns up the very moment I'm trying to break out, making a hell of a noise? Gun in his hand. It will whip him into a complete fury.

I think again of what happened in the cellar at home, that one time I made the mistake of challenging him.

I just don't know which is more dangerous. Triggering his unpredictable anger or playing along with this gruesome charade a bit longer. Keeping him as calm as possible? We need to get out of here, away from that gun, but I need to know he'll be away from the caravan long enough for us to break down both doors.

It's agony trying to make these decisions; to cover up my own fears for the girls' sake. I haven't explained about the fast to them yet. They're frightened enough already. They've complained of being hungry, but I've just told them there aren't any shops in the countryside so we've got to make the juice and the biscuits last all day. Split them fairly. Of course I haven't had anything myself. I just pretended to sip on the apple juice as we passed the carton between us. I gave the girls one biscuit each and the last of the raisins but it's not enough. And it leaves just one biscuit to split between them later.

I turn my head to take in Chloe's concentration. She loves colouring and it's a Disney book featuring her favourite films. She has distinctive green eyes, my daughter, which always remind me of her father. I wonder when she will ask me about him again. I fobbed her off the last time it came up.

He had to go away, darling.
Will he ever come back?

◆ ◆ ◆

I was only fifteen when I met Chloe's father. A naive and silly teenager prone to crushes on singers and actors. I'm not streetwise, I know that. And in my teens, it was worse; I was so unused to freedom. Unused to boys. I had a best friend back then called Julia but my father told me I was to stay away from her. He said she was a bad influence. Wild. Which is precisely why I both loved and envied her too.

Julia was everything I was not. Savvy and confident. Outgoing and funny. She was allowed make-up and had her ears pierced and had all these plans. She didn't get on with her father but for entirely different reasons. He drank. Got loud and argumentative. She used to talk about running away to London to get a job in a bar and start to live for real. She hated school.

I was the opposite. Little miss goody two-shoes. The swot who did well at everything. High grades and a father with ridiculously high expectations. Doing well at school kept my father calmer. Back then he was taking tablets though I never knew what they were for. His moods were still up and down but not quite so bad. He had these weird punishments if my grades dipped. Made me take cold baths in my pyjamas, using the kitchen timer. Five minutes for a B grade. *You could have got an A.* Fifteen minutes for a C. I quickly learned to put in the hours; to make sure the school reports were good. It made my life so much easier.

And then it was Julia's sixteenth birthday and her mother was buying her a record player for her bedroom. Julia was into all things retro and had started a vinyl collection. There was a record shop in town and I decided to save my pocket money and buy her a record as her birthday present.

So that's where I met him.

His name was Daniel and he looked to me like a musician. Hair to his shoulders. Designer stubble. Tight jeans and a white shirt. Oh, and those eyes. Piercing green eyes.

I was so naive, I blurted this out almost immediately – *You have really unusual eyes* – which made him laugh at me. Looking back, he must have thought I was flirting but I really wasn't. Because I went to an all-girls school and I had no idea how to even talk to boys. My father just wouldn't let me go to pubs or clubs or anything. It never occurred to me that someone like Daniel would be interested in me.

He said his father was French but his mother was Irish. They lived on the outskirts of Paris. The green eyes were from the Irish genes. He said his mother had traced their family tree. Had it all typed up on the computer, going back generations.

I asked him a lot about Paris. I loved learning French at school and was blown away that he was bilingual. The idea of being able to speak two languages fluently thrilled me. He asked me for my name in French and I answered in French. The whole thing gave me butterflies. I gabbled in English about wanting to travel myself. Learn new languages. See the world. I told him about Julia and the birthday present and he helped me pick out the most fabulous record. Bright red vinyl. Beautiful. Her favourite band.

He asked if I would be calling into the shop again and that he'd really like it if I would. I felt hot. And strange. And also conflicted because I just knew deep down that my father would be absolutely horrified to think of me chatting like this to a boy who was a few years older than me. *You don't know what boys and men can be like.*

But I didn't care. I loved how it made me feel, standing in that shop with Daniel smiling at me with his lovely green eyes. So I said I would be back the next week. And I lied. When he asked how old I was, I said I was sixteen. Just a bit older than my friend . . .

'I'm hungry. When are we having proper breakfast?' Chloe puts the colouring pencils down and pouts. 'I want to play. Or watch a film. Or go outside or something.'

'I know it's hard, honey, but we'll just stay here for now.'

'But when's Grandad getting back? When are we going to *eat*?'

'Soon, sweetpea. Soon.'

Amelie rolls on to her side and I can see that she's crying again. It hits me suddenly that I need to stop with all this dithering. It's not fair what I need to ask of these girls; they're too young. But the truth is I need to start preparing them for what I need to do. I need to explain, as gently as I can, that my father's 'illness' is becoming a serious problem. Which means the time for playing along has passed. I need to get us away from him.

And so I need them to be brave.

CHAPTER 40

MELANIE – Day Four

One cup of coffee and Melanie's mind is racing as she prepares for the team's breakfast update. She FaceTimed George again while he munched cereal and he says the arm's not too painful but she's still feeling horribly torn as she jots notes for the meeting.

The headlines? Adam Meadows is being brought to Devon for questioning again, under arrest this time as he's been lying and concealing evidence about his wife. Local police are doing a second full search of his properties. The bank's now confirmed that Dawn Meadows has an active bank account still listing the marital home with Adam, despite his protestations otherwise. They're checking her card records and are to provide details of any purchases or ATMs used. Hopefully that data will be in later in the morning.

Statements have been taken from the two drivers identified by Matthew from the overnight review of the car park footage. One's potential dynamite. The driver says he saw a man carrying a girl in a green dress across the car park. The witness asked if they needed help but the man said no. He said his daughter was diabetic and had just fainted. She'd skipped breakfast and just needed some orange juice from the car and her mother to take her readings again.

The witness said he was worried but the man seemed on top of the situation. Reassuring. *Don't worry. We've got this. She'll be fine. Just needs some sugar.* But infuriatingly, just like Zak and the canal sighting, the driver did not see where the girl was taken. The car park was L-shaped and the man carrying the girl walked around a corner out of sight so the witness could not identify the car.

I'm sorry. After checking they were OK, I went to my own car and didn't see where they went. I feel terrible now but at the time I remember being impressed at how calm he was. I have two kids myself and thought – I'd be a nervous wreck if one of them had diabetes. Never occurred to me he might be lying. You just don't think like that . . .

Melanie pauses. Narrows her eyes. So the update is Amelie definitely tried on the green dress as suspected. She somehow wandered through the rear security door by the canal. It was supposed to be locked but was used sneakily by staff from the shop for a quick smoke and hence was unlocked. One of the staff has since admitted they put the bag over the security camera as there had been a memo warning them not to use the rear path for smoking. The staff didn't want to get caught.

So why did Amelie walk out of the rear door instead of joining her mother at the front? Was she trying to steal the dress? Or did someone distract her? Adam Meadows? Was he the man who carried her across the car park? And how did he knock her out? Some kind of drug? Was Dawn with him? Was that it? All planned?

Melanie taps her pen against the lined paper as she makes notes. She scribbles – *update on all Matthew's past cases.* It's important to keep an open mind. Not get tunnel visioned. Matthew has convinced himself that Dawn Meadows is behind Amelie's disappearance. And maybe she is. But Matthew's laser focus on the Meadows is partly driven by his own sense of guilt about the death of Jacob Meadows, and she's seen one-track thinking go wrong in too many investigations.

She sighs. Rubs her nose which is suddenly itching. She can feel adrenaline pumping as she moves into performance gear. She needs everyone chasing the other drivers in the car park in case someone can describe the car that took Amelie so they can track it. She needs her team upbeat. Firing on all cylinders today. Amelie has been missing for far too long.

Melanie puts her notebook in her pocket and takes out her phone to take in the screen saver of George. Smiling at the beach. She feels a powerful internal lurch. That longing again to just get in the car and be with him. She breathes in and out slowly to ride the discomfort, blows her son a kiss. Then she closes the phone, leaves the small office which has become her overnight camp and heads out into the main corridor.

'Morning, boss.' Alison, the detective, passes her with a take-away coffee in hand. 'Sorry. I would have got you a cup if—'

'It's fine,' Melanie says, finding a smile.

And then Sam suddenly emerges from the main office, eyes wide.

'Boss. Big news.' He lets out a huff of air. 'We've found Dawn Meadows.'

CHAPTER 41

OLIVIA – Before

I was so naive when I fell pregnant with Chloe. You read about these girls who have sex once and end up with a baby and some people just don't believe that can happen. *Don't we teach sex education these days? Make teenagers put condoms on bananas?* But guess what? I'm here to tell you, you absolutely can have sex just once and get pregnant.

Of course the problem with naivety, by definition, is you don't know that you are. Worse – you accidentally mask the fact, turning your naivety into a timebomb. People ask you questions that you don't understand and you cover up your lack of knowing and you lie and you smile. You want to appear cool and grown up and so you dig a deeper hole for yourself. That's certainly what happened with me and Daniel.

Much later, when my periods stopped and it all blew up, Julia asked me if Daniel forced himself on me. *You saying he didn't use a condom? Did you actually say – yes?* She said that if I didn't, we could go to the police and he would be charged because of my age.

My father ranted and raged and said the same thing: *I want his name and I'm going to the police.*

But the truth was not what they imagined. It didn't feel bad, what happened between me and Daniel. I don't remember saying 'yes' specifically but I certainly didn't say 'no' and so I had to hold my hands up and tell them that *it wasn't like that.*

And it really wasn't.

After that first meeting when I told Daniel I was sixteen, I never took it back. The lie. And I never realised the significance properly until it was too late. I went to see him again the next week like he asked, telling my father that I was doing some research for a school homework project in the library. I'd never bothered lying to my father before because it was so much easier to just go along with his weirdness. But meeting Daniel was like this massive awakening. It shocked me how much I wanted to see him again. And it shocked me how easy – and exhilarating – it was to lie to my father to make it happen.

The religious thing with my father had grown bigger and bigger. I kicked against it at first but that just made him angry. Borderline frightening. So in the end, I just tried not to trigger him. But the older I got, the more protective, weird and suffocating my father became. The prayer sessions and the handwashing got really bad as soon as I moved to secondary school. Sometimes he'd have me washing my hands dozens of times a day. I noticed that there were no tablets on the kitchen worktop anymore. I asked him about that because they seemed to have helped his moods in the past. But he said God had told him not to take the medication.

Meantime his disapproval of Julia also grew and grew. By the second year, aged around twelve or thirteen, Julia started to roll the waistband of her skirt to make it shorter. Everyone did it. I copied her, of course, correcting the length before I got home. But one day, I got caught out and this led to a huge row with my father. Unbeknown to me he'd turned up to pick me up from school instead of me catching the bus. Looking back later, I realise that he was starting to monitor me. Watch me more closely.

He told me to stay away from Julia. Which of course made me want to spend even more time with her. I had a phone but a basic one. My father put some weird software on it to filter out things he didn't want me to have access to. And he limited the data. He said that social media was the path to disaster. *It drives teenagers to suicide. And sin. Don't you watch the news, Olivia? Understand what social media can do?* Every night he looked at the phone to see what I'd been googling and accessing. I simply wasn't savvy enough to bother to work around all that.

And because he was a teacher in another school, my father had a lot of teacher contacts. Out of the blue, he kept me off school for a few days, claiming I was sick. He wouldn't say why. But when I returned, Julia told me they'd done sex and relationship education. I challenged my father and we had another massive row.

They talk about it as if it's all fine. Teenagers having sex. Ordinary. Sex is for after marriage, Olivia. You don't need to know about all of that at your age. All you need to know is that the Lord says it's sacred. For marriage only.

Of course I eventually figured out how to google round at Julia's. We giggled when she told me about practising with condoms in the class I missed, but what I didn't share was that I was secretly horrified. Sounded so embarrassing.

I wasn't allowed to school discos. Or outings. Or any activity beyond scouting and sailing classes which my father helped to both organise . . . and police.

So the excitement of meeting Daniel and his apparent interest in me was not only unexpected but heightened – and made more risky – by my lack of experience. And lack of knowing. I confided in Julia about him after giving her the record on her birthday and she was thrilled. She was the one to then encourage me to go back there to see him again.

I can't.

You can.

So the second visit to see Daniel was a Tuesday and I had never felt anything like it. The thrill to see his eyes fixed on me as I walked into the record shop. He was just so relaxed and chatty and happy to see me.

He said that he finished work at five and could I stay so we could go for a coffee or a burger? The shop was walking distance from my house but I knew it would take twenty minutes at least to get home and I couldn't risk being late.

Then I remembered that my father got home later on a Wednesday. So I switched my 'library day' to Wednesdays and started to visit Daniel every week, knowing I had a couple of hours at least. We went for a coffee or a burger after his shift ended at first. We talked mostly. He let me practise my French. We talked about books and the cinema, and to be honest, it was all quite sweet. He kissed me on the cheek when we parted and I definitely got the whole butterflies in the stomach thing so that when he kissed me properly on the mouth on the third week, I was beside myself.

Back home afterwards, I lay on my bed in a sort of trance, worried that I hadn't done it right. The kissing. That he would realise it was the first time I'd ever kissed a boy. But he didn't say anything. He just asked if maybe I would like to visit him at his little studio flat the following week. He offered to make me a meal instead of a burger. A proper French recipe that was a family favourite. Of course, I said yes – no clue what I was really signalling yes to. I was naive, remember. Fifteen, going on twelve.

So I went straight to his little studio from school. It was sparse and surprisingly tidy, with posters on the walls and a huge collection of vinyl along one long shelf. And he really did cook for me.

Chicken in a rich sauce with a salad. Plus wine that I wasn't used to. And here's the thing. I thought we'd just do more kissing. But when we did kiss, I got my first and overwhelming experience of true lust. This powerful feeling deep in my gut and then down below. He pushed his body against mine and I happily pushed back. The whole thing overwhelmed me and the truth is I just gave in to it.

He asked me if it was OK to move to the bed. He did ask. *Are you sure?* He also asked me if it was safe and fifteen-year-old me didn't understand the question. I thought he meant – would anyone find out. I thought he was worried that my dad might suddenly turn up, looking for me. Naive me did not realise he meant contraception.

So the truth is I sort of gave consent because I got carried away and I didn't realise where it would all lead. I was one of those people who assumed you couldn't get pregnant the first time you had sex. Looking back – yes; Daniel was pushing his luck. Taking advantage? But he was genuinely shocked by the blood on his sheets. *You never done this before? You should have told me you had never done this before. You are on the Pill . . . yes?*

I said I was fine. A lie. I was shell-shocked. One little part of me was excited that I'd managed to have sex before Julia. Most of me was just numb. It had hurt. And once it started hurting, the lust diminished immediately because I was too embarrassed to tell him it hurt. Instead, I shrank inside myself until it was over.

He had a little en suite shower room. Absolutely tiny. I had a quick shower and said I needed to get home. He asked to see me the following week but I said I had exams, which was another lie.

I remember how flustered he was. Kept raking his fingers through his hair. Agitated. *Are you going to be OK?*

My period was supposed to start about two weeks later. I was like clockwork. When it didn't come, I hoped it was just stress. Julia said her dates were all over the place around exams.

Looking back, I think I realised quite early on that I might be pregnant. I knew that periods stopping was the first sign. But a bigger part of me just thought it was impossible. One time. Really? I felt OK at first. Just a little tired. And so stupidly I played ostrich. Let the weeks roll by.

By the time I finally started to feel sick and also to show, my dad challenged me. The showdown was horrible. A blur. A lot of shouting. Absolute fury on his part. Absolute shock on mine. I tried to defend what had happened, shouting back at him, but he slapped me hard around the face. I was stunned by how much it hurt. Then he marched out the front door, slamming it behind him and I just sat at the kitchen table crying.

He came back about half an hour later with pregnancy tests from the chemist. He told me to do one. Then a second one to confirm. And then when both tests were positive, he just took over. Barking questions and demanding answers. He said the Lord would forgive me but he was only human and would take much longer. *My princess. You were my princess and now look what you've done.*

He demanded details and stupidly I told him. I said that Daniel was a decent person and it wasn't his fault. I had this ridiculous notion that Daniel would stand by me. That maybe I would move into his little studio flat and we would become a little family.

Absolutely . . . ridiculous.

My father went to see Daniel. He was gone a long time. And when he got back, he was just quiet. Sort of depressed. He said that Daniel swore he thought I was older and that I implied I was on the Pill. He was too young to take on the responsibility of a baby. He wanted me to have an abortion and had offered to pay for it.

What kind of person says that? my father asked. *A bad person, Olivia. That's who.*

Daniel then texted me about having an abortion. Said he would take me secretly to a clinic if that was what I wanted. I didn't reply. I waited a long time before I finally worked up the courage to go to the record shop to see him.

But the owner was behind the counter. He said Daniel had suddenly let him down. Also his landlord. Quit the job and the flat and disappeared back to France.

The owner stared at my bump as if it all suddenly made sense. He said he didn't have Daniel's address. Only knew that it was in the Paris suburbs.

I looked for Daniel on Facebook and other social media a few times but the ridiculous thing is I didn't know his surname and I was too embarrassed, standing there pregnant in front of the record shop owner to admit that and ask. So I never found him.

When Chloe started asking questions about her father, I was always vague.

Too ashamed to admit it was my fault. That I'd messed up. And her father had done a runner.

I have grown to love Chloe so much that I don't ever want her to see herself as a mistake.

An accident – yes. A product of my ridiculous naivety. My first crush.

But *never* a mistake.

CHAPTER 42

MATTHEW – Day Four

It's 8 a.m. before Matthew finally makes it home. No way did he want to head home sooner and pretend to sleep. He's been driving round and also grabbed food in an all-night café.

It's a relief that Sally now has Carol to support her. He finds them together in the kitchen – dressed but both looking exhausted.

'Carol,' he says. 'It's good you're here. Thank you.'

She just nods. Face grave.

'Any news?' Sally is at the breakfast bar.

'Only what I told you in the text. The things from the CCTV we're following up.' Matthew takes in his wife's pale skin. 'You didn't sleep again?' He reaches out to touch Sally's arm, tilting his head and locking eyes. They've stopped hugging this past twenty-four hours. *Do you mind if we don't hug.* It was Sally who said it first, lying fully clothed on their bed. A part of him understands – hugging no longer a comfort. A bigger part cannot bear it.

Sitting in that all-night café, he was wondering what will happen to them. Him and Sally, the couple who cannot bear to hold each other, if . . .

Matthew closes down the thought. Keeps his gaze fixed on Sally, his hand still rested on her arm. Finally she pulls back and shakes her head. 'You look as if you didn't sleep either. Where have you been? I've been worried.'

'Driving. Liaising with the team.'

'Let me make you a coffee and you can tell me more about this CCTV.' Sally pushes back her bar stool.

'I'll do it.' Carol springs to her feet and heads over to the espresso machine but Sally moves too. 'No, really. I'd like to do it.'

'Don't be ridiculous. I'm here to help.' Carol flicks the switch on the machine but Sally interrupts again. 'No really, Carol. Let me.'

There's an awkward pause and both Sally and Matthew stare at the ground.

'Oh, right.' Carol glances from one to the other. 'No problem. Of course. I'm sorry; I'll give you guys some space. Grab a shower.'

Both Sally and Matthew keep their eyes fixed on the kitchen floor tiles as Carol leaves the room. They wait for footsteps on the stairs. The sound of the guest room door and then the bathroom door.

'She's been great,' Sally says at last, looking up.

'Yes. I've found it a big help, knowing she's with you. What about the FLO? Molly?'

'She's coming back a bit later. Ten, I think. I told her to take her kids to school today. She has two boys, you know. I feel bad that she's away from them. The long hours.'

Matthew doesn't answer. He feels that surge of jealousy which is becoming common every time he thinks of anyone with their own family. It feels bitter and wrong, the jealousy. But he can't help himself.

He looks at the light on the coffee machine, waiting for it to turn green.

'I worry about you driving around at night.'

'I know. But I promise I'm careful.'

'So, tell me everything. What's the latest on the car park witness? And the CCTV. So brilliant that you found something on the tapes.' Sally's voice is thin. She's trying to sound upbeat, optimistic, but for all the pretence, the tone is strained. Distant. Just filling the silence between them. The numbness which he is so afraid will swallow up everything he has always loved. Amelie. And now Sally too?

'It's being followed up today. The driver saw a man carrying a girl in a green dress. I told you that on the phone.' He waits as Sally nods. 'But he didn't see which car they went to. The cameras didn't pick it up. Out of their range.'

'Why didn't the witness step in? Do something? A man carrying a girl. Surely—'

'The man gave him a story about diabetes. Said the girl was just a little faint. Needed some sugar. He was convincing. The witness feels terrible. Mel is following it all up again today. She's holding a big breakfast briefing with the team and will update us. At least it's something. And I take it they have a description of the guy.'

'Yeah?'

The light flicks to green and Matthew places two cups under the spout. 'You want one too?'

Sally nods. 'Black please. So the description. Does it match Adam Meadows? What's Mel saying?'

'The description is quite broad. But they're interviewing Adam Meadows again and repeating the search of his property.'

'You think they might have missed something? Didn't do it properly?'

'No. Not that. But when there's a witness update like this, they tend to cross the t's and dot the i's. Run the checks again.'

Sally clinches her right hand into a fist and taps her lips with it. 'I've been googling.'

'Hey. I told you not to do that.' Matthew looks at his wife, feeling the stab of concern growing. 'It's a rabbit hole. It won't help.'

'No. Googling stories that turned out OK. Positive stories. Missing people who turned up.'

'Right. I still think it's best to stay away from the internet, Sally.' Matthew turns back to the machine and lets the two cups fill and turns off the switch, carefully passing one cup to his wife, whose eyes suddenly look wilder. He's afraid to ask what she's been reading. There's a huge range of stories out there. Some of them terrible. He knows because he googles every day himself.

'One of the stories said a girl was found years later. But she was never the same. And I was thinking—'

Matthew reaches out with his left hand to touch Sally's shoulder. And then her face. He can see that she's going to cry. Again, he badly wants to hold her tight but instead keeps his hand on her shoulder. 'That's what I mean. It won't help. Raking over other cases. We just have to hang on to hope. Keep ourselves focused on our Amelie.'

And then suddenly his phone rings. Matthew takes it from his pocket. 'It's Mel.'

He puts the phone straight to his ear, Sally's eyes still wide, clearly trying to read his face. He can hardly believe what Mel is saying.

'They've found Dawn.' Matthew speaks over Mel, leaning in toward Sally and putting his cup on the kitchen surface. 'Sorry, Mel. Yes. I'm still listening. Just updating Sally. She's right here with me.'

Mel won't give details. Keeps the call short. She shares that both Adam and Dawn will be brought in for questioning. She

210

promises the whole team's in overdrive. She'll update if there's any news. Anything at all.

Matthew is putting the phone back in his pocket when it buzzes with a text. He reads it on the locked screen and tries to keep his face neutral.

'What is it? Mel again?' Sally's eyes are unblinking.

'No. Nothing important.' Matthew puts the phone back in his pocket and realises he doesn't have long.

To decide.

CHAPTER 43

MELANIE – Day Four

Waiting for Dawn and Adam Meadows to be arrested and brought to the station is purgatory for Melanie. Every minute dragging out like elastic stretched and stretched until you know there's pain coming – dreading the recoil. The sting against your flesh.

She spends the time in her office pacing and calling the search teams over and over. Melanie's biggest fear is that Amelie has been at one of Adam Meadows' building site projects in the Rugby area all along. Locked away somewhere. Afraid and all alone. That the first round of searching missed something.

The geography's also tricky. Dawn Meadows has been found in Somerset, just over an hour from the incident room in Maidstead. But Adam's still much further away, en route from Rugby. The decision to have them arrested locally but brought to HQ for interviews – while search teams again check all their known properties – is hers. She's still not sure it's the right call but it's never a simple decision.

Now, as she waits and plans the interview with Dawn in her head, she realises it's crunch time over the most recent anonymous letter. The one she didn't share with Matthew. Sam is still the only one on her team to know about it. Melanie's plan now is to confront Dawn with the letter, hoping it will spook her. Get her talking. She will then tell her bosses this is why she's kept the letter quiet all along.

This isn't true, of course. A sweep of shame and nerves passes through Mel as she thinks of it. But she has to at least try to cover her back; to explain why she didn't declare this letter earlier to the whole team. She's already had one dressing-down from her senior officer over the vigilante trouble out on the Park Estate. Melanie's biggest worry is she may now be hauled off the case. And how will that help Matthew and Sally? And Amelie.

However this interview with Dawn goes, the most recent letter will have to go straight on to the digital case file. And there's a strong chance the inquiry team and then the suits upstairs will start asking the obvious question. *Why didn't we know about this new letter before?*

Will they bring in another senior officer? Melanie deeply regrets not telling Matthew about the letter. Not pushing for it to be more thoroughly investigated earlier. Trying to find Dawn much sooner to confront her with it. But it's too late for regret. For hindsight.

Deep breath. Melanie stands, fires her empty coffee cup into the bin and marches from her office into the main incident room. All eyes turn towards her bar one sergeant, Richard, who's on the phone. Suddenly he stands and raises his hand, turning to her also, eyes wide and horrified.

'I have the SIO here now. I'll put her on.' Richard holds the receiver ready for her. 'It's bad news, boss. Matthew Hill is at Dawn Meadows' house.'

CHAPTER 44

MATTHEW – Day Four

The biggest shock as Matthew pulls up to Dawn's bungalow is he's the first to arrive. No police cars. No cordons.

A friend inside the team tipped him off – the same friend who tipped him off about the dive team. But it never occurred to Matthew that he'd make it here before local uniforms.

The realisation as he leaps from the car and runs to the door, that it is all down to him now to get Amelie out of there, is completely overwhelming. He feels a surge of adrenaline. And panic. And fear. He rings the bell, imagining his sweet Amelie somewhere inside. So afraid. Maybe bound. Gagged? Day four . . .

By the time Dawn opens the door just a little, Matthew has lost all reason. All control. He pushes the door so hard that Dawn is slammed backwards between the door and the hall wall.

'Amelie! Amelie! Where are you? Daddy's here.' He starts charging from room to room. The kitchen. Nothing. The utility. Nothing.

'Get out of my house!' Dawn follows him, fishing her phone from her pocket. 'I'm calling the police.'

Matthew moves through the dining room and sitting room, then back into the hall, swinging open any cupboard door that looks large enough to conceal a child. Finally he is in what looks like Dawn's bedroom with huge double doors to a dressing area. He swings them open and swishes back rows of clothes, frantically searching the corners and the floor area. A huge laundry hamper.

'Amelie. Are you in here? Call out to Daddy.'

Nothing. He swings around to see Dawn dialling. He grabs the phone from her hand and throws it on to the bed.

'The police are already on their way. Now – you tell me where my daughter is or I swear to God I will kill you.'

Dawn looks frightened. Backs away. And then suddenly there are voices – *police, we're coming in* – and two uniformed officers are in the room.

'What the hell—' The taller and older of the two speaks first, striding towards Matthew.

'This is Matthew Hill. He forced his way into my home. Threatened me.' Dawn is now in the corner of the room.

'Don't listen to her. This woman has my *daughter.*' Matthew lunges forward but the taller PC is quickly between him and Dawn. He's big. Looks strong.

'You need to calm right down, sir, and stay right where you are.' The PC spreads his arms as a shield in front of Matthew. 'So you're Amelie's father?'

'Yes.'

'Well, you have no place here today. This is our job, not yours.'

'No, no. You don't understand. I need to check the loft. And the sheds. I need to find Amelie *myself.*' Matthew tries to push the officer away to carry on searching but the PC is stronger. Fast. Well trained. He twists Matthew to face the wall and pins one arm high up behind his back while his colleague radios for backup.

'I'm warning you again that you need to calm down. And let us do our job.'

Matthew keeps struggling and keeps shouting – *Amelie, it's Daddy. I'm here*. But he's held in too firm a lock, the image still exploding in his head of Amelie somewhere in this house. Bound. Gagged. *Waiting* for him . . .

CHAPTER 45

OLIVIA – Day Four

'OK, girls. So I need you to be really brave and to trust me.' I stand up alongside the bed. Both Chloe and Amelie lift their heads from their books. 'You do trust me?'

The girls exchange a worried look then stare at me and finally nod. My father is still not back so I need to break us out of here. I think of his gun. Those voices he hears. No choice now. It can't wait.

'OK. So my father – Grandad to you, Chloe – is obviously unwell.' I pause as they take this in. 'Much sicker than I realised.' Their expressions darken and it's awful to watch the anxiety growing in their eyes.

'You're clever girls. And I'm so sorry that this is really upsetting. But you can both see that the illness in his head is making him do things and say things which are a bit frightening. And *wrong*. The truth is I don't know why he brought us here and what he's planning. Most important, this has to be our secret, me talking to you like this. But we need to get out of here and maybe to try to get him some medical help so he can have a really good rest and get better.'

'How do we get out? He's locked everything.' It's Amelie who looks towards the padlock on the window.

'I'm afraid I'm going to have to try harder to break the door down which is going to be noisy and difficult and upsetting for you. But I think it's for the best. I just need you to move back a bit.' I pause. 'So – will you let me do this and try to be brave girls for me?'

Amelie nods, eyes wide, but Chloe looks very confused. 'Can't we just wait for Grandad to get better, Mummy? Can't we just wait? Maybe get him some tablets? Or give him some Calpol?'

'I don't think so, poppet. I think this illness is bigger than that. And the thing is I don't know how long he'll be away each time and we need to be able to get to the toilet. And to fresh air. And to get help. Do you understand?'

Chloe seems to think for a long time and finally shrugs her shoulders.

'Good. So I want you to shuffle back on to the pillows and pull the blanket up in front of your faces in case any bits of wood or splinters fly about when I bash into the door. Can you do that for me?'

Chloe suddenly looks terrified. I give her a kiss on the cheek and I feel this surge of gratefulness to Amelie who helps Chloe shuffle back against the rear wall of the caravan. Amelie then lifts the spare blanket up in front of both of them.

The only tool I have is a metal pen which I use to bash and lever the hinge of one of the cupboards on the side wall. It takes a lot of blows and leverage attempts – bruising my fingers in the process so that both hands now hurt – before it finally starts to break. A few more manoeuvres with the pen in the weak spots and at last the cupboard door comes away with a creak.

'I don't like this, Mummy.'

'It's OK, Chloe. I'll be as quick as I can. Stay back now.'

Next, I use the severed cupboard door to bash at the main bedroom door, swinging it with all my might. First the handle area, then the hinge area. I also kick, first with one foot and then with both feet, my back pressed into the edge of the double bed. I alternate this onslaught for a while. Bashing with the cupboard door from various angles to try to loosen the hinges and lock in turn, then kicking at the door with all my might, braced against the bed.

'Can we stop, Mummy? I don't like it.' Chloe has her hands over her ears and is shrieking.

'It's OK, Chloe. I've got you, I've got you. Come here.' Amelie's voice is high-pitched, clearly also nervous, as she puts her arm around Chloe's shoulder and lifts the blanket shield higher in front of them. 'Try to think of something nice.'

I turn to smile at Amelie, so grateful again for this little girl's strength. Trying so hard to be brave. To help Chloe. Then I continue with my bashing and pounding. The door starts to yield a little, especially with the blows using the cupboard door. It seems as if the hinges are giving a little with each blow and I am just starting to feel optimistic of success when there's a thundering bellow from the other side.

'What the hell is going on in there? You stop that right now!!'

I freeze and raise my hand to signal to the girls to keep still.

I'm so shocked and afraid that I fear I am going to wet myself. Right in front of the girls. *Stupid, stupid, Olivia.* It was the one thing I hadn't considered. That the noise of trying to break out would cover the noise of his car returning. My father continues shouting and swearing as Chloe bursts into tears. Amelie hugs her close. I hear the rattling of keys. I put down the cupboard door and move closer to the girls, sitting in front of them as a shield, my arms outstretched.

When the door is finally opened, my father peers into the room, his face puce with fury. Eyes wild. 'I asked you what the hell is going on in here. Who did this?'

'It was me. My fault.' I feel my heart pounding as if it will burst through my chest. 'I'm sorry. I really needed the toilet and you weren't here. I didn't want to have an accident in front of the girls. Upset them. I didn't know how long you'd be.'

'Amelie. You get out here – now!' He spits the words, jabbing his finger towards her. His expression dark.

'No, Dad. It was me who damaged the door. Please. Don't frighten the girls. It was me. I'm sorry. I needed the toilet and I didn't know what to do.' I'm now frantic.

'Shut up, you,' my father says, pointing right at me now.

He walks backwards out of the room towards the front door and reaches behind him to pick up his shotgun. Chloe begins to wail and I clasp her close. 'It's OK, darling. It's all going to be OK.'

'Amelie. I'm waiting. Come on out here.'

I've never seen my father's face look this wild. This angry. Amelie's eyes are wide with terror and her whole body starts to shake.

'Stay where you are. I'll go.' I push Chloe towards Amelie then turn towards my father and stand. 'I'll come. Whatever you want. Make it me. Not the girls. You're scaring them.'

'No need for anyone to be scared.' He lifts the gun. Cocks it. 'I'm only going to say this one more time, Amelie. You come with me.'

CHAPTER 46

MELANIE – Day Four

'If I had anyone else free to take over this inquiry, you would be off this case this very minute. You understand me?' The superintendent's face is puce, a vein bulging in his neck as he speaks. 'But I don't have anyone else sadly. So I'm going to ask you straight one more time. Did you give Matthew Hill Dawn Meadows' address?'

'I didn't, sir. I swear. I did not give Matthew Hill any information which would compromise the inquiry. I would never do that.' Melanie had expected a dressing-down but it's been worse than she feared. 'But I will find out who did—'

'Oh no, you won't. There will be an independent inquiry into what's happened here. An inquiry that will expect your full cooperation. Your phone. Your computer. Your WhatsApp messages, the lot. Yes?'

'Yes, sir. Of course, sir.' At least she's not off the case. Not yet . . .

'Meantime, I have no choice but to let you press on with this Dawn Meadows interview. Get this sorted. You think she did this? Took the girl?'

'I don't know, sir. Personally, I don't think so. But I'm going to find out. *Today*.' Melanie is still thinking of the new anonymous letter. Whether it will help the interview with Dawn who is ready in the interview suite downstairs. Or make everything ten times worse with the superintendent down the line. *You're now telling me you concealed a threatening letter?*

'Well, if she's innocent, we're in an even deeper hole. You report back to me straight after the interview. I need to know if we're any closer to finding this poor girl. And also if Dawn Meadows wants to press charges against Matthew Hill. What a stupendous mess, DI Sanders. Get out of my sight.'

'Sir.'

Back in the incident room a few minutes later, Melanie has the super's anger still ringing in her ears. The atmosphere unbearably tense across her team. Accusatory glances bouncing around the room like pass the parcel. The whole station rumbling with theories over who really tipped Matthew off. Whether it will now leak to the media.

She read them the riot act before she met the super. *I'll find out who it was, you mark my words.*

But for now, Melanie has to park her fury over the leak. Press on. The truth is she knows she's unlikely to get the name. Loyalty code and all that. It's the arrow unfairly pointing at her that's the real problem.

'Still nothing from the search teams?' She's already phoned the officer on the ground in charge of the repeat searches of both Adam and Dawn's properties. She's ordered them to check for a lock-up and to go over once again every address that may be linked to Adam's building business.

Several heads are shaken around the room but no one meets her gaze. They will all guess what's gone on upstairs. 'Any news, you interrupt me – even if I'm in the interview room. Update me straight away. Yes?'

'Of course, boss.'

'Right. I'm leading. Let's do this.'

◆ ◆ ◆

In the larger of the interview rooms available, Dawn Meadows, seated next to her tall and slim male lawyer, is not what Melanie expects. A very different woman from the picture in the newspapers and on the television all those years ago when her son Jacob's death on the railway hit the headlines.

Back then Dawn's hair was almost black. Shoulder length. She was overweight. Her voice as she delivered her curse and her threats – the clip that Melanie has watched over and over – was firm and bitter. Chilling.

This Dawn is another woman entirely. Shrunken. Skinny now to the point of looking not just frail but unwell. Her hair is short and grey. Eyes blank.

Melanie takes a breath to regroup. The lawyer is going to give her merry hell over Matthew storming into Dawn's house but there is nothing yet to prove this woman isn't capable of abducting Amelie and hiding her somewhere – or worse. The clock is ticking.

Mel opens with the standard courtesies, starting the tape and naming those in the room.

'So. Dawn Meadows. You've been informed that there will be a full and separate inquiry into Matthew Hill visiting your home.' Melanie keeps her tone neutral, keen to mask her fury over Matthew's madness and press on. But the solicitor is looking smug alongside his client and leans forward.

'Wait. We have some questions before we go forward as to how Matthew Hill was given my client's address. You can imagine how distressing this has been for her.' The solicitor clicks his pen, notebook on the table.

'Understood,' says Mel. 'And your questions will be fully addressed as part of our inquiry. But *right now* we have a young girl missing and *that* is my priority here.' Melanie meets the solicitor's gaze, unblinking, and turns to Dawn. 'You understand why you're here. Amelie Hill is still missing. The daughter of a man you are on record as having personally threatened, threatened in the following terms: "I hope you *do* have a child and I hope that child dies so you will know what this pain truly feels like." Now, Matthew Hill's eight-year-old daughter has been taken from her family. I'm going to ask you straight, Dawn. Where is Amelie Hill?'

'How would I know? I've got nothing to do with it.'

'Did you take her?'

'No.'

Mel pauses for a moment. 'So why did your husband Adam lie to us? Why did he say you were divorced and had no contact? When it turns out you're still very much married, albeit living separately. And we've since traced phone calls between your mobile and his this very week. Why lie if you have nothing to hide?'

'He was just trying to protect me.'

'And why would he need to do that? If you've done nothing wrong.'

Dawn glances at her solicitor and then back at Melanie. 'You're wasting your time. Sending Matthew Hill to my house to scare me. Sitting here, persecuting me when you should be out there, doing your job. Finding that girl.'

'I did not send Matthew Hill to your house. I told you. That will be looked into. I agree with you that should not have happened. But that is entirely separate. So I'll ask you again. Why did your husband lie about your relationship? Why are you using your

224

maiden name in Somerset? I'm assuming that was to stop us finding you. Finding Amelie.'

'Look.' Dawn fiddles with her hair, tucking strands behind her ear. The cut is barely long enough and the hair immediately springs back to its original curl. 'My husband was genuinely trying to protect me. He knew when this girl, Matthew Hill's girl, went missing, you would put two and two together and make five. Come looking for me. He was trying to spare me the upset. That's all.'

'You made serious threats against Matthew Hill when you lost your son Jacob. You made threats against any future family he had. Which means Amelie. So I'm asking you again. Do you have any information on the disappearance of Amelie Hill? She's an innocent child. You of all people should know that she needs to be safe—'

'You really think I would take a child? Hurt a child? After what I've been through?'

'You were the one who made the threats, Dawn—'

'Oh, *please*. That was *years* ago.'

'This wasn't.' Melanie takes the photograph of the most recent anonymous letter from her file and places it in front of Dawn. Her heart is racing. She has no idea how this will go. 'For the tape I am showing the suspect a print of an anonymous letter, the words cut from magazines. The letter was sent to me recently – precisely six weeks ago – and it reads . . . "Matthew Hill is a child killer. You take him back on your team and you will all be sorry." Did you send me that letter, Dawn?'

Dawn says nothing but she looks shaken for the first time, glancing at her solicitor.

'I understand you have a crafting room at your bungalow. That you like cutting things up. With scalpels. Making cards and montages. You should know that my forensic team is checking that craft room inch by inch as we speak. My guess is we'll find the magazines and the matching glue to prove you made this letter. Sent this letter.' This is a long shot. But Melanie's best shot. There *is* a crafting room but no forensics yet to link to the letter.

Dawn colours then looks away to the wall and slowly back at Melanie. 'OK, OK. So I went mad for a bit. Sent some stupid letters. So what? I didn't mean any of it.'

Melanie feels a rush of relief. She can hardly believe it. So the letters *were* Dawn.

'I have an alibi for when Amelie went missing. I tried to tell Matthew Hill when he turned up at my house but he was too busy, marching around, shouting like some madman. And I told the officer who arrested me too. I have an alibi—'

'And you also have a husband who's a proven liar. And who *doesn't* have an alibi.'

'You leave my husband out of this. He's a good man. OK – so it was stupid of him to lie. He wasn't thinking straight. He was just trying to protect me.' Dawn takes a long, slow breath and tilts up her head. 'All right then. I'll tell you about the letters.' Again she plays with her hair. 'And the rest.' Melanie holds her breath. 'But I swear we don't know anything about Amelie. *Nothing.*'

'I don't call the threat in that letter nothing.' Melanie pushes the letter closer to Dawn. 'So did you send the other letters too? The earlier ones?'

'So what if I did? The letters were just me letting off steam. Angry to see Matthew Hill in the papers again. Like some local hero when my Jacob is still gone. I didn't *mean* what I put in those letters.' Dawn sniffs and fishes a tissue from her pocket. 'The truth? I didn't even know what I was saying. In those letters, or after that inquest either. I was just so angry. And so sad. I needed someone to blame and I took it out on Matthew Hill. But it was hot air. That's all. You've got this all wrong. I have no idea where Amelie is.' Dawn looks again at her solicitor. 'So what do I do? Do I tell her? *All* of it?' He holds her gaze then nods slowly. 'OK, then.' Dawn takes a deep breath as she continues. 'There's a reason I've never been able to let it go. Why I *really* said that stuff about Matthew Hill at the inquest.' Another pause. 'But it's not what you think.'

CHAPTER 47

SALLY – Day Four

'You think they'll get a breakthrough. With Dawn Meadows?' Sally's rocking to and fro, seated on one of the high stools at the breakfast bar that divide the kitchen area and the large dining room cum family space.

'Let's hope so.' Carol is leaning against the kitchen worktops. 'You want some toast, honey?'

'No. Not hungry.'

'Well, I'm making some for myself. Maybe try a half piece? You have to eat, darling.' She twists her body to take bread from the ceramic bread bin, dropping three slices into the toaster and depressing the lever. 'No word from Matthew?'

'No nothing. It's odd. Him dashing out. Not answering texts. With so much happening.' Sally is still rocking but more gently. 'Apparently, they're going to show Adam Meadows' photo to the witness from the car park. See if he was the guy carrying the girl who might be Amelie.' The hugeness of this statement makes Sally sit up straighter. 'So it could be today.' Sally taps the palms of her hands together. 'It really could be today, Carol.'

She finds it so difficult to sit still. Never knowing what to do with her hands. Her arms. Her body no longer comfortable in the space around her. Before he left earlier, Matthew tried to encourage her to take a bath. To relax her body. But she keeps trying to tell them all – Matthew, Sally and the FLO Molly: any attempt at relaxation or rest feels like a betrayal. Like the hugging. She pushes the bar stool back and starts to pace the room.

'How do you think she'll be holding up?' Sally pauses. 'Amelie, I mean. How do you think she'll be coping? Matthew won't talk to me about that. Finds it too hard.'

'She's a strong girl. Didn't you say she had had counselling to try to build her resilience. After that cathedral case. The shooting?'

'Yes, she did.'

'Well. That will help her.' Carol's tone is steady as the toast suddenly pops up.

She's referring to the sessions organised after the Hill family were caught up in a cathedral shooting a few years back. A graduate was shot at the very moment her certificate was handed to her. Matthew and Sally and Amelie happened to be in Maidstead and saw the panicked crowds running away from the cathedral. Matthew told Sally and Amelie to run to safety but he turned back towards the drama. His police training kicking in. Sally had begged him not to go but he wouldn't listen.

Afterwards Amelie had nightmares. Was afraid to go to school. And refused to return to Maidstead for a long time. But the counselling, which included art therapy, made a real difference. She was taught to use a 'worry jar'. To write down her worries and put them in the jar. Pack them away. It had helped a lot. Week after week there were fewer notes in the jar until eventually it stood empty on the kitchen windowsill. Sally thinks of that jar and remembers how it made her sigh with relief every morning she came downstairs to make coffee. To find it still empty.

'And she's older now,' Carols adds as she moves to the fridge for butter. 'She's very bright. You're always saying how pleased her school is. Her amazing reports. And she knows how very loved she is. You have to stay strong, Sally. To believe she'll do OK.'

Sally takes her phone from her pocket as Carol moves across the kitchen space to place a plate in front of her with half a piece of buttered toast. 'It's weird he's not answering messages,' Sally says finally. 'Do you think I should phone Mel?'

At that very moment there is the doorbell. It's the FLO. Sally stands and hurries to the door. 'Let's see if Molly knows anything.'

CHAPTER 48

OLIVIA – DAY FOUR

Amelie stands stock still for a moment, her hands trembling. But then very suddenly she tilts up her chin and steps forward.

'No, Amelie,' I say, holding her back. 'You stay behind me. I mean it, Dad. Take me outside. The girls are going to stay in here.' I am absolutely petrified but I have it in my head that he is less likely to shoot me. And I *have* to save these girls.

'No,' says my father, still gripping the shotgun. 'Step out of the way, Olivia. Amelie knows to do as she's told, don't you, Amelie?'

Amelie nods, then she turns to me, her eyes unblinking. 'The Lord will want to keep me safe, won't he, Olivia?'

I'm broken. Confused and stunned that this girl, this poor child – so desperate and so obviously terribly afraid – is managing to play along like *this*? But it's a dangerous ploy and I can't allow it.

'You're right, Amelie. The good Lord will want you to be safe so you stay here.' I turn back to meet my father's eye. 'See. She has faith, Daddy. Amelie is a good girl. You let her stay and take me instead. We can talk. I can—'

'You be quiet!'

I lunge forward but he points the gun right at me. 'Stay back, Olivia. I mean it.'

I freeze. Chloe bursts into tears.

'Amelie, get a move on.' He swings the gun back towards Amelie then signals to the door with the barrel of the shotgun. 'Outside, Amelie. That's right, you go first. See that wood, just across the meadow? I want you to walk straight towards it. Olivia and Chloe, you stay in the bedroom. No more of your nonsense or you will make me *very, very angry*. Do you understand?'

'Please, Dad. I'm begging you. Take me.' I move forward again but this time my father swings the gun to point it at Chloe who is sobbing with terror.

'I told you to step back, Olivia.' His eyes are wild with anger and I remember again what happened in the cellar. What he's capable of.

There's a split second when I consider diving for the shotgun or trying to kick it from his hand. An upward kick? But with the weapon now pointed at Chloe, I just can't risk it. And the moment's lost as my father turns the gun away from my daughter and points it at Amelie's back as she opens the caravan door and steps outside.

Chloe's still crying as her grandfather slams the door behind him and locks it. 'Where's Grandad going?' she asks. 'What's he going to do with Amelie?'

I can't answer, my own body trembling. Terror gnawing at my insides. Too late, I'm wishing with every ounce of my being that I'd at least tried to grab the gun. Or kick the gun. Again I've got it wrong. Failed the girls. What was I thinking, trying to break out of the bedroom? It's only made him angrier. More dangerous. Why didn't I stop him from taking Amelie with him?

I want to rewind. Get a second run at it. I go back into the bedroom and sit on the bed, my whole body shaking as I pull Chloe close to me. There is a deadly silence all around. A minute passes. Two. Three. And then a single shot pierces the silence. Chloe screams, then starts sobbing ever more loudly. I clutch her even closer, the echo of the shot reverberating around inside my head. There's a pause and then a second shot.

And then nothing.

CHAPTER 49

MELANIE – DAY FOUR

'I mean it,' Dawn says, looking around the interview room. 'You're wasting your time here. You should be out there, looking for that poor girl.'

'I'll be the judge of that.' Melanie leans forward. 'So go on. You were about to explain why you really threatened Matthew Hill. Said those terrible things at the inquest? And then sent those letters.'

Again Dawn turns to her solicitor, who lets out a huff of exasperation and finally nods.

'OK. So carry on, Dawn. We don't have all day.' Melanie tries to keep the frustration out of her tone. Day four. Time's ticking.

Dawn is suddenly sitting very still as if reconsidering. Melanie knows this could go either way. She dreads the possibility she'll change her mind. Clam up.

'I've never even told my husband,' Dawn says at last, fiddling with the cuff of her blouse, pulling at a stray strand of cotton.

Melanie waits. Then stands. 'I've had enough of this—'

'Look. I caught him smoking, alright,' Dawn says suddenly, pulling herself up straight.

'Caught who smoking?'

'My son Jacob. I smelt it on him. Found cigarettes in his school bag. We had a terrible row. I didn't tell Adam because he hated smoking so much. His father died of lung cancer. It was long and slow and horrible. I knew he would lose it with Jacob if he knew he'd started. So I grounded Jacob. And I stopped his pocket money. I thought' – she takes a deep breath – 'that if he didn't have any money, he wouldn't be able to carry it on.'

Melanie feels a shift in her stomach and sits back down.

'Anyway. A few weeks passed. Jacob was too young to get any kind of Saturday job. He tried but they all said to come back when he was older. He absolutely *hated* having no money at all so he started to ask me if he could earn pocket money. Wash the car. Mow the lawn. Any other jobs around the house. I said no because I knew what he wanted the money for.' There's a break in her voice now. 'Like I say. I had this stupid and stubborn idea that if he didn't have any money, he wouldn't be able to smoke.'

Melanie suddenly begins to understand. She gets an image of the boy in the shop. Grabbing the two packets of cigarettes. Bolting. Matthew outside unaware of what was happening. And what had gone before. *This*. It's like imagining it all from an aerial replay in slow motion. Dawn back at her house, pottering in the kitchen. Her son, furious with her. A split-second decision. Just being young. Not wicked. Just young.

'Do you see now? The reason my boy – my Jacob – stole those cigarettes was because I stopped his money. He was every bit as stubborn as me. And I pushed all his buttons. Backed him into a corner. So I blamed Matthew Hill and I lost the plot at the inquest because I needed someone else to blame. My heart was completely broken and I didn't want to face the truth. And I didn't want to have to tell my husband the truth – that what happened wasn't Matthew's fault at all.' A pause. 'It was *mine*.'

Melanie clears her throat. Alongside her Sam shuffles the papers in front of him. The solicitor shifts in his seat.

'This doesn't change the fact that you made serious threats against a police officer whose daughter is now missing. Threats in person and then threats in anonymous letters.'

Melanie struggles to keep her tone neutral. She must keep pushing. Be absolutely *sure*. But the truth is she believes Dawn. It's a surprise and unbearably sad what she's just heard and she can feel a change inside her – the hollow disappointment that her gut instinct was right. That this interview, this person is not to going to bring her the breakthrough she longs for.

All of the theories and the hope falling away . . .

'Don't you get it? I could never hurt a child,' Dawn adds. 'I said terrible things at that inquest out of guilt and I'm sorry now that I wrote those letters. But I would never wish this life on anyone.' She stops to fish in her pocket for a tissue to blow her nose. 'When your Matthew Hill came storming through my front door, shouting and screaming for his daughter, you know what?' Another pause in which Dawn at last looks straight into Melanie's eyes. 'I was afraid – yes. I thought he was going to hurt me. But only for a moment. Once I realised he wasn't going to hurt me, I watched him running from room to room, banging doors and cupboards and shouting her name, I felt something I never dreamt I could feel for him.' Another sniff.

'I actually felt sorry for him.'

CHAPTER 50

OLIVIA – DAY FOUR

I lie on the bed, trembling for a long time. The weird thing is my teeth are chattering as if I am cold. Shock? All I know is I'm too dazed to move, to make any kind of new escape plan. I'm petrified that if I push it again, he will take Chloe outside . . .

Alongside me she keeps asking when Amelie will be back. *Is she alright, Mummy?* I lie and say that everything is going to be fine until at last she falls silent, her body clinging to mine. Not asleep, just numb.

I feel numb too and through the numbness, I think of Julia. How I wish I'd listened to her. Gone to London with her when she begged me. *You need to get away, Liv. We both need to get away.* If I had just been braver sooner and gone with Julia, none of this would have happened.

Julia and I both had very different problems with our fathers but she was always so much braver. Her father drank and when he was drunk, he pushed her and her mother around. Sometimes Julia would turn up at school with a bruise on her face. The tutor arranged a special meeting once and she lied. Said she had become clumsy and kept bumping into things. She'd read stuff online about a condition called dyspraxia and said her mum was so worried that she might have it, that her parents were taking her to the doctor about it. The school bought it. Julia used to pretend to trip up when teachers were watching. No more special meetings.

Julia started to plan to run away not long after I got pregnant. *I'm going to London. I'll get a job in a hotel. Live in if I can. You can come too.*

Of course it was a ridiculous idea. Beyond ludicrous and typical Julia. How could I work with a small baby? Julia said we could get different shifts and take turns to look after the baby. *Bonkers.*

She started to research hospitality agencies and she started saving too. Stealing from her dad's wallet when he passed out from the booze. She also got a job as a waitress at the local gastro pub. I was so envious. Money and freedom. Things I could only dream of.

As my pregnancy began to show, I was taken out of school and my father arranged a sabbatical from his teaching to home school me for a year. A nightmare. His religious rantings were getting worse and worse. It's when the hand-washing ritual went nuclear, sometimes dozens of times a day. He said that I needed to cleanse myself; to ask God's forgiveness for my mistake.

Julia was allowed to visit me at first but my father felt even more strongly that she was a bad influence. One evening, I caught him listening at the door to our whisperings and so we would play music to drown out our voices. That's when Julia told me she'd had enough and was going to London very soon. She had it all planned out.

She reckoned the experience of working in the pub would make it easier to get a job in a hotel. She spoke to an agency, lying about her age, and they said they could get her a live-in position for a fee. I warned her that it sounded a bit dodgy to me. I'd read about the sex industry. People-trafficking. Girls ending up as virtual slaves, cooking and cleaning. Worse. But Julia said I was being hysterical. She was on cloud nine.

London. I'm going to London, Liv. I wish you'd come with me.

Because she was only fifteen, Julia said she'd use a false name. Buy a false ID online. She swore me to secrecy and offered to get me a false ID too but I knew it was madness. I needed medical support to have the baby. A roof over our heads. Much as I loved Julia, I knew she couldn't take care of me. And I just didn't have her bravery.

But what broke my heart is the fact that she went without saying a proper goodbye. There, one minute and then gone the next.

She just sent a text.

I've done it. Gone to London. Will B in touch.

But she never was.

I tried searching for her on social media but I didn't have the new name she was using with her false ID. And my father got himself in a state. I think he was worried she would be in touch and I would follow her. He changed my phone. He said it was a better model but I knew why; it was so I had a new number. I had Julia's number in my old phone and stupidly I didn't write it down separately.

A part of me thought I should have been prepared for it. Hardened to it. The hurt of someone you really care about leaving. After my mother, I mean.

But it cut me deeply – Julia going to London. I tried to be pleased for her. And I lied to the police for her. Her mother reported her missing and she ended up on one of those sad posters. I told the police she might have gone to London but I didn't tell them about the hotel job plan or the false ID.

The truth is I didn't want them to find her and haul her back to be pushed around by her father. As the weeks and then months passed, I tried to think how much better it was for her to be away from her dad. But the selfish part of me missed her so badly. My Julia. My only confidante. My only real friend.

I keep my eyes closed, picturing Julia. All my regrets. I lie dazed on that bed with Chloe for quite a long time. And then something odd happens. I can hear the echo of Julia's voice. *You need to do something, Liv. Get away from him.*

She said that to me so often in the past. But here on this bed with my body trembling and my teeth chattering, it's as if she's talking to me right now. Right here. In the caravan. And I realise suddenly that Julia – brave Julia – is right; was *always* right. I can't just lie here in shock. Take it. Do nothing.

Slowly and carefully, I get up from the bed, whispering to Chloe to rest. My father has locked the main door. A wave of dread goes through me as I think again of the shots. Two shots. I have no idea how long he'll stay outside but this is the first time I've had the run of the caravan. I push the bedroom door to and start rummaging around the kitchen. I try all the drawers again. No knives. *Damn.* He must have hidden them. But there are forks and so I grab two.

Next, I check the cupboards. Mostly empty but there's a small frying pan. Heavy. Yes. I move quickly back to the bedroom to push the forks and the pan under the bed out of sight. Things I can use. Then I move back to try all the other kitchen cupboards. There's nothing much that will help. I'm still searching when I hear footsteps outside.

Fear courses through me. He is so strong. I need to feign cooperation and work out how to surprise him. I dart back into the bedroom and lie down alongside Chloe again. I don't like her breathing. It sounds different. *Wrong.* But I think of the forks and the heavy pan. And how I'm going to use them . . .

CHAPTER 51

MATTHEW – Day Four

Matthew sits in the interview room waiting for Mel.

He taps his foot on the floor very fast. He can't breathe properly, but for some reason this makes him think of holidays in Cornwall with Amelie, water swirling over their faces as they tried to body board. He closes his eyes. That too had the sense of not breathing properly, water gushing over their faces. But back then it was funny – being dunked and tossed around in the relative safety of shallow waters. Amelie would splutter and cough and then stand up and laugh and he remembers exactly how that felt, to have her so close and so happy. This sensation, this inability to get quite enough oxygen, is *completely* different. The waves of unease and fear so unpleasant, rolling in over him again and again. Deep water. Choking. Drowning, not laughing.

He tries to breathe in and out more slowly, afraid that he'll have the embarrassment of another panic attack. That Mel will see.

Mel. He dreads how she'll be with him. And yet he doesn't regret what he did. How can he regret trying to find his daughter? The only thing he feels sorry about is undermining Melanie. He'd imagined – stupid or arrogant, he can't decide – that he would find

Amelie in some shed or log store or the like, the ends justifying the means. That Mel's anger would be diluted with the happy ending. That moment of ringing Sally – *I've found her.*

Now he just feels hollow. And numb. The worry over how Mel will handle this overshadowed by the deeper despair over where Amelie really is. Where the Meadows have hidden her.

Matthew checks his watch. Practises for the moment Mel enters the room. Should he look at her? Look away? Speak first? Wait?

He thinks of their younger selves. They trained together a lifetime ago. Drank together. Became coffee snobs together. Became ambitious and very serious about the job together, each respecting the other's natural talent.

Once, just once and very early on, he made the mistake of making a pass at her. It was a moment of madness, when they were still recruits, years before the magic of meeting Sally. Long before he knew what love could truly be. Mel was mortified and so was he. Too much wine. He worried it would be the end of their friendship but thankfully it just set the terms. Mel was never interested in him in that way. And so in the end, he came to see her as a friend only. The colleague he admired above all others. The one person he could be honest with about the ups and downs and horrors of the job.

And now? *I've blown it.* The same feeling of dread that consumed him all those years ago when once, just once, he tried to kiss her.

At last the click of the door handle. Matthew looks up, wondering if a more senior officer will be with her. Overseeing. Interfering. But Mel walks into the room alone, closing the door and sitting opposite him. Two things strike him. She won't look at him. And she has a thick file.

They sit in silence a while. Matthew has no idea what to say.

'There's to be an inquiry, Matthew.' She pauses. 'And they very nearly took me off the case. They think I gave you Dawn Meadows' address.'

Her tone is distant, and he hates that she used his full name. 'Mel. I didn't mean to undermine you—'

'Well, you did.' At last she looks up. There is hurt in her eyes. 'Why couldn't you just trust me?'

'I do trust you.'

'No, you don't. If you trusted me to do my best to find Amelie, you would have looked after Sally and let me look after the inquiry. Like you *promised*.'

He closes his eyes.

'No. Open your eyes and look me in the face, Matthew.' She waits and Matthew takes a long, slow breath before meeting her eyes. 'I need to know who on the team tipped you off.'

'Come on, Mel. You know I can't say.'

Melanie lets out a huff of exasperation. 'Look. I can't even imagine what you're going through. I just don't want you to face charges on top of everything you're going through. But that could happen.'

'They want to charge me?'

'Quite possibly. For now we're concentrating one hundred per cent on finding Amelie. But the suits are worried about the media. If they find out what you did. If Dawn kicks off. Gives interviews. If that happens, who knows? Obstructing a police officer? Threatening behaviour? I could make a list.'

Matthew bites his bottom lip.

'I'm doing this for Amelie. I gave up my holiday for her. And for you. Jeez. I have a son with a broken arm who I haven't even seen—'

'George broke his arm?'

'Never mind.' Melanie waves her right hand in the air as if she didn't mean to mention the injury.

'I'm really sorry about George. And I'm sorry about all this. But I don't care if I'm charged. What about the Meadows? The search? Where are we at, Mel? Did they find anything? I didn't get a chance to do a full check myself. Check the loft. The shed and so on.'

Melanie's expression changes. He watches her eyes snap into professional mode. 'That's why I'm really here, Matt.' He feels a shot of relief. *Matt.*

'It's not the Meadows.' She meets his gaze as he takes this in. 'Forensics are all over Adam's car and all over both properties. I'm still waiting for the full report but the preliminary is crystal clear. There's nothing. Amelie's DNA is nowhere to be found. Dawn has a cast-iron alibi too. They didn't do it. Also – the witness did not identify Adam Meadows as the man in the car park, carrying the girl. We're working up a photofit. But it's not Adam.'

'But they could be very clever. Lying. Covering their tracks—'

'I did the interview with Dawn myself and I'm telling you, it's not her, Matt. I wish it was and we could fast-track to where we want to be. But it's not her. And we have to let that go and focus on the other possibilities. Which is why I'm going over all your other cases again. One by one.' She taps the file in front of her but Matthew is frowning.

Not the Meadows. He rakes his hand through his hair as the awful possibility lands. That he's made an unforgivable mistake. One-track thinking. A determination to make the facts fit the theory, rather than following the evidence. Methodically and with an open mind. He's remembering all those lectures at police college. The warning not to lose focus and to disappear down rabbit holes. Is that what he's done?

'How sure are you it's not them?' Matthew is checking her response closely. 'Like I say, they could be very good liars. We've both seen it before. Maybe the search wasn't thorough enough. Maybe—'

'I'd stake my career on it, Matt. It's not Dawn and Adam Meadows,' she interrupts with a steely determination then pauses until he looks at her again. 'But there is something else I need to tell you.'

'What?'

Melanie clears her throat. Seems hesitant suddenly. 'Dawn Meadows has admitted sending those anonymous threatening letters when you had cases in the papers.'

'But I thought that was all checked out with her years back. That she was interviewed and it came to nothing. No evidence.'

'That's right. But she sent another letter more recently to me. Over the coverage of you joining my team.'

'You didn't tell me that—' Matthew can't believe this. Can't quite take it in. 'Why the hell didn't you tell me?'

'I don't know. Turns out we've both made mistakes.' She sniffs and colours, her neck turning pink. Then her face. 'I was trying to protect you. You and Sally. But I realise now that I should have told you and I'm apologising for that. But the fact is I put the new letter to Dawn Meadows and she caved. The letters were nasty, Matthew. A crime. But they were empty words. She didn't put anything into action. The Meadows don't have Amelie.'

'So will she be charged over the letters?' Matthew is furious. He's remembering all the nights of Sally worrying. Agonising over whether him rejoining the force would make things worse. 'Those letters really frightened Sally.'

'And you really frightened Dawn Meadows, storming around her house. I'm told her solicitor is looking for a deal. A caution for her in exchange for no charges against you.'

'Seriously?'

'That's how it's looking. And I have to be honest, it would work all round. Because I get the distinct feeling the inquiry into who gave you Dawn's address will quietly go away if there's no court case against you. It's the optics they're really worried about. They don't want the leak discussed in open court.'

'Right.' Matthew pauses. It's a shock to confirm Dawn sent the letters. And that Mel would keep something from him. But his bigger worry is this extra pressure Melanie's under because of him visiting Dawn. 'So the heat will be off you too? Over the leak?'

'I guess so. Hope so.'

'Well, let's hope they do the deal.'

'And you won't mind Dawn not being charged over the letters?'

'Well, it's not ideal.' He pauses. He thinks of Sally and has no idea how the hell he will tell her all of this. 'But I guess if it gets the super off your back, it's needs must.'

'Good. But that's for later. Right now I need you to tell me that I can trust you from here. To *stop* meddling and let me do my job. To find your daughter. What I need from you is to help me look over your past cases again and that's it. That's your sole input from here.' She doesn't blink. Doesn't waiver. Holds his stare with absolute resolve. And sadness. And a question that he also needs the answer to.

'Are we still friends, Mel?'

She tilts her head. Sighs. 'Of course, we're still friends.' A pause. 'I made a mistake too.'

He clears his throat. 'OK. So let's do this. Let's go over all my cases again. What's the latest on the search for any more car park witnesses?'

'We're going to do another TV appeal. I'll lead the Q&A. And I have another difficult request on that.' She holds his gaze.

246

'You want Sally again? Oh no, no, no. Why can't I do it? Now we know it's not the Meadows. That seeing me won't trigger anyone.'

'It can't be you because the super is a whisker away from booting me off the case. And he doesn't want you anywhere near the team and especially anywhere near a microphone. Non-negotiable.'

CHAPTER 52

OLIVIA – Before

I will probably always torture myself over why I didn't get away from my father sooner. But for so long, I had no money. No confidence. No independence. I simply had nowhere to *go*. And once I was pregnant, I had the baby to consider.

It was after Julia left for London that I first decided to try to find my mother. To see if she'd help. I had no idea if my mother *would* step up – she'd left me after all – but she was still sending me birthday cards so I figured she must still care.

My father gave up trying to hide them. The cards. I started setting my alarm early in the week of my birthday and creeping downstairs every day to get to the post first.

So my plan after Julia left was to find my mother and throw myself on her mercy. Her guilt. Her maternal instinct. Whatever. To *plead* with her to take me in, at least for a little bit, while I had the baby and sorted myself out. I rehearsed in my head that I would share how seriously weird my father was getting. The spiralling obsession with religion. The controlling and suffocating behaviour. A part of me wondered if that was why she left? The reason she fell for another bloke. I wanted to ask her straight. *Was it Dad's weirdness? And if so, why didn't you take me too?*

The pregnancy was progressing OK but I had terrible bouts of exhaustion. I told my father I was seeing the doctor for anaemia blood tests, but instead I went to see a local private detective on the outskirts of Oxford.

I'd found her online. She had a swish website and I had no idea that counted for nothing. The reality was a shock. Grubby office with papers everywhere. No receptionist and the PI was offhand. All the same, I showed her the birthday cards and the postmarks. I shared my mother's details and her maiden name and everything I could think of. She interrupted me quite quickly to talk about fees and I realised it was all a pipe dream. The quote was ridiculous. I had no work back then and there was no way I could raise the money.

I asked her about her success rate next and she became quite spikey, clearly wanting me out of the office. I realised then that even if I could find a way to raise the money, I didn't have confidence in her. So in the end I parked the whole idea and decided I'd try to find someone else after the baby was born.

Of course, I had no clue what was coming. Chloe arrived two months short of my sixteenth birthday. And it was a nightmare. I did feel love for Chloe from the off. She was tiny and perfect and so innocent. But the bigger part of me was just in complete shock. I was too young. All I did was feed her and change nappies. Make meals. Do the shopping. Worst of all, with no Julia around, I was desperately lonely. Isolated. Tired all the time.

I remember having a conversation with my father that now makes me feel ashamed. I said I couldn't do it. I asked him if we should consider putting Chloe up for adoption. He hit the roof. Said she was our flesh and blood and I had a responsibility to bring her up as a child of God. To make amends for my 'mistake'. He also said something that I would only later come to see for what it really was. He said that it was his job to protect me and Chloe too *from the world out there. From the sin out there.*

When I think how much I came to love my Chloe, it feels terrible to admit how hard that first year was. But I was just a kid myself. And my father wouldn't let me go back to school. I'd passed a few GCSEs and wanted to try A levels but instead he enrolled me in some teenage mother education programme which I realised was just a scam. Home schooling by another name. I had group sessions once a week with other young mothers but most of the time we were left to our own devices. No mention of A levels.

It was only once Chloe was much older – once I'd grown to love her properly and learned how to both look after her and enjoy her – that I started to think again about finding my mother. Another option for us. An *escape* . . .

By this time, Chloe was in school and I was doing waitressing shifts at a local gastro pub in the evening while my father babysat. Just three evenings per week but I saved all the money. My father was back teaching full-time but I got the impression our finances were tighter after his time off, home schooling me while I was pregnant. It was the only reason I think he let me work. He knew I couldn't and wouldn't leave or run away because of Chloe, I suppose.

I lied about how much I was being paid. I told him I was keeping some money for clothes for Chloe whereas in truth I was squirrelling away as much as possible. He still checked my phone and restricted my life. He made Chloe do the hand-washing nonsense, the chanting and also Bible lessons. *I'm not going to make the same mistake with her that I made with you. No boys. None of that* . . .

I pretended to go along with it all, while secretly saving every spare penny and researching better private detectives. It's how I found out about Matthew Hill. All his cases in the papers.

And then the cellar happened. And everything went very dark in my life.

It happened just before I went to see Matthew. The desperate trigger to somehow get Chloe to safety.

I was taking extra shifts at the pub when I could, trying to squirrel away money for the search for my mother. My father seemed to be OK about me working. Well. Not OK. He was never OK about anything. But he seemed to have come to grudgingly accept it. He'd bought a new car, a black Volvo, on a loan the previous year and I got the impression our finances were trickier. He kept tutting when letters arrived. Bills in brown envelopes. He seemed to be more stressed. The mortgage had gone up, he said. Energy and shopping bills too. And it had drained all his savings to take the year's sabbatical when I had Chloe.

So I sensed that it helped for me to contribute, working a bit at lunchtimes and while he looked after Chloe in the evenings. I lied about how many hours I worked lunchtimes when he and Chloe were at their schools. I also lied about my hourly rate so that I could put more aside for my search fund. But my father was still worried about me meeting another man at work. Kept warning me that he didn't want a repeat of what had happened with Daniel. That I owed it to him to be pure. Be grateful. *I need to be sure you will always stay with me. So that I can protect you. You and Chloe.*

The upshot was he bombarded me with messages throughout each of my evening shifts and always grilled me when I got home about the other staff and customers. Who I'd been talking to. Who was on shift with me. Had anyone behaved inappropriately towards me? He checked my phone too, though I'd learned by then to delete messages and my searches.

And then one evening shift I did something stupid. It was one of the bar staff's birthdays. A guy called Mike. I didn't fancy him or anything like that but he was genuinely nice. A sunny personality.

Always smiling and always pleasant to me. He said he was buying a round for everyone at the end of his shift and he asked me to stay.

I never joined in with anything like that. Not worth the fall-out with my father. But this evening, I was tired and fed up and I thought – *why not. One drink.*

Of course, one drink turned into two. Then three. I sucked mint after mint as I walked home, well aware it was going to cause a big row. Me being later home. But I had enjoyed myself and I honestly had no idea what was coming.

My father was in the kitchen and stood glaring as soon as I made it into the hall.

'Where the hell have you been?'

'Offered some overtime to prepare for a wedding tomorrow.'

'Let me smell your breath.' He marched towards me and sniffed. 'Mints? You've been drinking, haven't you? You think you can cover that up with mints?'

I should have kept up the lie. But I was tired and so fed up with my life. And it was probably the alcohol that made me bold. Stupid.

'OK – so I had a drink or two. It was someone's birthday. Big deal. You should be glad I have a job. Can contribute.'

Chloe was in bed. A good sleeper. But what happened next shook me to the core.

'Come here.' He grabbed me by the arm, opening the door down to the cellar off the hallway, and dragged me down the first few steps.

I was used to all his nonsense, the weird hand-washing and the prayer stuff, but this was new. He had never been so physical with me before.

I shouted at him to let me go.

'No. I need to talk to you somewhere Chloe won't hear us. I don't want her upset by arguing.' His voice was so cold. So angry.

And so stupidly I let him drag me down the rest of the cellar steps. He was so much stronger than me anyway. He flipped a switch and a light bulb flickered on, then he sat me down on an old wooden chair in the middle of the space. Dusty boxes and shelving units along the wall.

I was expecting a long lecture on the evils of drink and men. The usual stuff about how hard he was trying to keep me and Chloe safe from the big bad world. I was feeling cocky. Emboldened by the alcohol. I was in the mood to answer back. Give him a piece of my mind.

But I never got the chance.

He started pacing. I folded my arms. Rolled my eyes. He walked behind me and I thought, *Here it comes. The big lecture about sin.* Instead, the next thing I knew he pulled down my chin and stuffed a cloth in my mouth. And then wrapped something around my face to hold the gag in place.

I couldn't believe it. The shock of it and the speed of it all. I could only breathe through my nose. My eyes wide, I tried to struggle against him, take the gag away, but he pulled my arms back behind the chair and tied them up with something. More cloth? Something soft but tight.

It was horrible.

I started thrashing about and trying to free myself, all the while screaming for help through the gag, but he just stood in front of me. Calm as anything. His eyes strange.

'You think I *want* to do this?' he shouted. 'You think this isn't as hard for me as it is for you?'

I screamed through the gag.

'You need to calm yourself down, Olivia. And think about your behaviour. All I have ever wanted is the best for you. To keep you with me. Safe and protected. And what do you do? You get yourself pregnant. You have a baby out of wedlock. And now you start drinking and throwing yourself at whoever comes along next, and let's be very clear.' A pause. 'We all know where *that* will lead.'

He stared at me for a while as I continued to struggle. Then he walked behind me and I could hear him opening something. The clinking of glass? A bottle? Next, he put a new rag on to the gag with something wet soaking through. A horrible smell. I felt instantly woozy. Sort of drifting and falling as I heard him walk up the creaking steps and turn out the light. Close the door. Draw the bolt across so that I was locked in. Trapped in the dark.

I don't know how long I was out of it, down in the cellar. Or what was on that cloth. But when I came to in the darkness, my head was pounding and I felt sick. I listened: the house was quiet. I thought he would surely have calmed down by now. I imagined he would eventually come back. Untie me. And I had it in my head that the moment I was free I would get Chloe up and dressed, pack all our things and leave.

But he left me there all night. In the dark. After what felt like a lifetime, I finally heard footsteps above. I found out later that he got Chloe up, made her breakfast and took her to school. He told Chloe I had gone out with a friend and didn't bother to come home. She was distraught.

After what seemed like an eternity, I heard the bolt go back and he opened the door and turned on the light, coming down the stairs to stand in front of me.

'Have you learned your lesson?' he said.

I nodded, desperate to be set free. My arms were hurting, my wrists sore. My face ached from the gag.

He looked at me for a while, as if deciding what to do. 'If you ever behave in such an ungodly way again, Olivia, I will bring you down here again. Understood?'

I nodded.

'And don't even think about telling because nobody will believe you. I would simply tell them the truth. That you abandoned Chloe to stay out drinking. That you aren't fit to be her mother. That I may need to seek a court order to take my granddaughter into my own protective custody. And who do you think they'll believe, Olivia? The teenage mum who stays out after hours drinking with strange men, or me, a respectable teacher? The father who sacrificed his career because his daughter got pregnant at fifteen. The grandfather who has to look after Chloe while you stay out all night.'

I was petrified. My head spinning. I wanted to pack all our things – mine and Chloe's – right that minute. But the horror of having absolutely nowhere to go, no friends and no support, made me feel even more sick. How could my father treat me like this? How could I protect Chloe? And my father's threat. What if he *did* convince the authorities that his lies were real?

I was terrified of losing Chloe.

And so instead of doing the right thing – going to the police or social services – I did the wrong thing.

I promised to behave. I begged for his forgiveness. Later, I prayed with him. And I washed my hands with him. Over and over. Then in secret I made an appointment with Matthew Hill. He worked miles away – in Exeter – but he'd been in the papers and had such a good track record, I was sure he was the only one who could save us. Find my mum. So I arranged the sleepover for Chloe. And a hotel for me.

I lied to my father on the phone that I would be working late at the pub and I might have to stay over with a friend to volunteer for a breakfast shift the next day for extra cash.

He flipped. But I didn't care. Not after the cellar.

I just hung up on him and said I'd see him after I picked Chloe up. I knew he'd take it out on me when I got back but I also knew that I needed to be brave and see this through. Get another option in place for me and Chloe. So I caught a train and went to my meeting with Matthew Hill.

I knew that I now *had* to find my mother. To throw myself on her mercy. And get me and Chloe the hell away from my father.

CHAPTER 53

MELANIE – DAY FOUR

When FaceTime connects and they appear – George sat on his dad's knee with his arm in plaster – it is almost too much. Melanie feels something shift inside. Not guilt. Something else.

'Hello, darling boy. How are you?'

'It itches.' He holds up his arm closer to the phone camera and Melanie realises it's relief she feels. That her son, this boy even with his broken arm, is safe.

While Amelie . . . *Day four.*

'We're all packed. Ready to set off for home,' Tom says suddenly. 'So you can show Mummy all your signatures very soon.'

'I got lots. All the cousins and the man who runs our favourite café here signed it too. He drew a picture of an ice-cream cone. Look.' George moves his cast closer to the camera.

'Quite a good artist.' Melanie clears her throat, pushing down the shame of her relief. Her little family. *Safe.* While Matthew and Sally . . .

'I can't wait to see you, sweet boy. Give you a big hug.'

'Well, you can't squeeze too tight.' He widens his eyes, tone matter-of-fact. 'You'll hurt my arm.'

Melanie laughs. 'I promise not to squeeze too tight but you're getting a snuggle. No arguments.'

George smiles. 'And a present? For being brave?'

His tone is cheeky and Melanie smiles, pleased to see he's definitely doing OK. 'As soon as I finish this case, we'll have a treat. All three of us. And yes, of course you get a present for being so brave.'

'Have you found Amelie?' George asks suddenly, his face more serious. Melanie realises it was inevitable that he'd figure out what was going on. Her picture everywhere. Newspapers and TV and social media. But it hurts to see his concern. His worry.

'We're still looking, darling.'

'And how is all that going there?' Tom asks, his face also more serious.

'Still busy. But I'll be home with you tonight. And I'll stay overnight at home from here on. Try to get more sleep.'

'Good. So we'll see you later, then?'

'Course. Hope you have a good journey. Not too many burgers on the way.'

'Sorry, Mummy. Boy time. What happens on the drive, stays on the drive.' Her husband is smiling as he speaks, trying to lift the mood for George, but the smile doesn't quite reach his eyes. He looks tense. And tired. It's obviously been a lot – holidaying without her and then the complication of the accident.

'Bye, Mummy. Will you sign my arm?'

'Course I will. I'll sign it this evening. Bye, darling.'

As the call disconnects, Melanie lets out a long sigh. She breathes in and out slowly several times to steady herself as she thinks of George and Amelie in Matthew and Sally's garden. Amelie on the swing and George kicking a football around. Finally she pulls herself up straight. She picks up her jacket from the chair and puts it on before striding from her makeshift overnight camp cum office back to the main inquiry hub.

One of the team has been on a bakery run. A box of doughnuts on a central table. And one of the younger detectives is tucking into some kind of hot pastry – a croissant with a cheese filling which is drawn into a long, hot string as he pulls back, fanning his mouth with his hand.

Melanie skipped lunch and is just acknowledging that she feels hungry herself when Sam strides towards her from across the office. 'Another lead from the press appeal. A second guy reckons he may have seen the man carrying the girl in the car park.'

'A new witness?'

'Yes. I asked him to come straight in. He's downstairs. You want me to handle it?'

'No. I want to hear this. Front desk?'

'Yes.'

Melanie heads straight through the CID corridor and takes the stairs two at a time. At the front desk she updates that she's taking on the new witness personally. She's given the name, Malcolm Bell, from the logbook and calls it out. In the waiting area, a tall man stands with a golden retriever on a lead, the dog's tail wagging furiously.

'Hello. I'm DI Sanders. They didn't mention the dog. He's a beauty.'

'She actually. I was on a walk when I phoned in. They asked me to come straight here. Is the dog a problem? Shall I come back later without her?'

'No. Absolutely not. You bring her through and follow me.' Melanie uses her pass to open the security door alongside reception.

'Sorry. Sorry, boss. The dog?' The constable on reception looks thrown. Melanie realises she's not up to speed on the rules. Animals.

'Guide dog,' she says quickly. 'Pop it in the logbook as a guide dog.'

'Seriously? You're saying you have a blind witness, guv,' the constable says sarcastically as he writes in the log.

'Write what you like. The dog's coming in.' Melanie holds the door for the tall witness, winking at him. 'This way.'

Upstairs in her office, she asks if the dog would like a digestive biscuit, rummaging in her desk drawer for her supply.

'Oh no,' says Malcolm. 'Sophie's on a strict diet. Golden retrievers are terrible pigs,' he says, smiling. 'She has this look she gives me and I'm afraid I'm a soft touch. Give in too often. The vet says she must lose weight.'

Melanie looks at the dog and likes her even more. 'I feel you,' she says, smoothing the top of her head. She then grabs her notebook and turns back to Malcolm. 'Right. So tell me what you saw.'

'OK. I feel awful actually. As if I should have done something. But a few days back, I saw this guy, carrying a girl in a green dress across the car park. It worried me a bit as she looked conked out. Too big to be carried, really. Not a toddler, I mean. Maybe about eight, nine.'

'What did she look like? You've seen the pictures of Amelie on the news? Was it her?'

'I couldn't say a hundred per cent it was Amelie, the missing girl. Her head was sort of tucked into the man's chest so I didn't see her face properly. But she had brown hair. Long hair. So it could have been. I was thinking I should go across and offer to help or find out what was going on but another guy in a black leather jacket went up to them. It looked as if he was offering to help so I watched. They chatted a bit. Everything seemed to be OK. The man in the leather jacket raised his hand in farewell. It seemed relaxed between them, so I assumed everything was OK. The man then carried the girl around the corner.'

'You saw which car he took her to?' Melanie feels her pulse increasing.

'Yes. It was a black Volvo. An estate.'

'And he put the girl in the car?'

'I'm so sorry. I guess so but I didn't actually see that. I turned away and walked into town.' He pauses, stroking the dog. 'Like I say, I feel terrible. When the appeal first went out, I was thrown because they said the missing girl was wearing a pink hoodie.'

'The man carrying her. He wasn't carrying her hoodie. Anything pink?'

'No. But he did have a bag with him. It could have been in there, I suppose. It was only when the new appeal mentioned the green dress, I realised I should have phoned before. I feel just awful.'

'OK. Don't feel bad. This is really helpful. I don't suppose you noticed any of the letters on the number plate. The black Volvo.'

'I'm so sorry. I knew you'd ask that. I've been trying to picture it but I just didn't look closely.'

'OK. But the man. What was he like?'

'He was tall and very stocky. Looked strong. Brown slicked-back hair. Forties.'

'Do you think you could sit in with our sketch artist, work up an image of the man? The other witness did that. We can put your two photofits together.'

'Yes. I think I can do that for you. If you think it might be important?'

'Thank you. I do.' Melanie feels a sweep of cold as she thinks again of Amelie, knocked out in some way, and carried across that car park.

'I really do think it could help us.'

CHAPTER 54

SALLY – Day Four

When Amelie was tiny, the breastfeeding didn't work out and Sally switched to bottle feeding after just a couple of weeks.

Lying flat out on her bed, staring at a now familiar mark on the ceiling, Sally remembers all the paraphernalia she once needed in the bedroom. A bottle warmer, plugged in and ready to go, and a special cold-storage container with the next bottle made up so she wouldn't need to traipse down to the fridge.

Baby Amelie would make this strange little grunting noise as she woke up for a feed. Fidgeting and grunting for about thirty seconds, a minute maximum, before breaking into a proper wail. But what was strange is that Sally always woke before Amelie.

It was the same each time. Sally's eyes would open with a start. She would turn to the Moses basket on its stand, right alongside the bed. Sally would listen. Amelie would be still. Silent. But Sally would flick on the bottle warmer all the same and get things ready. And within just a few minutes, Amelie's familiar fidgeting and then grunting would start.

Sally felt guilty about the breastfeeding not working out. But she loved that she seemed to know when Amelie needed feeding, even before her daughter did. Matthew teased that it was her body clock, getting used to the rhythm of the night feeds. Or maybe Amelie fidgeted before she started to grumble for the bottle.

But that didn't quite explain it. The gaps between feeds varied with Amelie in those early weeks and yet nine times out of ten, Sally would wake just ahead of the baby. It felt like a little bit of magic between them. An invisible thread.

Sally's thinking of all this, staring at the ceiling, when suddenly the room is much darker, and it takes a beat to realise she must have dozed off and Carol's turned out the light.

Next comes this terrible feeling of dread. It's crushing, like those dreams where you feel pinned to the bed in pitch darkness, unable to move.

She reaches out to turn on the bedside light but the strange thing is nothing seems to change. As if the light can't quite reach her.

'Carol. You need to come. *Carol!*'

It's not long before Carol is in the room, eyes panicked. 'What is it, honey? What's happened?'

'It's still dark.' Sally can't understand it. 'Put the big light on.'

Carol quickly flicks the switch. Sally can see the bulb glowing overhead and yet it makes no sense.

'It still feels dark, Carol. I don't understand.'

'Probably dreaming, darling. Give yourself a moment.'

'No, no. It's Amelie, Carol.' Sally casts her head from side to side, terror coursing through her.

'I can't feel her anymore, Carol. Oh my God. *I can't feel her anymore.*'

CHAPTER 55

OLIVIA – DAY FOUR

The noise of footsteps outside the caravan seems to go on forever. *What's he doing?* I pray that he'll take the car. Give me another window to smash my way out of here. But instead there's suddenly the sound of the main door being unlocked.

I quickly check again that the metal frying pan can't be seen under the bed. I slip one of the forks into the pocket of my sweat-pant bottoms, praying he will not see the bulge. Then I stand in the bedroom doorway so that I will be between him and Chloe.

He steps inside the caravan and leans the gun against the far wall. Seeing it again makes the echo of those two shots boom once more inside my head.

'Where's Amelie?' I stare at him but he won't look me in the eye. I stare at the caravan door, willing her to appear. Nothing. I wait some more. Still nothing. Instead, my father moves to the sink and starts to wash his hands, chanting his prayers.

'I wash my hands in the name of the Lord. To cleanse my flesh and to cleanse my soul.'

'I need to know where Amelie is.' I cough. My throat parched. So long since I had a drink.

He dries his hands on the tea towel for a moment, as if considering what to say. 'Amelie ran away,' he says finally.

Everything inside me seems suddenly then to drain downwards. Blood in my veins. Air from my lungs. It is as if gravity is all at once in overdrive; a distorted pull on the whole of my insides. I feel giddy and have to reach out with my hand to steady myself as I sit on the bench.

'I heard shots,' I say. 'Two shots.'

'Rabbits,' he says.

'But you said we were fasting. Why would you—'

'Enough questions, Olivia. You were wrong about Amelie and so was I. I thought I could save her. I thought that was why I was told to take her. But she was a very foolish and ungodly girl. She would not do as she was told. And she ran away.'

'Was? You said *was*—'

'Enough with your questions, Olivia. You need to conserve your energy.'

'I feel giddy.' I don't mean to say this out loud. But my vision is blurred.

'Good. That's the fast working. Purging. Like I say, you need to be sensible and conserve your energy. Go and lie down with Chloe.'

'No.'

'You will do as you're told, Olivia.'

I stare at him and start to cry. But it's pretend crying. I reach into my pocket as if looking for a tissue but instead grasp the fork and then I swing with all my might, aiming for his face. His eyes. He shouts in shock and clutches at his face first, then at me. He has hold of my right wrist so tightly that the fork pings on to the floor and he kicks it away.

He has blood on the side of his face but to my horror, it's just from his ear. I missed his face. Only caught his ear.

'*Why* would you do that, Olivia?' He looks not just angry but shocked. 'When all of this is for *you*. To save you.' He slaps me hard around the face so that my head is smashed against one of the kitchen cupboards.

'What's happening, Mummy? What's happening?' Chloe's voice. It sounds so scared but also weak. As if she's a long way away.

I think again of that time he locked me in the cellar. Gagged me. I'm terrified he'll do that again. I feel faint, the side of my head hurting so badly.

I'm so frightened I'm going to pass out. That Chloe's going to be all alone with him.

CHAPTER 56

MELANIE – Day Four

'Do you have any idea how many black Volvo estates are on the road?' Melanie is eating a slice of pizza, sitting with Tom on the sofa. George is already tucked up in bed, fast asleep. Tired from the journey and also from telling her all about the trip.

'You look exhausted, Mel. Can't you take a few hours away from the case? Just for tonight?'

'I am exhausted but no. I'm afraid I can't.'

He leans over to kiss her on the forehead then takes another slice of pizza from their shared plate. She notices he takes the piece with most pepperoni and smiles.

Melanie has her phone in her left hand and is checking messages and other updates on her laptop. Sam is on data watch back at the incident room, chasing the ANPR checks on the Volvo and cross-checking with the sex offenders' register nationally. He's holding the fort late tonight so Melanie can be at home with George. But the team is on a fresh new push now that Dawn and Adam Meadows have been discounted from the investigation. Melanie can't let the momentum slide. Not for a moment.

She won't say this to Tom, but she feels conflicted to be away from the office. The instant access to all the systems. Any new phone calls coming in.

A good overtime budget means she has rolling cover with the team now working on shifts. It feels good to be with George, but now she's reassured that he's doing OK she feels twitchy to be home when the Amelie case is taking a sharp new turn.

'Popular estate, the Volvo,' Tom says finally. 'No idea how many. You tell me.'

'Tens of thousands at a guess. And black is still one of the most common colours,' Melanie says. 'Apparently, they're going to stop making them. Switching to SUVs.'

'Really?'

'OK. So the witness said the Volvo we're looking for is in terrific shape. New or newish but he didn't clock the number plate so it could just be well maintained. I just wish it wasn't a black car. Needle. Haystack.'

'Who's doing the leg work? Checking the ANPR?'

'Sam's overseeing. A dozen black Volvos so far on cameras within a few miles of that canal car park at the time. The number's going up every time he messages me. It's going to be a slog. Chasing and checking each one. Lord knows how many black Volvos we'll have on the list by the morning. The nearest working cameras are a couple of miles from the car park. And that car could have been taking Amelie in any direction.'

'Is there not a camera at the car park exit?'

'Yes.' She pauses. 'Broken, would you believe.'

'You're kidding me?'

'No. It's as if the gods are against us. A bag over the camera at the canal and a faulty camera where she was somehow bundled into a car.'

'And what about the description? The photofits?'

'That's where things get more hopeful. I'm waiting for the update. The two photofits combined. Witnesses can be notoriously unreliable, but the latest message says it looks promising as their descriptions marry. First thing I will have the combined photofit and we start cross-matching that with our Volvo drivers. I'll also put the photofit out to the media for breakfast coverage. We're doing another press conference first thing. You never know. We may get lucky and someone will phone in.'

'Breakfast news coverage? So what time will you be getting up?'

'Best you don't know. In fact . . .' Melanie sucks pizza sauce from her fingers, drying her hands on another sheet of paper towel and stands. 'I need to get to bed. Day five tomorrow.' She pauses.

'You OK, love?'

'Not really. I never imagined it would run to five days, Tom. I honestly thought I would have found her by now.'

CHAPTER 57

OLIVIA – DAY FOUR

'Is Amelie all right, Mummy?' Chloe's voice is faint and she's looking really pale. I've given her the final drops of juice but can tell from the croakiness that she's parched too. And I know she's hungry, her hand pressed against her tummy.

'She ran away, darling,' I whisper. I don't believe this for one second, but what else to say? Chloe so little and so scared. 'Which means she'll be able to get help for herself and for us. We just have to rest now and wait.'

'Does Grandad still have his gun?' Her eyes are tired and swollen. We're back in the little bedroom together. I was terrified he might get physical with me again. Try to knock me out like he did in the cellar. His ear's still bloody from the fork injury but he's been strangely quiet. Ominously quiet.

He keeps washing his hands and he told me he's going to pray to find out what to do next. He let Chloe use the toilet again but she hardly passed anything. The dehydration. And the flush has stopped working which means the whole place smells even worse.

He has the gun close by him now, leaning right against the banquette seating. He's keeping the bedroom door open now to watch me.

'Best not to think about that, sweet pea. Like I told you, Grandad is unwell,' I whisper. 'We just have to stay calm. Do as he says. And wait for help.'

'I'm really hungry. Don't you have any more biscuits?'

'I'm so sorry, darling. Everything's gone. But we'll be OK.' I pull her closer against my body on the bed and stroke her hair. 'When help comes, we'll have a lovely big meal. What will you choose?'

'Lasagne with chips and Coke. And ice cream with chocolate sauce.'

'Good choice.' I stroke her hair again and she closes her eyes.

'Quiet in there. I'm trying to listen!' My father's voice.

'Sssh, honey. It's OK,' I whisper to Chloe. And then louder to my father, 'Sorry. We'll be quiet.'

I keep up the smoothing of Chloe's hair, enjoying the rhythm, and she finally stills. Not asleep but resigned to waiting. I keep my hand on her head and I think again of Amelie. What happened out there in the wood?

Why, oh why, didn't I do something *sooner*? Stop him forcing Amelie outside. I think of the second fork and the frying pan under the bed. I imagine hitting his head really hard with the metal pan. Or trying again with the other fork. But I can't risk reaching for them with him watching me so closely. He could so easily grab the gun faster than I could try to attack him.

I decide that I'll have to wait until he needs the toilet. He's not drinking either so it could be a while. But he'll pull the toilet door to for modesty and that will be my chance to move quietly. Try to catch him unawares. Strike him from behind.

I just need to be sure to hit much harder and more accurately next time.

CHAPTER 58

MATTHEW – Day Five

Matthew is exhausted. It's 6 a.m. and he's drunk too much coffee to try to counter the tiredness and psyche himself up to take Sally to the press conference. The upshot is he's wired from the caffeine but still anxious. Unable to still his body or his brain.

Last night he went out for two hours again, driving the streets of Maidstead while Carol stayed with Sally. It didn't help. He drives those streets now, not out of hope of spotting Amelie but out of sheer frustration. At home, he feels so excluded from the search. So useless. *Helpless.*

He begged Melanie to help overnight with all the urgent cross-referencing of all the new data. The black Volvo number plates. The photofit picture of the guy seen carrying a girl in the car park near the canal. Matthew has seen so many investigations come good over a dogged determination to drill and redrill this kind of data.

He's good at that kind of work and he's terrified other people will miss something that he would have spotted. But of course Mel won't let him anywhere near the incident room. She still has the super on her back after he stormed Dawn Meadows' house. Mel won't even meet him again for coffee off site.

Finally Matthew sits on the sofa by the sliding doors to the garden. He punches the cushion alongside him.

'You OK?' It's Sally in the doorway, still dressed in her tracksuit. Neither of them bother changing into nightclothes.

'Sorry. Just wired. Too much coffee.' He puts the cushion back in its place.

'Has Carol gone home?' she asks.

'Yes. She nipped back when I got in.' Matthew is so grateful that Carol lives in the same row of cottages. For her support for Sally.

Matthew checks his watch. Six fifteen.

'I heard your phone,' she says.

'Yes. It was a text from Mel on her way back into the office. Tom and George are back at home now, so she's been with them overnight. She's in early to get ready for the press conference.' Matthew pauses. 'Sure you're still up for it?'

Sally lets out a long sigh. 'I'll do it for Amelie. But you know I'm nervous again. Is there really no way you could do it instead?'

She asked this last night before he went for his drive and Matthew feels a wave of terrible guilt. A tingling through his whole body. He hasn't told Sally about going to Dawn Meadows' house. Can't face her judgement. Feels so bad for making everything worse for her. He wants to touch her. Hug her. Say a million sorries. But he can't risk upsetting her even more before the press conference.

'Like I said – you did so well last time. They want you again.' His stomach flips as he speaks the lie. Hates himself for the lie. He'll tell her the truth later.

'OK. I'll have to cope then.' She closes her eyes a moment as if imagining it. The media room. Then finally she opens them, her chin twitching. Nervous. 'So talk me through what Mel had to say. Her text.'

'They're looking for a black Volvo, going through all the cameras in the area,' he says. 'But it's a popular car so the big hope is they'll find a driver who comes close to the photofit. She sent it through. Thought you should see it before they show it at the press conference so it's not a shock.' Matthew reaches for his phone and skims to find the download. 'You ready to see it?'

'Sure.' Sally moves to sit beside him and he turns the screen towards her.

She immediately puts her hand up to her mouth.

The police image shows a man with slicked-back dark hair with a few specks of grey. Deep-set eyes. Ears close to the head. An oval face. Matthew feels a strange numbness as he takes in the picture again. The man looks ordinary. Unremarkable. The only thing that might be helpful is the photofit depicts a small mole above his top lip. Mel said this is assumed to be a mole but could just be a temporary blemish.

'You don't recognise him? Didn't see anyone like this in Maidstead that day? In the shop? In Freda's Fashions.'

Sally shakes her head. He is used to her looking tired but she suddenly turns even paler. She reaches out her hand to grip the corner of the nearest chair and suddenly darts from the kitchen to the downstairs cloakroom. He follows to hear her retching into the toilet.

'You OK in there, Sally? Shall I fetch a glass of water?'

'No. I just need a few minutes. Leave me, please.'

He stands and waits. The retching stops. The flush. He hears the taps running and finally the click of the lock on the inside. He steps back as she emerges.

'Sorry,' she says. 'Just hard. Imagining a real person. A man. I think it was easier when I thought it was Dawn Meadows. A woman. I thought. I don't know. It sounds stupid but I thought there was a chance a woman might be kinder—'

'I know.' He just stands and they stare at each other a while.

'I wish I could help you, Sally. I wish we could comfort each other.'

'I know. But it doesn't work, does it?'

They just stand there, holding each other's gaze. It's still dark outside, the lamp lighting just a portion of the garden through the glass of the sliding doors. Amelie's swing just visible.

'Was it a complete mistake, concentrating on Dawn Meadows for so long? Was that our fault?'

'We weren't wrong to be suspicious. Turns out it *was* Dawn Meadows who sent the threatening letters. Mel got her to admit that in the interview. We couldn't know she wasn't involved in this.'

'So it *was* her. The letters.' Sally's eyes widen. 'And she'll be charged for that? Yes?'

Matthew shrugs. 'I guess. I don't know.' He can't bear to admit yet there's a bargain being struck. Dawn's solicitor is apparently pressing hard to trade a caution so the police don't face the embarrassment of a court case against Matthew, detailing his threats at Dawn's house. And the leak of Dawn's address. No way will Matthew reveal the friend who tipped him off. But it's a mess now and he can't face telling his wife what he did. That Dawn probably won't be charged because of him.

Sally rubs her arm as if cold. 'So what time do we need to leave? I'll grab a quick shower.'

'About half an hour. They're going earlier than usual with the conference to try to catch breakfast TV.'

'OK.' She turns to leave the room and he hears her footsteps on the stairs. Matthew opens his phone to look at the photofit again. So much riding on it today.

The problem is Matthew knows that photofits are notoriously unreliable. There was a study done once, he can't remember where, which explained why. How the human brain naturally takes in a *whole* face for recognition, not designed to break down the parts. To notice the shape of the nose or the length of the face or eye shape in isolation. So that asking a person to describe a suspect feature by feature is pushing the brain to switch from pictorial 'whole face' recognition to verbal description. It tends to go wrong.

One experiment found suspects were recognised from a police sketch in only about 8 per cent of cases.

He looks out on to the garden again to notice a line of ants marching across the grey paving towards a drain. Just visible in the lamplight. The nest near the patio doors must be back. The Matthew Hill of two weeks ago was on a mission to napalm that nest. He'd tried boiling water and three different treatments from the nearest DIY store. He drove Sally mad, fuming about the patio invasion. He hated those ants so much.

Today's Matthew Hill simply draws the curtain so he can't see them.

CHAPTER 59

MELANIE – DAY FIVE

Melanie checks her watch again. Five minutes to go. She's nervous.

The communications lead Lisa has confirmed there's a good turnout in the media room. Not as many as the first press conference but good numbers for an early start. The BBC and ITV have both sent cameras, which is key. Sky have said they're on the way. And Sally and Matthew have just arrived, which is a huge relief. Coverage is always better when a parent's involved.

When Melanie crept out of the house early this morning, she left a note on the breakfast table for George. A silly drawing with several lines of kisses. She was wearing trousers and a jumper then, aware that the office would be cool out of hours. Now she's changed into the navy suit she brought in a smart carrier for the press conference.

It's a little bit tight. She hasn't worn it in a while. Melanie will have to sit up nice and straight to avoid unflattering side angles on television. It's not vanity; she doesn't want distractions. Snarky comments on socials when she needs everyone's focus on the appeal, not her stupid outfit. For just a moment she wonders if she should quickly change back into the jumper. No. Too casual. No time.

'You ready?' Lisa knocks on the already open door, stepping straight into the room.

'Sure. Is Sky here or should we wait?'

'Just setting up. We'll give them a minute.'

'Anyone going live with this? Or is this for bulletins?'

'Bulletins, I think. There's another flood rescue. Two kids on a roof with their mother waiting for a helicopter so that's getting all the live effort. But we should make the breakfast coverage. Important to stress how critical this breakthrough is, though.'

'Yeah, yeah. I'm on it.' Melanie glances at her notes. *Day five. Absolutely critical. Any information you have about a black Volvo driver who looks like this man could be our breakthrough. Please look at this face closely. Please phone in.*

'Let's go and fetch Sally. Check she has her script.' Melanie's suggested that Sally makes a personal plea for people to check that photofit. Phone in.

Melanie and Lisa move along the corridor to the side room and knock. Matthew opens the door, face drawn. 'She's ready.'

Sally steps forward, again clutching Amelie's pink rabbit. Melanie can't quite believe it's just three days since they did this together before. There have been numerous press releases and radio and TV interviews since then. But these bigger press conferences are key.

Lisa leads the way and Sally sits on the podium between her and Melanie. They wait for the familiar wave of camera clicking to die down a little. Then Lisa sweeps her hand to confirm everyone's ready. The TV cameras swing silently.

Melanie scans the faces and picks up a different vibe in the room. Some of the journalists are checking their phones. She's worried they'll be called away. Amelie's disappearance is a big story still but it's not the top story today. Two people have died in flooding overnight in their car. Others are still being rescued from rooftops. She makes a snap decision.

'OK. So in a moment I'll give you my full update on the inquiry. All the details. But first, I'd like you to hear from Amelie's mother Sally why we're here so early this morning. Why we need your help urgently to find *this man*. Our key suspect. Put the photofit up please.' She glances to Lisa who frowns but signals for the graphic with the face and the incident room number to be put up full screen behind them. 'We have digital copies for you all and it's going straight up on all our feeds.'

Melanie notices journalists glancing around as they take this in. The cameras start zooming in on Sally but something still feels wrong with the energy in the room. One journalist stands up as if to interrupt but Melanie raises her hand. 'Questions later, please. We need to hear from Amelie Hill's mother.' She then leans closer to Sally to whisper. 'Do you mind, Sally? Going first. You have your paper?' Sally looks thrown for a moment but then reaches into her pocket to take out her sheet of A4.

'Amelie has been away from us for too long,' she says slowly. 'This is the fifth day without her. And we need her home. Today we need *your* help urgently.' She stares towards the three TV cameras.

'We need to find this man.' Sally turns to look at the enlarged picture on the screen, the number of the incident room in bold digits beneath it. 'New evidence suggests he is . . .' Her voice breaks. Sally starts to cry. 'The police think this man has our little girl.'

Melanie reaches out to touch Sally's arm. 'It's OK. Thank you, Sally. I'll explain from here.'

'Two witnesses saw this man carrying a girl in a green dress across a car park very near the place Amelie disappeared. We have good reason to believe from her outfit and her distinctive shoes that the girl *was* Amelie.' She pauses for impact. 'We understand the man we're looking for drives a black Volvo. And this image was compiled from the matching descriptions of our two new key witnesses. I cannot stress how urgent it is for us to find this man. If you have any suspicion who it might be, please phone in. That mark on his face may be a mole. Or it may be a temporary blemish. But don't worry about making a mistake,' she adds. 'We can rule people out very quickly. And if you've noticed any unusual activity involving a black Volvo. Or a man who looks like this who drives a black Volvo. Again. *Please . . . ring the incident room number.*'

Melanie turns her head to Lisa who opens the floor for questions and only now does Melanie suddenly remember her tight suit. Sits up straighter. She's expecting questions about this breakthrough. This man.

But the tabloid journalist who stood up earlier is back on his feet. 'Is it true that Amelie's father Matthew Hill is facing charges for threatening a previous suspect? Dawn Meadows. That he was given Dawn Meadows' address? By someone on the team? That he forced himself into Mrs Meadows' house, despite her being totally innocent of any involvement. And that senior officers have lost faith in your handling of this whole inquiry?'

Melanie's stunned. There's muttering across the room. A loud wave of clicks as photographers smell blood. The TV cameras swing. Sally, still crying, turns to Melanie, her expression disbelief. And *panic*.

'Day five. Is hope lost?' another journalist asks. 'Have you mishandled this whole inquiry—'

'My team are working tirelessly,' Melanie says, her heart pounding in her chest. 'Every aspect of this inquiry is subject to scrutiny. And I take full responsibility for all aspects of this investigation. But this is *not* the time, not the day, for questions about previous suspects. Or losing hope. Today is about asking for help to find this man. The man we believe has abducted Amelie Hill. Look at the picture—'

'But have mistakes been made? We're day five, DI Sanders,' the tabloid journalist repeats, still standing.

Lisa suddenly stands too. 'This is not helpful.' Sally is now sobbing uncontrollably. 'Mrs Hill was very brave to come here. And she doesn't need this.' Lisa moves swiftly to help Sally stand and steer her from the room, the TV cameras swinging to follow her.

Melanie feels her phone vibrate in her pocket. It will be the super, watching on the livestream link. She feels her chest clamp tighter, wondering who the hell leaked this to the media. Dawn Meadows? No – more likely her husband Adam. He was *furious* about Matthew threatening Dawn. Or maybe he thinks this will clinch the 'no charges' deal for his wife. Whatever . . .

'I repeat that I will answer any questions about the broader inquiry at the appropriate time. But my absolute priority today is finding Amelie. Which means finding this new key suspect.' Her voice grows louder with her determination. 'I will take any questions about this new lead. But I will *not* have our focus today undermined. We have an eight-year-old girl still missing.' She pauses. 'And two parents whose hearts are breaking.'

CHAPTER 60

OLIVIA – DAY FIVE

I wake with a gasp. The sliver of light through the high bedroom window suggests it's morning proper now. I'm furious that I let myself fall asleep. Tried so very hard not to.

I turn to Chloe alongside me and am shocked at the change in her. It's freezing in the caravan bedroom but her hair is damp around her forehead. I press the back of my hand to her skin and she's burning up. *Oh dear God, no.*

'Chloe. Chloe,' I whisper. 'Are you OK, darling? How are you feeling, honey?'

'I'm so thirsty, Mummy.' Her breathing seems too fast. Shallow but much too fast.

'I know, darling. Wait. Wait a moment.'

I get up and dart across the small room to bang loudly on the door, checking my left pocket at the same time where I've hidden the second fork.

No response.

I bang again. 'I need to speak to you. Chloe's not well. We need to get help for her. And she needs a drink.'

At last there's the sound of movement next door. I bang again until I hear the jangling of keys.

Earlier in the night there was a terrible stand-off between me and my father. For a long time, he refused to let me pull the bedroom door to. He just sat on the banquette with the gun upright beside him. He said he was waiting to be told what to do next. I wanted to shout at him that voice in his head wasn't God. It was evil. Madness. But I kept thinking of the cellar and was terrified to tip things the wrong way. I was frightened he'd put me to sleep again. That Chloe would be left all alone with him.

And then? Without explanation at around 4 a.m., he suddenly locked our bedroom door again . . .

'What the hell is all the noise about, Olivia? I need to listen. And think. And how can I listen with all that racket?'

As he unlocks the door, I stand in front of Chloe on the bed, arms out and my pulse pounding in my ears. I had so hoped to use the fork or the heavy pan to assault him in the night – escape – but he just watched me for what felt like hours, holding his gun close. And then he caught me by surprise, locking the bedroom door so very suddenly. Tired? Afraid of falling asleep himself? Who knows.

'Chloe's not well,' I repeat as he swings the door open, standing there with the gun pointing right towards the bedroom. 'She needs something to drink. And a doctor. She's *burning up.*'

'And you seriously think I'm going to fall for that, Olivia? She's probably just adjusting to the fast. I told you. It's what the good Lord wants. Nothing to drink. Nothing to eat.'

'But she's too little. And I tell you she's *unwell.* There's something wrong with her breathing. Come and look.'

His head sort of twitches and his eyes narrow as if he's thinking. Or listening? He looks tired. In the night this gave me hope as I watched him, praying he would fall asleep so I could belt him with that pan. Knock him out and get us away. But now with the gun in his hand, his exhaustion terrifies me. What if the voice in his head says the *wrong* thing again?

'She needs a drink. And help. Come and see for yourself.'

'No way. I need to wait out here,' he says. 'To listen. It's not up to me what to do. And in any case. I'm not stupid. I know what this is *really* about.' He puts one hand up to his sore ear and signals with the gun for me to move back. 'You need to get back in there. And *shut up*. Let me pray. And let me listen.'

'*Please*.' I move forward, feeling again for the fork in my pocket, but he cocks the gun – a terrible click – and then kicks our bedroom door closed. I push against it but it's hopeless; he uses his weight on the other side of the door. Then there's the sound of jangling again as he secures the lock.

'No. Please don't lock us in. Chloe's ill, I tell you. She's ill!'

I kick the door over and over in my frustration then stand for a second, a wave of absolute despair coursing through me.

'What's happening? Where are you, Mummy?'

I dart back to Chloe and smooth the hair from her hot forehead. She has her eyes open but it's as if she's not seeing. 'It's OK, darling. I'm here.' I lift her top to do more checks. There's no rash but there's a strange pulsing in her chest, the skin dipping in and out in a triangular shape. I've never seen this before. I gently touch the triangle and feel the pulse. Rapid. Laboured.

'What are you doing, Mummy?'

'Just checking you, my darling.' I reach for my bag and quickly rustle through pocket after pocket in case I've missed anything. A final juice carton? In frustration I tip the contents on the floor but there's nothing. All gone.

I'm crying now as I lie down beside Chloe and stroke her hair. My mother used to do this when I was little and ill. Stroke my hair then brush it gently with a pretty silver brush which was a gift from her own mother.

I never met my grandmother but I remember how soothed and loved I felt by that hair brushing. So I lean down on to the floor to pick up my own very ordinary black plastic brush and I start to gently brush Chloe's hair.

'There, my darling. It's going to be all right. Help will come.' I can feel tears dripping right down my cheeks, my hand shaking. Angry and wretched and terrified and ashamed that comfort is all I have to offer my daughter.

CHAPTER 61

MATTHEW – DAY FIVE

'How could you? Is it true? That you went to Dawn Meadows' house?' Sally's voice is wild as she bursts back into the side room from the press conference along the corridor. Tears are still pouring down her face. Lisa, the communications officer, is a step behind her.

'I'm so sorry.' It feels as if all the blood in Matthew's veins is draining downwards. 'I was just desperate to find her. To *find Amelie.*'

Matthew is standing alongside the small livestream screen on its stand with Mel's voice, still defiant, bleeding from the speaker. She's trying to field questions but most of the journalists are now standing. Interrupting her. And interrupting each other . . .

Lisa darts across the room to turn down the volume on the stream. 'Sally. Take a seat. I'll get you some water – I need to get back in there. To support Melanie.'

'I don't want water. I don't want *anything*.' Sally puts her hands up to the top of her head and starts casting around, looking this way and that, then marching to and fro. Matthew is distraught watching her. She's flailing around just as she did in the car park the day Amelie disappeared.

'I'm so sorry. I should have—'

'How could you not tell me? I just can't believe you didn't *tell* me. You let me go into that press conference. And you didn't *tell* me what you did.'

'I'm so sorry. I should have. I didn't know the Meadows would speak to the media. I was waiting for the right time—'

'The right . . . time?' Sally's tone is incredulous. Lisa hurries to close the office door as if afraid people will hear. She moves to the corner table to pour a glass of water but Sally won't take it. She just keeps marching this way and that, her eyes wide and wild, glancing from wall to wall and finally looking straight at Matthew. 'So is it true that you threatened her? Dawn Meadows? After promising Mel and me that you wouldn't interfere. Rock the boat. Upset the search for Amelie.'

'I thought I was doing the right thing. I thought that Amelie was in there, in Dawn's house, and that I was the one who could find her.' Matthew's mind is racing. It's as if he's right back in Dawn's house, dashing from room to room, calling Amelie's name. No answer.

'But you didn't tell me. You let me go in there. You let me walk right in there, into all of that' – she points at the feed of the press conference – 'and you didn't tell me.'

'I know, I know. I should have. I made a mistake, Sally.'

'A *mistake*?' The look on Sally's face is too much for him. Not just anger but a look of real contempt. So that a bomb goes off in Matthew's head.

'Yes. A mistake. Like refusing to let her try a dress on. Taking your eye off her. *A mistake*, Sally.'

Even as the words leave his mouth, Matthew can't believe he's said them. Wishes he could rewind. Suck them back in.

'I'm sorry. I'm sorry. I shouldn't have said that. I absolutely don't mean that. Sally – come here. Let me—' He moves forward, his arms outstretched, but Sally recoils. Steps back with her arms up as if to protect herself.

There is a moment of terrible silence in the room. Lisa glances between them, her face shocked.

'I need someone to take me home,' Sally says at last.

'I'll bring the car round to the front.' Matthew, head down, is reaching in his pocket for his keys.

'No. No. Not you. I don't want to be near you. I can't be near you.' Sally's voice is shaking as she turns to Lisa. 'Can you arrange a car for me? I need to get out of here. I need to get home. *Please.*'

CHAPTER 62

MELANIE – Day Five

'Right. Well, that obviously didn't go to plan,' Melanie says as she marches back into the incident room. The team's gathered around the viewing screen, all eyes turning to her. No one says a word but their faces speak volumes.

'But we hold our nerve and we press on.' Melanie cannot let the team know how she feels inside. 'So, it was an unmitigated disaster in there. I can't change that. And I can't afford to let that distract us. All that matters *right now*, today, is Amelie. This new appeal. Whether we get calls on the photofit and the black Volvo. So let's get to it, shall we? Keep crunching that data. Cross-checking the Volvo sightings. And hope the media decide it's more important to help us find Amelie than stir up attacks on the force and on this inquiry.' She pauses. Sniffs. '*And me.*'

Melanie feels her phone buzz in her pocket and reaches to check it. Another message from the super.

My office.

She ignores it. The dressing-down can wait. Melanie's afraid that if she goes upstairs to face the music, she'll be taken straight off the case, no matter how short-staffed the force is. 'Sam,' she says. 'I'm putting you in charge of monitoring how this plays out in the media. Can you do that for me?'

'Sure.' Sam catches her eye. Looks worried. 'Is Lisa not on it?'

'Yes. But she's dealing with something else this minute.' To Melanie's surprise, Lisa didn't return to the press conference after helping Sally leave the room. Her text said there had been a big argument between Sally and Matthew. They left separately and Lisa was trying to shield them from the media. Was worried they might be followed by journalists. They'd agreed Sally should stay with her friend Carol.

'First I need an update on the Volvo drivers on our list,' she adds, staring at Sam. 'Can you follow me into my office, please.'

Melanie strides fast into her side office, shutting the door after Sam. She has her phone open still and presses the BBC news app. To her relief, a story appears. Brief but helpful. Under the headline – *Did this man take Amelie Hill?* – the story is just three paragraphs. But it includes the photofit and the incident room number. And no mention of the Dawn Meadows sideshow. *Yet.*

'The BBC are running it straight. The photofit.' She turns the screen to show Sam. He nods. Looks relieved. 'It's something at least. Right. So let's regroup, you and me.' Melanie turns to face her whiteboard. It's an old-school duplicate in miniature of the incident room's large digital board. Amelie's picture in the middle. The Meadows now have a cross through their photos. Ditto Sally's friend Carol. A list of locals on the sex offenders' register with ticks for each alibi check. A still from the security footage which caught a glimpse of the girl in the green dress being carried. Plus the latest two additions. The photofit and a still of a black Volvo.

Early this morning Melanie added her new Venn diagram. One circle for black Volvo drivers. One for photofit leads. Also anyone on the national sex offenders' register who drives a black Volvo. It's all about cross-matching now. She picks up a pen and moves to her board to write *Matthew Hill cases matching Volvo or photofit.* The pen squeaks as she writes.

'So, Sam. Where are we at on the black Volvos caught on camera Tuesday when Amelie disappeared. Anything more yet?'

'Nothing concrete so far,' he says, skimming his digital pad. 'Either men of wrong age, women driving or full alibis. A few we can't get hold of. Some addresses out of date. I've sent uniforms round to check the ones we can't get by phone. We're working through the list as fast as we can.'

'So who are the possibles outstanding at the moment?'

'A vicar of the right age. He's carrying out a christening as we speak. I spoke to his wife but his online profile pic doesn't look like our man. We've got a computer sales rep. I've asked his wife for a picture. Should be in soon.' He glances again at his tablet. 'We've also got a maths teacher in Oxford. But it's half-term so no joy with his most recent school. No picture on the school website and teachers don't tend to do socials so no luck there. Local uniforms have tried the house, but neighbours say they're away. Lives with a daughter and a granddaughter apparently. There are four other possible cars I'm still chasing. I'll update you the minute I get photos.'

There's a knock at the door.

'Yes?' Melanie turns to see one of the younger members of the team standing in the doorway.

'I have the super on the phone in the main room. He wants to talk to you.'

'Tell him you can't find me.'

'Boss?'

'I said tell him you can't find me. Now close the door please.'

Sam's eyebrows are raised as Melanie turns back to him. 'Please tell me you don't know who leaked the address to Matthew, Sam. It wasn't you, was it?'

'No. It wasn't me, I swear. And I don't know.'

'Good. Right. Fair enough.' She takes a long, slow breath, realising that at some point very soon she's going to have to let it go. The leak. Never mind who it was and never mind that she's cross, she needs to shut down this mess over the Meadows and the media, rebuild team morale and focus on one thing only. *Amelie.* 'Right. All good work on the Volvos. But I want to go back over Matthew Hill's softer cases. Is Alison still working on that?' They have checked all the serious cases he's worked on. But Melanie now wants all cases reviewed. No stone left unturned.

'Yes, boss. All the divorce and missing person cases. We have the list from the past six months. Nothing so far. Should we go back a year at least? Check *everyone* for black Volvo ownership.'

Melanie pauses. 'Yes. Good idea. You get back to the hub. I'll ring Matthew now and chase that.'

CHAPTER 63

MATTHEW – Day Five

'I'm sorry. She doesn't want to see you.' Carol, on the doorstep of her cottage, just two doors along from their own, looks shaken. 'She told me what you said, Matthew.'

'I know. It's terrible. And I will never forgive myself. I shouldn't have said it. And I don't think—'

'So why *did* you say it? You know that she already blames herself. How could you say that to her?' Carol has started to cry.

Matthew steps back as if slapped. For a while they just stand there, Carol crying and him dazed. And utterly desperate. Convinced in this moment that he has lost absolutely everything. Amelie. And Sally now too.

'If I could just speak to her.'

'No. She needs space. And I need to look after her.'

'Will you tell her that I love her and I truly didn't mean it and I'm so very sorry. I don't blame her. *Of course* I don't blame her.'

Carol stares at him, still crying, and finally gives a small nod, closing the door.

For a while longer, Matthew just stands on the doorstep. He thinks of Sally inside and presses the palm of his hand against the glossy red paint of the door. It feels that if he steps away there will be no point to anything anymore.

Finally, hand still pressed to the door, he sees a light go on upstairs. He imagines Carol comforting Sally. He stares at his hand for a minute, maybe two, and finally moves it very slowly from the door, turns and walks back to his car. It's parked in a nearby lay-by, hidden by hedges. Lisa, the communications officer, said to be careful. Journalists might know his car.

In the driver's seat, he takes out his phone from his pocket to see a message from Mel.

Ring me.

He's too afraid to call up news sites yet. To face the consequence of the disastrous press conference. Some outlets will worry about libel. They won't want to report the allegation about Dawn without evidence. But the tabloids might get bold.

Matthew dials and presses the phone to his ear.

'You OK?' It's Mel's voice.

'No. Sally won't talk to me. You?'

'I'm so sorry, Matt. Nightmare here too. Hiding from the super so he can't sack me. Do you need me to give you more time?'

'No. Shoot. What's happening?'

'I have the team doing a big push. The BBC have run the photofit and we have some calls coming in. I want the team to go over *all* your softer cases. Not just six months. The past twelve months. Check them against black Volvos and the photofit.'

'I don't recognise the photofit, Mel.'

'Sure. But there could be a link we're not seeing. Can you check your diary and your records again? Divorces, missing persons – the lot. Make sure we have every case for this past year.'

'Sure.' He feels hollowed out as he starts skimming his diary. Can't imagine this will help. They've already checked all the criminals he helped to convict. All still in jail or with rock-solid alibis. Matthew can't see how his less serious work could have anything to do with this. 'I'll keep checking and send you an update.'

Matthew continues to scroll through his diary as he speaks and is hit by a sudden realisation. '*Damn.*'

'Why – damn?' Mel's voice.

'Sorry. Just thinking aloud. Nothing important. Checking my diary and I realise there's something I forgot to do. Feel guilty, that's all.'

'A case you forgot about?'

'No. Not an active case.'

'Tell me anyway.'

Matthew calls up the diary entry. 'It was a young woman. Kid really. Just nineteen. Wanted me to look for her mum. She was in the office the day Amelie disappeared. When the call came from Sally, I had to usher her out fast. Said I'd bump the case to another PI. But I completely forgot.'

'Did you get a name? The young woman. The misper?' Mel presses.

'Yeah. Sure. Here somewhere.' Another pause as he calls up his notes. 'Only very basic details. Like I say, I haven't taken the case. Not officially.'

'But this was the day Amelie disappeared. Yes? We should at least check it.'

'Ah. OK. Here are my notes. Kid of nineteen. Mum left the family when she was eight. With another man apparently. Father a bit strict, a bit controlling, the kid said. She wants to find the mother to see if she can live with her with her daughter for a bit.'

'Any more on the father?' Mel sounds animated.

'Why?'

'Humour me.'

'Sorry. Not much. Like I say, no time for a proper interview because Sally phoned. Hang on. Here it is. A teacher, she said. Yes. Her father's a maths teacher.'

CHAPTER 64

MELANIE – DAY FIVE

'A *maths teacher*?' Melanie can't believe it. She marches from her office to the incident room. 'We may have something, people.' Her voice is so loud that several heads turn. 'Right. Stay on the line, Matthew.' She strides further, up to Sam's desk, and holds the phone in front of her.

'I'm putting you on speaker this end, Matt. I'm with one of my DSs – Sam. He's working through the black Volvo drivers caught on cameras within a few miles of the canal when Amelie disappeared. You said one was a maths teacher, Sam?'

'That's right. Neighbour confirmed occupation.'

'Look his name up, will you? We may have a link. And you look up the girl's full name, Matthew.'

'Olivia something,' Matthew says. 'I can't remember. Hang on.'

Complete hush across the incident room.

'Here it is. Olivia *Miles*.'

'John Miles,' Sam says almost simultaneously.

A beat of disbelief. Adrenaline shoots right through Melanie's body. She'd expected the breakthrough to come from the photofit.

It takes her a moment to accept it's been here all along. A note in Matthew's diary. A girl . . . *in . . . his . . . office.*

'Right. I think this may be our man, Matthew. I'll ring you back. Need to get everything going. He's not at home, we know that, but we'll do a full search of his house. Speak to the neighbours again. Check his Volvo across live ANPR.'

'No. Don't ring off, Mel. Where does he live?' Matthew's tone is desperate.

'I promise I'll ring straight back. The minute I have everything in play.' She's already thinking of a helicopter. An armed response team. The cascade of liaison. The search. Forensics.

Melanie moves to the front of the room. She needs to be sure the whole team's heard. 'OK. Listen up. We have a name, people. John Miles. Maths teacher. Oxford area. Sam will brief you. I'm getting everything going. This is it.' The words catch in her throat a moment. 'It's today.'

She leaves Sam to brief further and marches back to her office to put in the immediate calls so she can target support teams once she knows the geography.

She gets the search of John Miles' house approved first. Local uniforms and full forensics. Also a repeat visit to the neighbours to try to get information on where the family might have gone. Show them the photofit. She updates her superintendent with a voice message – not risking a phone call after the press conference – saying that for now ANPR is their best hope unless John Miles has switched cars. They have the Volvo number plate.

Melanie strides back into the main office. Sam is at his desk, the whole team on their phones. 'Anything?'

'Yes. Just coming up.' Sam swings his screen to share the ANPR report with Melanie. It shows John Miles' black Volvo picked up on several cameras Tuesday, travelling from mid Devon to Oxford. The day Amelie disappeared. Then again on several cameras Thursday travelling M4 west towards Bristol. About halfway between Swindon and Bristol, it turns off north towards open countryside and farmland. Disappears. No sightings picked up by any cameras since.

'Right. Let's get on the road. M5 north. Let's get the helicopter up, checking this area.' She circles a zone around Malmesbury. 'Chances are, he's stuck to rural roads since.'

◆ ◆ ◆

In the car with Sam heading north, Melanie gets an unwelcome update. A text first then full details on the system. John Miles has a gun licence. A shotgun held legitimately. Turns out he's an enthusiastic member of a local gun club. Attends meetings monthly. Melanie instructs her team to try for a photo from the gun club and to speak to as many members as possible to see if there's any clue where he might go for shooting practice. Any favourite haunts? Rural areas or farmland west of Oxford?

She watches the digital file for updates as Sam drives and then dials Matthew again.

'Right. Matthew. Sorry to leave you hanging. Shall I send a car? Or do you want to drive yourself? You need to head for Bristol. I don't have a location yet – and you know I can't give you the exact details. But we believe it's possible John Miles is in the Malmesbury area. That's east of Bristol. I'll update you when I know more. But you'll have to stay behind cordons. Yes?'

'Of course. And you know all this from cameras?'

'Yes. Last sighting Thursday so he's either not moving or sticking to rural lanes. I have a helicopter going up right now, looking for the car.'

'OK. I'll drive myself but can you send a car for Sally? She's still struggling . . .' Matthew has to pause. He can't bear to share the full truth. 'After the press conference.'

'OK. I'll do that.'

'Anything else, Mel? Any sightings of Amelie in the car?'

'Sorry. Nothing certain.' She's not ready to tell him about the gun. Not yet. Instead there is this terrible moment of silence and the fear and all the imaginings hang between them. A loudhailer. A line of police moving slowly side by side.

Melanie waits. She stares at the road ahead. There are no more words. And at last it is Matthew who ends the call.

CHAPTER 65

OLIVIA – DAY FIVE

The noise is deafening.

'Mummy, what's happening?'

I've never heard a roar like it. Or seen Chloe so scared.

'It's OK. It's OK.' I clutch her close, feel her forehead again. Still way too warm. Her breathing still too fast.

The noise comes again. Like thunder over the caravan. I frown and glance at the tiny window. Dry. I listen. And then I realise.

'It's a helicopter, Chloe. I think they're looking for us.' I wait and the sound moves closer. Clearer. Yes. It's definitely a helicopter. It seems as if it's circling now. Louder for a while and then slightly quieter. And then roaring overhead once more.

I feel this sweep of relief. This new hope that maybe Amelie *did* somehow run away. That she's found help for us. Found the police and sent them here. I try to picture her with the police this very moment, pointing out the caravan.

There is a rattle of the padlock and my father swings the bedroom door open.

'You two need to get out here,' he says, his face puce with panic. The shotgun is in his hand.

'I told you. Chloe's not well. You need to go out and speak to them. It's over, Dad. It's best you—'

'No way is this over, Olivia. You started this and now I have to do as I am told.'

'I didn't start anything.' I feel furious. Emboldened. But also confused. What does he mean – *do as he's told*?

'You took Amelie,' I say. 'You did this.'

'I only took Amelie because the Lord saw how like you she was.' He's shouting now. 'He wanted me to save her too. You and Chloe and Amelie. All of you. Do you not see that I have to do as He asks?'

I feel overwhelmed. All Amelie and I have in common is our colouring. Same hair. Same blue eyes. Is that what he means? And why is he talking about her in the past tense again? I take in the wildness in his eyes and I see that this madness goes beyond anything I can try to understand. Or reason with. This has nothing to do with religion.

This isn't religion. This is something twisted and evil. And *mad*.

'She looked like you when you were little. Do you really not see it?' He is rambling now. Eyes blazing. Turning his head this way and that, his gun still in hand, pointing at the ground. 'When I'm given a task, I have to accept it.'

Suddenly there is the roar again of the helicopter, moving back closer. Right overhead again.

It is difficult to hear what my father says next but he is crossing himself as if praying. He reaches inside his shirt collar for the crucifix he wears around his neck and puts it to his lips.

He lifts his gun and clicks it into position. He points it towards us – me and Chloe. And then comes the loudhailer.

'This is the police. We need you to come outside with your hands in the air. All of you.'

CHAPTER 66

SALLY – DAY FIVE

Sally thought she had known the worst that fear could be. But standing on the high ground, looking down at the caravan, she realises that only *now* does she understand the true darkness fear can deliver.

It's so paralysing, this new terror, that she can imagine her heart stopping. The blood unable to pump. All the muscles and all of her insides numbed. Inert.

On the drive, Matthew sent a voice message: 'Sally. I am so ashamed and so sorry. I will never forgive myself for what I said to you. I didn't mean it. I lashed out because the truth is I blame myself. Not you. *Myself.* I failed to keep you both safe and that is completely unbearable to me. I love you, Sally. And I'm so sorry.'

She played it over and over as Molly drove them here. To this awful place. This vantage point. The grim and dilapidated caravan below them in a clearing near a wood.

The helicopter has just moved away. There are police marksmen positioned all around. Uniformed teams too.

Matthew is several yards to her right, being guarded by an officer. He's already tried once to surge forward and been restrained. Molly has warned her too that she mustn't move forward.

Sally looks across at her husband and takes in the agony on his face. She thinks of his message. Of so many pictures of him with Amelie over the years. Up on his shoulders at the beach. Him swirling her around in her dance tutu. Something inside her breaks and so very slowly she walks across to him. Molly follows.

For a moment Sally and Matthew just stand side by side. Tears start dripping down Sally's cheeks as they just stare at the scene, numb and terrified. Waiting and willing a glimpse of Amelie. And then very slowly she reaches out with her hand. To take his.

They don't say anything at first. But after a time he turns his head. 'I'm so sorry. What I said—'

'Shhh. It doesn't matter. None of that matters now.' She squeezes his hand, and he grips it back tightly and lets out a sort of moan.

'Is he armed?' Sally asks at last. She looks at the caravan again. A rusty and neglected structure. She imagines it cold and damp and dirty inside. Imagines Amelie cold and damp and dirty inside. Seeing the police all around she thinks that the kidnapper must have a gun. *All . . . these . . . marksmen.*

'Yes. He's armed,' Matthew whispers. Then suddenly he tries again to surge forward but this time the officer intervenes much more firmly. Holds him tight.

'I told you, sir. You *must* stay here. DI Sanders' orders. This is your last warning. Or I'll take you back to the cars.'

Sally reaches again to take Matthew's hand. Understands better. If she had been given Dawn Meadows' address, she would probably have gone there too. This waiting and this watching – this sense of being so helpless and useless – is completely unbearable.

Truth is she wants to run down there herself. To pound on the door of that dilapidated caravan. Tell the man that if he wants to shoot someone, *shoot me. Not her. Take . . . me.*

She looks down and sees wildflowers in the grass. Their delicate colours – pink and yellow against the myriad of greens – all wrong. She puts her left foot over them and twists her heel. Turns back to the scene.

Every now and again the loudhailer voice punches through the silence.

'No one will be hurt. If you come out slowly with your hands up. All of you.'

It is not Mel's voice. Matthew whispers that it's a trained negotiator. John Miles' phone is either out of battery or he is refusing to pick up. He's been getting snippets of information from the police guarding him. In touch by radio.

'They've spoken to the farmer who owns the land,' Matthew adds. 'He says the caravan has no electricity now. Hasn't been used in years.'

'Oh no. She'll be so cold.'

Matthew puts his arm around Sally's shoulder and meets her eyes. She doesn't pull away. He tells her more of what he knows. That the farmer used to let it to John Miles and his wife when their daughter Olivia was small. He had known Miles' father, also a farmer, when they were younger.

The caravan was left on site while the owner's family made a decision whether to diversify. Invest in more caravans and a shower block. Or clear the old one away. No one noticed the Volvo. No one noticed that anyone was on site at all.

'How long will they wait before going in, Matthew?'

'I don't know. I honestly don't know.' This time he doesn't look at her as he speaks. His gaze fixed on the caravan.

Sally watches Mel, in the middle of a police huddle behind a van some distance from the caravan. The command position? Mel seems to be on her radio and Sally wonders what she's saying. Terrified they will storm the caravan. Imagines gunshots and screaming.

There was a drone earlier when she and Molly first arrived. They watched it float on the air like a hawk, circling the caravan after the helicopter left. Matthew tells her it was trying to get a view inside the caravan but there's been no word what it found. All the curtains drawn.

Now the loudhailer again. 'We can send a drone to the door with a phone. What else do you need?'

There's no reply. One minute. Two. Three. And then suddenly a man's voice. 'We don't need anything!' He shouts something else but they can't make it out. Matthew asks the policeman to check on his radio. *What did he say?* But the policeman puts his finger to his lips.

Then very suddenly the door of the caravan swings open.

CHAPTER 67

OLIVIA – DAY FIVE

'You are going to have to drive the car.' He barks this at me as he kicks the main door open, the gun in his hand.

'I can't do that. You know I can't.' It's been years since my lessons.

'You can and you will, Olivia.' He throws me the car keys from his pocket. 'Chloe, come here and walk in front of your grandad.'

'No, Chloe. You stay where you are.' I move to pull her close to me but he's faster. Grabs her arm and wrenches her towards him, the gun lifted. Cocked ready now.

Chloe, face white, bursts into tears as he pulls her in front of him. 'Mummy!'

'It's OK, darling. It's going to be OK.'

We are back where we were with Amelie. Once more I have no idea how to stop this. So afraid he will shoot.

'She's ill. Chloe's *ill*. And they said they wouldn't hurt us, Dad. Any of us. We just have to go outside with our hands up.'

'No, Olivia. He's saying we have to get away from here now.'

'*Who's* saying that?'

My father winces. Narrows his eyes. 'Shut up. Shut up. I'm listening.' A pause, his forehead furrowed. Face twisted. 'You two have to do as I say. We are going to walk to the car. You are going to drive. And I am going to sit in the back. That is what is happening. Chloe – you start walking towards the car.'

'Mummy. What do I do? What do I do?'

I see it now. He is mad. Lost. But he knows they will not shoot him if he has the gun on Chloe.

'Do as he says, darling. I will be right behind you.'

'I can't move, Mummy. I'm too tired. I can't do it.'

'Yes you can, my darling. I am right behind you.'

At last Chloe steps from the caravan, my father behind her pointing the gun. 'You walk alongside me, Olivia. Nice and slow. No silliness.'

The fresh air is a shock. And the brightness. The stretch of sky. The green of everything. Trees. Fields.

I see now that the caravan is in a dip in a field. Woods to our left. A line of trees shielding the view to the fields ahead of us. There are police vehicles over by the trees. I see several armed police, holding different positions. I will them not to shoot. Fix my eyes back on Chloe.

'Keep walking, Chloe. Over to the car.' My father's head is twitching as he speaks.

I feel for the fork in my pocket. Dare I? And then Chloe, so clearly still unwell, suddenly collapses to the ground. I twist my body and this time I do it. I kick the shotgun from his hand. Upwards. And at the same time stab at his face with the fork. The gun goes off instantly.

I dive towards Chloe, to cover her body on the ground with mine. But my father is fast. Face bloodied, he stretches left. Has the gun back in his hand again and there is a shot.

And for a time I cannot tell, in the blackness of this moment as I arch my body over Chloe and the sound explodes inside my head, whose gun has fired.

Who has been hit.

CHAPTER 68

MELANIE – DAY FIVE

In the freeze frame, Melanie is thinking that it happened too fast. No matter the planning and the training and the agonising over all the options, it always in the end happens too fast.

In a single beat she is ordering the armed officers forward to check the body on the ground. An officer lifts John Miles' gun into the air. Another checks his pockets. *Clear. Ambulance required.*

Others on the team quickly check first Olivia and Chloe – *mother and daughter – ambulance needed –* and then inside the caravan.

The ambulances parked on a bridlepath move quickly forward, and then, from behind, Melanie hears Matthew calling.

'Amelie? Amelie!'

She turns her head to see him punch his police guard on the chin and run down the slope towards the caravan.

'Amelie! Amelie!'

Eyes turn. Guns turn. 'It's the father. Matthew Hill. Don't shoot!' she barks into her radio. 'Tall, fair man. Amelie's father. Don't shoot.'

Melanie is holding her breath as all eyes turn back to the caravan. She's waiting for the officers to come out of the caravan, but Matthew keeps running right up to the door where two uniforms grab him. Hold him. *Oh, dear God no*, she thinks. Eventually the search team emerges but they are shaking their heads. 'Caravan clear.'

Something terrible twists inside her. Still Matthew is struggling and shouting.

'Amelie! Where is Amelie?'

Up on the hill still, Sally has fallen to her knees.

Melanie moves forward as Chloe is lifted on to a stretcher, her mother leaning over her, crying and stroking her head. Matthew is casting his head around, still held by two officers.

'Check the car,' Melanie orders on her radio as she strides to the first ambulance to speak to Olivia.

'Olivia?'

'Yes.'

'Do you know what happened to Amelie?' She tries to mask her panic, to keep her voice gentle as Olivia steps up into the ambulance alongside Chloe.

'Is she not with you?' Olivia looks horrified. 'He said she ran away. I thought she found you. That she brought you here.'

'No. She didn't.'

'Oh my goodness, no. He took her into the woods. I'm so sorry. I tried to stop him. I really did try to stop him.'

'Can you tell us anything else? Help us to find her?'

'There were two shots.' Olivia is sobbing now, hand over her mouth. 'We were in the caravan. We couldn't see. I'm so, so sorry.'

CHAPTER 69

OLIVIA – AFTER

For my father's court case, they let me give my evidence by video link.

It's impossible to explain how that felt because I don't even understand it myself. The Olivia in that caravan and who travelled in the ambulance is sorry her father survived. She wishes him dead. Wishes the police had shot him in the heart and not the shoulder.

But there is another Olivia who creeps into my dreams uninvited. The girl who remembers when she was very little, when both her parents were around.

And this other Olivia has so much confusion, trying to figure out if her father was *always* bad. I keep remembering laughter from a very long time ago – mine and my mother's too – and that haunts me. Makes me feel so bad about myself. My part in this whole story. So I try very hard not to think and not to dream about the past at all now.

I've changed my surname and that helps. Olivia Barnett. My mother's maiden name. *Sarah Barnett.*

That first day in the hospital with Chloe, I still clung to the notion, the fantasy, that we might find my mother and live with her. I imagined she would see all the stories on the news and get in touch. Surely? I kept looking at the door of the high dependency unit and could see her arrive. *There you are.*

I pictured the reunion and wondered if she would look the same as I remembered. The hugs and the tears. I imagined her fetching food and drinks for us and making plans so that once Chloe was better, I'd see a path out of the nightmare.

But that isn't what happened. Instead, I sat alongside Chloe's bed, and watched on the television news all those white tents go up at our home. Forensic teams with dogs. It was surreal. And even before DI Sanders came to confirm it all, I think I *knew* deep down.

Chloe was so poorly. It was a viral pneumonia, triggering asthma. I had no idea she even had asthma. There had been no wheezing or other signs, just a bit of coughing at night which I thought was a cold. The doctors told me not to beat myself up. *It can come on at any time.*

Melanie Sanders tried so hard to be gentle about it all in the hospital. But I still puked. I didn't even make it to the bathroom. I threw up in the bin right alongside Chloe's bed. I remember a nurse came with some of those cardboard sick bowls and I sat with one on my lap while DI Sanders told me the rest.

They found three bodies in the footings of the decking of our house – a raised outdoor dining platform that my father built himself. DI Sanders had a lot of questions about that decking and I remembered it was extended in stages. My father told me it was to catch more of the morning sun. Now we all understand the truth.

My mother's body was found beneath the first part of that decking. Julia and Daniel's bodies were under the extension.

I was hysterical for a while. I shouted that my mother could not be dead because she sent me cards. *She sends me cards.* I tried to push DI Sanders out of the ward door. In the end they sent someone 'special' to help me. And I'm still seeing someone 'special' – may have to for the rest of my life.

The forensic pathologist said it was difficult to determine exact dates of death but my father, under questioning, filled in the gaps. Because the biggest horror is he is not ashamed at all. Not of any of it.

His psychiatric assessment, put to the trial at the point of sentencing, suggests a rare form of schizophrenia with religious delusions and dangerous psychotic episodes. Some call it religiosity. He believes he is some kind of prophet and hears the voice of God speaking to him directly. I've read so much about it since, trying to figure out when exactly it started and how it spiralled the way it did.

I wondered how he held down his job after his delusions got bad. Turns out he didn't. That year off to support me when I was pregnant? It wasn't his choice. He was suspended after parents of his A-level pupils complained. He was apparently fixated on finding an equation 'to explain God' to unbelievers and tasked his pure maths group with helping him.

HR asked him to get professional help and he lied that he was on treatment. He was allowed back part-time with close supervision but that didn't work out either. So he was later put on part-time sick pay and benefits. I see now that we really were broke. That's why he allowed me to work.

I have no idea where he went when he claimed to be going to his school. DI Sanders said he spent a lot of time in the local library, working on his mad equation. And he also went on trips to dupe me over the birthday cards.

Imagine? He sent the cards from faraway towns then hid them in the bin, knowing I would find them, adding a level of pure cruelty to his evil.

He said that God made him do all of it so he could carry out God's work. Stop the police finding out what he was doing. *Save Olivia. Keep her close.* Every year he took trains to different towns to use my mother's bank card and to post my birthday cards to keep the lies alive.

The police's best guess is he killed my mother in a row because she was going to leave and take me with her.

He says that was why he killed Julia and Daniel too. *They were going to take Olivia away from me.* He strangled them.

He was tracking my phone messages, which is how he knew about my meeting with Matthew and followed me to Devon. He planned to force me back home. Had the chloroform that he used on me in the cellar with him. But first he found Matthew's address from his agency details at Companies House and spied on his family. When he saw Sally and Amelie, he was struck by how much like me Amelie looked. So he followed Sally and Amelie instead of Matthew and he said God spoke to him, told him, 'Take this child and keep her *safe from sin.*' So that's what he did.

He called Amelie to the canal path and said her mother had been taken ill. Had asked him to get her home safely.

Imagine how that makes me feel. His story that he abducted Amelie because of *me*.

My counsellor says – no, Olivia; he did it because he was ill. The rare but worst possible combination. Schizophrenia and high intelligence. It's a clinical subgroup that isn't well understood. Most patients with schizophrenia have a lower IQ and are not violent. But a minority of schizophrenics are very violent. And some do become killers.

My father still hears voices in prison, apparently, refusing treatment because the voice of God says the prison doctors are the devil.

I try not to think about Julia and Daniel. What exactly happened. We know now that my father had been tracking my phone for years. Using spyware to read my messages. And when he killed Julia and Daniel, he took their phones and sent false messages to throw me and their families off.

Daniel's mother came to court. It was so hard to look her in the face but we've kept in touch. She dotes on her granddaughter Chloe. She said she had a message from Daniel's phone to say that he had fallen out with the owner of the record shop and was going early to Morocco. That had always been his plan – moving on to Morocco. My father must have found that out from earlier messages on the phone. So Daniel's mother didn't report him missing for quite a while. And only with the police in France and in Morocco, not in England.

Daniel was her only child and she wants to be involved in Chloe's life. I find that both difficult and nice at the same time. One of the many things I'm slowly trying to unpack with the counsellor.

'How do I stop feeling guilty?'

That's the question I still ask her every single session. I have her tick list. I have my journal and I have her strategies all burned into my brain. But still I feel it. Still it haunts my dreams.

Julia coming to our house en route to the railway station to run away to London. Demanding to see me.

Daniel in his studio flat, facing my father.

Amelie in that wood.

Two gunshots.

EPILOGUE – PART ONE

EIGHT YEARS LATER

MATTHEW

'The ants are back.' Matthew stands in the garden by the smaller barn, watching the creatures march towards his vine.

Ever since they moved to France, the ants across the region seem to have conspired to mock him. He imagines them having little meetings in their horrible little anthills. Laughing at him. *Let's go torture the Englishman.*

Sally strides across from her herb patch and leans forward. 'There aren't that many. Come away.'

'There are *millions*, Sally. Did you not read that article I sent you?'

Just last week, Matthew had found a newspaper feature about a town in the north-west of France which had become completely overrun by ants. Nasty, bitey ants. An infestation lasting years. It was like something from a horror movie.

Sally starts to laugh.

'Don't laugh at me. This is serious. This is going to affect the value of the property. And the rental potential, if we really are going back to Devon.'

But she carries on laughing, tilting her head and shielding her eyes from the sun. And as he watches her with her golden tan and her soft freckles, he forgets himself. Thinks, as he so often does, how much France suits her. And soon he is sighing. His mind drifting.

And then finally smiling too.

'Come inside and have some wine. I can see Mel's car. Look.' She signals to the road winding from the distant farm and Matthew lets out a huff. Mel and the family visit every summer and they've had cherished times. Healing times.

They've been on a day trip, he doesn't remember where, and it's their last evening so Sally wants to spoil them. A supper outside in the courtyard with candles and the fairy lights she's strung across the mellow stone of the larger barn which is their home. She will go to a lot of trouble as she always does for Mel and Tom and George. He can already smell the beef stewing in wine. And Sally is carrying a basket of edible flowers to dress the salad. Berries for the cheesecake. Grapes for the cheese board.

She loves the garden here. All the different things she can grow in the warmer climate. The many flowers this sunshine nurtures. The rich orange of the campsis (he calls it 'the triffid') weighing down the pergola over the courtyard dining table.

Hard to believe the difference from eight years back. It was a complete wreck when they bought this place. He remembers telling the estate agent they were looking for a 'doer upper' but when they were first shown around he whispered to Sally that it was more of a 'falling downer'. Two barns, one large and one much smaller, with a courtyard between and two acres. But it was what they both needed back then. A project. A fresh page. Something to fill their days. And their minds.

He's done a lot of the building work himself, enjoying the hard labour and the company of the tradespeople he's employed to help along the way. The plumbers and the electricians. The plasterer and the ironmonger who's done special commissions for them. A beautiful black gate into the courtyard and large hooks for the hanging baskets. Many of the builders have become new friends who congregate in the courtyard for Sally's Friday night suppers.

She's returned to property management these past four years. Set up her own little company which manages the rental of their second converted barn and some other local properties too. It's worked well.

They thought at one point that they would stay for good. But apparently not.

◆ ◆ ◆

Matthew puts his hand to his forehead to shield the sunshine and watch Mel's car wind its way along the narrow approach road. She remains his best friend in the world. But sometimes when he sees her, it is hard. It all comes back.

That moment when the police team came from the caravan near the woods.

And shook their heads.

EPILOGUE – PART TWO

AMELIE

I watch from my bedroom window and see Mel's car getting closer. Good. I'm starving and supper smells super-scrummy. Also, I need to talk to Mel again. And Mum. About how to handle Dad.

Tomorrow, I get my exam results. Eek! Sooo nervous. But I'm excited too because I worked hard and I want so badly to get everything going now. Out in the open.

I think it surprised my parents that I want to go back to Devon for my sixth form. I haven't had the courage yet to tell them why. My big plan. I tried to talk to Mel last night because I need her help. But she said – *You need to talk to your father first, Amelie. Promise me?*

So tonight's the night.

It's going to be hard because I love him so much and I know this is going to scare him to death. But I also feel it's time. And I need Mel's help before she goes home. To make Dad see that it really will be OK.

When we moved here, I think Dad imagined we would stay forever. Put the past behind us. I did too. At first we were all just in shock. Wanted to feel safer. It felt the right thing to be somewhere completely different. And I've loved it, I honestly have. The great weather. The great food. And yes. Feeling safe.

It's cool to be bilingual too. Like a superpower. And so much easier than I expected. I picked an international school so I could study in English for GCSEs. None of us realised how quickly I'd become fluent in French.

But being here, as lovely as it is, has come to feel like a bubble. Not quite real. Like *hiding* now. And sixteen-year-old me wants something more. I've figured it all out in my head now. Which is why I need to explain it to my dad.

I tried telling him a couple of years ago that I want to be a detective. You should have seen his face! The blind panic. He closed the subject down; said I could be anything I wanted. He didn't want to talk about it because I could see that it terrified him.

My father has this idea, you see, that he is to blame for all the bad things that have happened to our family. He thinks he can fix that by hiding us away in rural France. And giving up the work he loves.

But I know that he misses it. His old work. I see it when he talks to Mel. Asks about her cases.

I've tried to talk to Mum about it all and I think she gets it. But she's scared too. *Be patient with us, Amelie.*

The problem is they both want to wrap me up in cotton wool. But I'm nearly an adult now. They can't keep me safe forever. Very soon that will be *my* job. Not theirs.

I think the biggest problem between the three of us – and I've only figured this out properly in this past year – is I haven't told them yet what happened in the wood with Olivia's father. I've been too afraid. I knew it would hurt them, the detail, so I used to shut it down. And when they asked, I pretended not to remember. But that isn't true.

I think about it all . . . the . . . time. And it's why I've made up my mind. That I'm going to do my A levels in England. I am going to do a degree in criminology.

And I am going to become a detective.

What my father doesn't realise is that it's because of him I'm here at all. He thinks it was his fault I was in danger. He doesn't realise the truth. That he *saved* me.

When I was in that wood with John Miles, I wasn't brave at all. Not at first. I was so afraid, I wet myself. He made me march alongside him deep into the wood. I was certain he was going to shoot me and when he lifted the shotgun and cocked it, I turned to face him. I don't know why. Not bravery. Just instinct.

I thought – *this is it*. And I remember worrying how much it would hurt. And I was thinking about my parents. How awful it would be to never see them again.

And then he surprised me.

'Run,' he said.

I didn't move. I was too scared.

'I'm going to let you go, Amelie,' he said. 'Now run. *Run!*'

That's when it all changed. And clicked in my brain.

I looked into his eyes and I just *knew*. He had no intention of letting me go. I could read his face. His weird and horrid face. He was a coward, that's all. He didn't want to shoot me while I was looking at him. He wanted me to run so he could shoot me in the back.

I remembered two things. Like this flash of pictures. First a video on socials of a big cat chasing a guy along a dirt track. I was sure it was going to kill him. But the man walked backwards, throwing rocks. He kept facing it and in the end, the big cat ran away. I googled it. Big cats like to pounce from behind. They don't like to be looked in the eye.

That's when the much bigger second thought landed.

You need to run, Amelie. Go on. Run.

I remembered my dad and the cathedral. It was as if I was right back there. So little, in town with Mum and Dad and all these people running down the High Street. They were shouting there was a gunman in the cathedral. Everyone yelling. *Run. Run away.*

I was petrified. Dad told Mum to pick me up and run to safety. But he didn't run with us. He turned the other way. He pushed his way back through the crowds towards the cathedral. *Towards* danger. To see if he could help.

At the time I hated him for that. Selfishly, I wanted him to run away with us.

But he refused. And he saved people that day.

So in that wood, when Olivia's father gave me one last chance to run away, I turned to him and said, 'No.'

He looked confused. 'I mean it,' he said. 'You need to run, Amelie.'

'*No*,' I said again. I stared him right in the face and I thought of my dad. '*I won't.*'

His face was *so* angry. He pointed the gun at me and I waited for the pain. I waited and waited. I tried to believe in heaven; that I would see my parents again in heaven one day. But I didn't move.

He seemed not to know what to do. His face changed. Suddenly he raised the gun and fired two shots into the air. Then he grabbed me roughly by the arm and marched me back to his car. He put a gag on me and bound my hands and threw me into the boot. And that's where the police found me.

So now I think – and as I watch Mel's car pull up, I know that I need to find the right words to explain this to my father tonight – that the only reason I survived what happened with Olivia's father, is because of *him*. The man who doesn't run.

Which is why I've made up my mind.

I am going to be a detective.

And all the mad and the bad and the sad excuses for human beings out there with evil on their minds had better know this.

I am my father's daughter.

And I will . . . not . . . run.

ACKNOWLEDGEMENTS

Oh my goodness, I feel quite bereft as I finish this novel.

When I wrote *I Am Watching You*, my first psychological thriller published in 2017, PI Matthew Hill sauntered into my writing room with a big grin and I had a good feeling we'd be firm friends. But I had no idea that he'd change my life! That book has sold over 1.5 million copies across the world and I have never stopped being grateful to all the readers who have so kindly championed it.

I Am Watching You was a standalone thriller – as are all my psych thrillers – but Matthew Hill kept poking his nose around my study door, winking as I was writing something new. And I would say, '*So you're in this book too, are you?*'

I became so fond of him, I ended up giving him a role in all my standalone thrillers. Sometimes just a cameo role. Sometimes a much bigger part. My thrillers are not a series per se, and you certainly don't have to have read any one of them to enjoy the others. But I have personally loved writing about Matthew, his wife Sally and their daughter Amelie.

And then one day I got the flash of *this* story. Amelie missing. And, although this is fiction, it shook me to imagine how much it would hurt Matthew and Sally. I put off writing the book for a few years because I knew that in this story Amelie needed to be eight, going on nine. And it would see Matthew leaving detective work behind him.

Also – a part of me really didn't want to write this story (but that's actually how I know a story is strong enough. When it's going to hurt). I finally knew I was ready when I pictured Amelie at the *end* of the novel. I listened to her voice (it always feels as if my characters tell me what to write!) and I felt so relieved. And proud of her. That in the end, this difficult story would give her agency, taking her from a little girl to a strong, young woman with a strong future.

As always, I have so many good people to thank for helping me to the end of another story. First my family, who are so supportive and patient always when I disappear for long hours into my writing room.

I must especially thank my publisher Thomas & Mercer and my fabulous editors Kasim Mohammed and Ian Pindar who made SUCH a difference to this book, helping me with so many ideas to shape this story to the very best version of itself. And thanks as ever to my superstar agent Madeleine Milburn and her whole wonderful team.

Finally, my heartfelt thanks go to you for reading *Close Your Eyes*. I feel so blessed to have such wonderful readers. And if you have enjoyed the writing, I would greatly appreciate a rating or review on Amazon as they really do help other people to find my books.

Also – feel free to say hello. You can find my website at www.teresadriscoll.com where you can sign up to my newsletter. You can also say hello on X @TeresaDriscoll or www.facebook.com/teresadriscollauthor and Instagram @tkdriscoll_author.

I really enjoy chatting to readers and will be delighted to hear from you.

Warm wishes to you all,

Teresa

ABOUT THE AUTHOR

Photo © 2015 Claire Tregaskis

For more than twenty-five years as a journalist – including fifteen years as a BBC TV news presenter – Teresa Driscoll followed stories into the shadows of life. Covering crime for so long, she watched and was deeply moved by all the ripples each case caused, and the haunting impact on the families, friends and witnesses involved. It is those ripples that she explores in her darker fiction.

Teresa's novels have sold more than two million copies and have been published in twenty languages. She lives in beautiful Devon with her family. You can find out more about her books on her website (www.teresadriscoll.com) or by following her on X, formerly Twitter (@TeresaDriscoll), Facebook (www.facebook.com/teresadriscollauthor) or Instagram (@tkdriscoll_author).

Follow the Author on Amazon

If you enjoyed this book, follow Teresa Driscoll on Amazon to be notified when the author releases a new book!

To do this, please follow these instructions:

Desktop:

1) Search for the author's name on Amazon or in the Amazon App.

2) Click on the author's name to arrive on their Amazon page.

3) Click the 'Follow' button.

Mobile and Tablet:

1) Search for the author's name on Amazon or in the Amazon App.

2) Click on one of the author's books.

3) Click on the author's name to arrive on their Amazon page.

4) Click the 'Follow' button.

Kindle eReader and Kindle App:

If you enjoyed this book on a Kindle eReader or in the Kindle App, you will find the author 'Follow' button after the last page.